The story line in *Green Underwear* is a basic primer of a ranger's day-to-day labors to conserve and develop the forest's natural resources, both for recreation and for commerce. It is a primer that leaves the reader with an understanding of civil service from the perspective of a career professional. The book reveals the dedication of foresters to basic principles that have lasting importance to our forests and the environment, while dealing with the challenges of transitory politics. The reader will revel in the happy and rewarding lives of children growing up in a family guided by solid ideals of honor, respect, work, and achievement.

—The Honorable Richard E. Ransom,
Chief Justice, New Mexico Supreme Court, retired.

The author has captured in tone and tint—the hue, texture, and composition of life as a forest ranger during the last decade of the twentieth century. It is fiction but based on real events, philosophy, and ethics. It is accurate and authentic. This story is for the student, historian, academic, and yes, the politician. It is also for the romantic, for here is a story of what life is like managing the "high country"—the nation's national forests. It puts the reader in a "green uniform."

—Don T Nebeker
Forest Supervisor, Uinta National Forest, retired.

These stories brought back vivid memories of an exciting and enjoyable life on a ranger district in the good old days when land management direction was based on professional, scientific, and good judgment concepts instead of political agendas.

—Mac Thomson
former Middle Fork District Ranger and Regional Law Enforcement Officer, retired.

Green Underwear is a great story with a great title! It vividly portrays several important "family" aspects. Personal family, Forest Service family and community family come through as an integrated whole in Ranger Larry's life.

—George A. Olson
former Forest Supervisor and Regional Director of Recreation and Lands, retired.

This is an interesting, enjoyable, and complete account of every aspect of a district forest ranger's job in on-the-ground management of the forest.

—Ray Connelly
Forest Service Equipment Engineer, retired.

Green Underwear

Green Underwear

by

Stan Tixier

Illustrated by Judy Harris

BONNEVILLE BOOKS™
Springville, Utah

ISBN: 1-55517-572-4
v.2

Published by Bonneville Books
Imprint of Cedar Fort Inc.
www.cedarfort.com

Distributed by:

Typeset by Kristin Nelson
Cover photo by Jan Tixier
Cover design by Adam Ford

Illustrations by Judy Harris
Printed in the United States of America
10 9 8 7 6 5 4 3 2 1

Library of Congress Control Number: 2001095261

Printed on acid-free paper

TABLE OF CONTENTS

DEDICATION

This book is dedicated to four special people in particular and to an untold number of people in general.

My wife, Jan, and our children, John, Joe, and Ann were my support and inspiration throughout a long and rewarding career with the Forest Service. Without complaint they made the moves as I was transferred to different and various assignments and accepted the fact that I was not always there when they had special needs. They have my undying appreciation and love.

Many other forest officers have had this same sort of support from their families in their careers. This book is dedicated to those families as well. The Forest Service has always been a "family," but it all starts with the family at home.

ACKNOWLEDGMENTS

A good many people have been very helpful in getting this book into final form, and they have my sincere appreciation. These include Judy Harris, artist and illustrator, and her husband Dave; professional copy editor, Delpha Noble and her husband, Ed, a retired forester; my daughter, Ann Bingham, who was a great help to me in getting past the mysteries of the computer and such things as the data disc; my wife, Jan, a concurrent reviewer, critic and supporter throughout the project. Other helpful reviewers within the family included my mother, Dorothy, and sons, John and Joe.

Several friends were kind enough to review the draft at various stages and provide critique and suggestions. These included: George Roether, retired director of timber management for the Intermountain Region and former forest supervisor; John Burns, former supervisor of the Targhee and Salmon National Forests and his wife, Ruth; Rex Cleary, former BLM district manager; Bill Hurst, retired regional forester of the Southwestern Region; Don Nebeker, retired supervisor of the Uinta NF; Larry Lassen, retired director of the Intermountain Research Station and his wife, Julie; Dick Ransom, lifelong friend and retired chief justice of the New Mexico Supreme Court; Jim Suhr, engineer and inventor of the Choosing by Advantages decision-making system and his wife, Margaret; Ruth Monahan, Ogden District Ranger, Wasatch-Cache NF; Mac Thomson, retired regional law enforcement officer and former district ranger; George Olson, retired regional director of Recreation and Lands and former forest supervisor; Ray Connelly, retired FS equipment engineer; and Max Peterson, retired Chief of the Forest Service, who wrote the book's foreword. Many thanks to each one for their time, efforts and considerable help.

FOREWORD

by R. Max Peterson, Chief Emeritus,
U.S. Forest Service

Green Underwear is an authentic and realistic account of life in a western National Forest Ranger District. It captures life and real-world events that typically take place on a ranger district that could only have been written by someone who has "been there and done that!"

Stan Tixier is a former district ranger, forest supervisor, and regional forester, as well as a staff officer who spent a career as part of a cadre of dedicated Forest Service professionals who make sure that things get done on the ground seven days a week and 365 days a year. From that perspective Stan has been able to capture and bring to life the exciting as well as the mundane activities so necessary to accomplish the agency's work within tight budgets and at times difficult circumstances, including terrain and climate. In doing so, he has managed to make the book both entertaining and educational as he explains, through typical ranger district activities and events, the frustrations as well as the sense of satisfaction realized as challenges are met and actions completed. The political pressures, debates and opinions expressed show the human faces of people both inside and outside of the organization and how Forest Service people carry out their duties even in situations where policy rationale may not be fully understood either by local people or employees.

The book vividly explains the district ranger's role in

increasingly difficult and many times controversial situations where different user groups vie for a larger "slice" of National Forest land and its natural resources. Getting people to share these lands and resources is a continuing challenge and the resulting polarization reverberates not only on ranger districts but throughout the Forest Service, public and private organizations, Congress, and in recent years, increasingly in the courts. Although written as fiction, the book provides historically accurate accounts of typical events as well as some local, regional and national debates as enumerated in Chapter VI, *The Speech*. This book should be required reading for foresters and other professionals who are interested in a career with the Forest Service.

As the eleventh Chief of the Forest Service, who spent almost thirty eight years with the agency, I was privileged to know and work with a host of dedicated Forest Service people like Stan Tixier. The agency's mission of "Caring for the Land and Serving People" requires thousands of loyal and dedicated people who for more than a century have assured that National Forests provide a variety of goods and services for the American people.

Forest Service people both active and retired will be stimulated as they recall with nostalgia the times they spent in the field doing some of the things described in this book. Members of the public who use the National Forests in ever-increasing numbers and those agencies and organizations who have cooperated with the Forest Service in various "partnership programs" will find these accounts interesting, enjoyable and educational.

Now sit back and enjoy reading this interesting and insightful book, and then pass it on to a son, daughter or friend. I did!

PREFACE

This is a story about a Forest Ranger, Lawrence E. Weaver III, about his family and about his organization, the Forest Service, an agency in the U.S. Department of Agriculture.

The setting is a ranger district where the work of the Forest Service is performed. The District is the basic, on-the-ground unit of the National Forest System and the most important, despite opinions that might exist in the National Headquarters, Regional and Forest offices.

The story is fiction, but it is based on a number of true-life experiences. Larry Weaver and the Elk Creek Ranger District of the Rio Verde National Forest, and the small town of Elk Creek (population 3,000) in Adams County, are fictional. Some 96 people, 13 horses, and 5 mules are all fictional. I hope you'll enjoy getting acquainted with all of them.

The time-period is the early 1990s. Obviously, references to the administration in Washington D.C. must be based on reality. However, the Vice President in Chapter X and his float trip are fiction. The float trip's location, the Middle Fork, is real; it is the one exception.

One character in the book is real. Some readers will know immediately. Others will have to guess which one.

Chapter V, The Parade, is based on a true story as told by Joel Frandsen in his book, Forest Trails and Tales, as well as a poem, "The Parade," in my book, "A Good Lookin' Horse," "Cowboy Poetry and Other Verse."

This book tells a story of how things are, or perhaps how they might be—or used to be, on a true-to-life ranger district. It should be understood that ranger districts come in a wide variety of sizes, shapes and work-loads. Some are located adjacent to cities and often feature outdoor recreation as a predominant activity. Some contain large and valuable stands of timber, mineral deposits or expanses of rangelands, so that work-load, staffing and management emphasis tend to reflect those resources. Some are remote, with the ranger station located "in-the-woods" rather than in a community. Some have large acreages of designated Wilderness or Wild and Scenic River corridors. All support wildlife populations, and all rangers have the challenge of balancing user demands and public priorities within the multiple-use context. Rangers have a great deal of responsibility, comparable to managing a complex business. And rangers have, or at least used to have, considerable delegated authority to make important decisions regarding land use without seeking approval at higher levels in the Forest Service.

The fictional Elk Creek Ranger District in this story may or may not be "typical" within the entire National Forest System; it may not be possible to depict a truly typical district, because there is so much variety. But it does represent a realistic, well-balanced work-load district, with normal problems, challenges and management opportunities.

I do not apologize for my ardent support for the Forest Service and for the concept of multiple-use management of the National Forests. It is the law of the land, although recent administration policy has moved in other directions. And I acknowledge a blatant endorsement of Foxtrotting horses. This breed, developed in Missouri and now used extensively on ranger districts in the west, represents the most versatile pleasure horses found anywhere.

Some of the terminology may be unfamiliar to some readers. A Glossary of Terms is in the back of the book to provide definitions (the symbol * is used in the text).

A "Cast of Characters" will help readers keep track of all the people; an "Organization Chart" explains the different administrative levels; references to other books are available as background; and a map is included to assist readers who want to visualize the Elk Creek Ranger District and places mentioned.

I hope you enjoy this story and perhaps gain a better understanding of the mission of the Forest Service and the duties of a forest ranger.

CHAPTER I

THE TIMBER SALE

The telephone ringing in the Elk Creek Ranger District Office that Monday morning in late April seemed to have more urgency than usual, but no one was answering. District Business Management Assistant Mildred Bronson had taken the morning off for a dentist appointment, and Receptionist Rita Vigil was busy making photo-copies of a report due in the forest supervisor's office the first part of the week. Apparently the voice-messaging machine was turned off or not working, because on about the tenth ring, Ranger Lawrence E. (Larry) Weaver III called out, "Isn't someone going to get that?"

District Forest Ranger Larry Weaver and one of his three primary assistants, Tom Cordova, who handled timber, fire, lands and minerals, were huddled over a drafting table reviewing the layout of the proposed Bear Hollow timber sale.

On the twelfth ring, Wildlife Biologist Beth Egan picked up the phone. She was on her way out to read browse transects* on Horse Mesa, when she realized that no one seemed to be answering the persistently-ringing telephone.

"Boss, it's Peggy on line one, and it sounds urgent," Beth announced.

"Must be, thanks," said Larry, "she hardly ever calls me at work."

"Hi, Hon, what's the problem?" he asked, trying not to sound critical.

"It's Ernie," she said, "he's been expelled from school for fighting!"

"Fighting?" Larry asked in surprise, "That doesn't sound like our Ernie. He normally gets along just fine with everyone."

"Principal Matthews said that he and Billy Crawford had a bloody battle on the school steps just before the bell for first period. And there were a couple of others helping Billy by grabbing Ernie and holding him from behind. He's all skinned up, but Mr. Matthews says that Billy and the other two are in worse shape, and he thought that Ernie must have been the aggressor, although all four have been expelled!" It was apparent that Peggy was very upset.

"Hold on a minute, catch your breath, Peg," said Larry. "Do we need to take Ernie to the doctor?"

"I don't think so," Peggy answered, "It looks like iodine and band aids will take care of the surface. I've already cleaned him up with soap and warm water, although he objected to being treated like a little kid. But he's been expelled, Larry, and he doesn't even want to tell me what happened!"

"Sounds like he's acting like a little kid," Larry replied. "Billy's dad is Bill Crawford, the foreman at the sawmill. I think I can guess what it's about. Do you want me to come home right now?"

"No, I don't think so," she answered, "but we're supposed to meet with Mr. Matthews tomorrow afternoon along with the Crawfords and the other parents. I don't even know their names."

"Okay then," said Larry, "but I'll come on home at noon. We're working on this sale revision, and I need to go by the mill and take some forms to Clark. See you after a while. And tell that son of ours to spend the day with schoolwork. This shouldn't be just a day off for him. Doesn't he have a big science report due this week?"

"He does, if he gets back in school," his wife replied. "Okay, I'll see you in a while," and they hung up.

"What was that all about?" asked Tom, as he stayed busy with the sale area maps.

"Oh, I guess maybe our timber controversy is spilling over into junior high school," Larry answered. "Ernie's been kicked out of school for fighting with Billy Crawford and some other kids."

"Not Ernie!" Tom exclaimed, "Not our future forest ranger, who is a friend to all. I wonder if Bill Crawford has been telling his kid it's our fault that the mill has had to cut back?"

"I should know more about it tomorrow," Larry answered, and he grabbed his hat and stepped toward the door.

"I'll be back this afternoon, Rita," he told the receptionist, "I'm going by the mill and then home for lunch."

"Okay, boss. Sorry about the phone. I'd forgotten that Mildred wasn't here, and I had my head down and locked over that copy machine."

"No problem," Larry said as he headed for his pickup.

Larry Weaver was a vigorous, thirty-eight-year-old, lean and athletic at six-foot-two, and 190 pounds, with thick brown hair and dark eyes. His face was tanned from an abundance of outdoor activity. A Vietnam veteran, he had served on an aircraft carrier in support of the Navy's air attacks. He seldom talked about that experience. After discharge, he went to forestry school at Colorado State on the GI Bill to prepare for the Forest Service career he had always planned.

Larry reached the truck in about ten long strides, started it and buckled his seat belt as he reached the street, driving north toward the Alliance Sawmill.

The sawmill was about a half mile out of town, and Larry pulled into the employees' parking lot near the scaler's shack. The Forest Service stationed a scaler at the sawmill to measure government logs as they went into the mill. His duties were to check the length and diameter of the logs to determine volume, and to deduct the defective portions of each log to arrive at the net volume upon which payment to the U.S. Treasury would be made by the timber company.

District scaler Clark Brightfeather had a workbench in the corner of the shack, and when there was free time or delays in the mill, Clark would often work on his silver and turquoise jewelry, simply keeping track of the time involved in doing such personal work and recording it accordingly. That was just what he was doing when Larry tapped on the door and called, "Anyone around?"

"Sure, boss, come on in," answered Clark, "I was just finishing-up this squash blossom. There's been about a dozen logs go though all morning. They're working with a cut-back crew at about quarter speed. Gives me time to fit some stones."

Clark's dark eyes sparkled, revealing his cheerful nature. Short and stocky, with black hair and bronze skin, Clark had the classic high cheek bones, but not the typical lean frame of his ancestors.

"Let me have a look," Larry said as he examined the necklace. "Wow, that's a beauty, Clark! You should enter it in the state fair and get a little free advertising."

"I'm not sure I need the advertising," Clark replied. "The Trading Post in town buys everything I bring them now. And they keep asking for more."

"Yeah, well maybe you could raise your prices some with a blue ribbon to show them," said Larry, "Think about it. But hey, the reason I came by, besides the chance to admire your jewelry, was to bring you these accident forms to fill out. When that bandsaw broke last week, you were lucky not to lose an arm or worse. The saw operator was lucky too, even if he did end up in the hospital with a chewed-up arm and, I guess, the loss of a good deal of blood. Have the investigators reached any conclusions about the spike in the log they were sawing? And how in the world did a spike or nail get through the metal detectors?"

"It was a ceramic nail, Larry. They found it countersunk well into the log. The debarker didn't even clip it," Clark answered, "but it shut down the mill for five days. Guess that was the objective."

"Yeah, I'm sure it was," said Larry. "Anyway, you can drop the forms by the office when you're done. If you need any help with them, just ask Mildred or Tom. See you later, Clark. And you take care!"

"Okay, thanks boss, see you later," Clark replied as Larry hurried out.

Larry turned back toward his truck and nearly bumped into Bill Crawford, who was fast-stepping toward the mill. "Hey Bill," said Larry, with as friendly a greeting as he could manage, "how's it going?"

"It's going pretty slow if you want to know," Crawford snapped back. "Our single shift is going in slow motion, and the log deck is just about empty, did you notice? And we've fished all the sinkers* out of the mill pond."

"I sure did notice," Larry replied, "and I know the accident last week didn't help either."

"That was no goddamn accident, ranger. It was a deliberate act of sabotage by those 'eco-freaks' from Wilderness Plus. They're doing their best to put us out of business by cutting off our log supply with their stupid appeals. And now by terrorizing our sawmill. And this time they've used ceramic spikes to get past our metal detectors," Bill Crawford scowled.

"I doubt if Wilderness Plus did the spiking, Bill," Larry said. "They're bent on stopping or at least slowing down our timber sale program, but I don't think that malicious vandalism is part of their 'MO'."

"Think what you want, ranger," Bill snapped back, "I

think they'll do whatever it takes. I heard your forest supervisor got a phone call from the White House telling him to withdraw a sale over on the Granite Peak District. The Vice President gets his orders from those well-organized tree huggers, and they're calling the shots! You'll be lucky to get the Bear Hollow sale on the market. And even if you do, by some wild chance, we'll be lucky if we can buy it. Everyone needs logs!"

"Well, Tom's working to finalize the Bear Hollow sale now," said Larry. "And if we're lucky, as you say, we should be able to advertise it in a couple of weeks. The environmental impact statement has been out for several months, and we've addressed all of their concerns. As you know, it's mostly bug-killed and fire salvage,* and the appellants have just about run out of reasons to question it. I'm hoping the forest supervisor will turn down the appeal."

"By the way, Bill, did you hear from your wife or the junior high this morning?" Larry asked. "Seems our kids got into a scuffle and got sent home."

"Yeah, I heard about it,"answered Bill. "Mary called and said Billy has a broken nose and a split lip, and two of his buddies are banged up too. How 'bout your kid?"

"Peggy says that Ernie will be okay," Larry replied. "Do you know who the other two were? Do their dads work here at the mill by any chance?"

Bill responded with a scowl, "Yeah, they do, as a matter of fact, or they did before we had to cut back to one shift. Why do you ask?"

"Oh, I just have a hunch they may have been arguing about the Forest Service timber sale program, or lack of it. It's a shame that this issue has to impact even our kids, if that's what it was," Larry said. "Guess I'll see you in school tomorrow," and he got into his pickup and started it .

"I agree with you on that one, ranger," Bill said into the

pickup window, "Kids need a chance to be kids without worrying about such things as timber sales and sawlogs."

Lawrence Ernest Weaver IV used his middle name, because he figured that there were enough Larrys or Lawrences in the family. Although he was just a fourteen-year-old eighth grader, he was big for his age. He was already nearly six feet tall and gangly as a typical teenager. He had known what he was going to do with his life ever since he started school. He was going to be a fourth-generation forest ranger; at least that was his plan. He had visited the forestry school at the state university, and he understood what he needed to do in high school to be accepted. Ernie went with his dad to the ranger district as a formally signed-up volunteer whenever he got the chance. He could shoe a horse (not many rangers in the region could do that anymore; his dad was an exception). He knew how to cruise and mark timber,* and he certainly knew how to clean a campground and build a trail. There was probably no other eighth grader anywhere as well prepared for a career in forestry.

His mother, Margaret Blair Weaver, called Peggy by her friends, was thirty-six, tall at five-foot-nine and slender, with light brown hair and pale blue eyes. Active with her family, their church and in the community, she was a rarity, a stay-at-home mom.

Peggy and Larry had met in college at a dance at the Newman Center. They were both juniors, he in forestry and she in business administration. It was a classic "love at first sight" situation and they were married within a year, despite some early objections from her parents, who were concerned that she might not finish school. Being married, Larry's GI Bill check increased enough so that with her scholarship, his part-time job in the school cafeteria, and low rent married-student housing, they got by in their senior year without help from either of their parents, although it had been offered. After graduation Larry took a job as a "junior forester" on a heavy workload ranger district in northern Idaho, and Peggy became office manager in a small law office in the same town. When Lawrence Ernest Weaver IV, Ernie, was born two years later, Peggy's business career and their relatively comfortable income were both put on hold. In another two years, Jill was born, and soon after that Larry got an assistant ranger's job in Montana with promotion. This helped solidify Peggy's status as a stay-at-home mom. Another assistant ranger assignment, with additional responsibility involving a major recreation-river in southern Idaho, helped prepare Larry for a district ranger position, the job he had wanted from the start. After just three years as ranger on a small district in Wyoming, he was selected for a larger workload district, and so they had moved to Elk Creek seven years ago. They considered it their best move yet despite the timber controversy that plagued the district.

When Larry walked into the kitchen, after kissing his wife, he looked at Ernie and asked, "You're a mess; what does the other guy look like?"

"Oh, you're terrible!" Peggy exclaimed, "You're supposed to be upset, not joke about it! This is no joke. Your son has been expelled for fighting in school."

"I know," said Larry, "it's a serious matter, but it's not the end of the world. What happened, son, what were you fighting about? And don't tell me, 'nothing'."

"Well, dad," Ernie said reluctantly, "you know that everyone in school knows that I'm planning to be a forest ranger when I'm grown. Well, Billy Crawford and a couple of his pals stopped me on the way into school and said that by the time this administration gets done, there will be no Forest

Service and no National Forests. They said I might as well figure on being a park ranger, or maybe a park custodian. That's not true is it, Dad? We'll always have National Forests won't we?"

"Is that when you hit him?" asked Larry.

"Well, no," Ernie said, "But when he kept going on about it, I just pushed him a little. That's when his buddies grabbed me, and I just started swinging. Before I knew it everyone was swinging and ducking and pushing. Then a couple of teachers and the principal started hollering and grabbing us. The next thing I knew, I was sitting in the principal's office and he was calling Mom on the phone. I didn't really pick a fight, dad, it just happened."

"Well, I can't fault you too much if that's how it happened," Larry responded, "but it's a serious business, getting kicked out of school. That could crimp your plans for high school and college—and beyond."

"You know I'm not going to let that happen, Dad," was Ernie's reply. "I'll do whatever it takes to straighten this out. I'll even apologize to Billy Crawford if I have to. He's not a bad kid, really, he just pulled my chain this morning and I lost my cool."

"You may well have to apologize, young man," interjected Peggy, "and serve detention time too, and no telling what else Principal Matthews may have in mind. You'd just better stay humble!"

"Oh I will, Mom, but those guys better knock off that park ranger stuff; that's not a joke either, not to me."

"You're a little thin-skinned, aren't you, pal?" Larry said. "There are times when you're going to be kidded in this life, and you need to be able to take it."

"Oh, I can take it, Dad, but Billy wasn't kidding. He said something about the sawmill closing if there aren't more logs, and it's the Forest Service's fault. Is that so, Dad?" asked Ernie.

"Well, you know the trouble we've been having getting timber sales through the appeal process and on the market," Larry sighed. "They can say it's our fault if they want to. It's a fact that this administration has made it tougher to do our job. They seem to side with our environmental critics on every controversial issue. I don't know which is worse. A few years ago we had an Agriculture Department that wanted us to offer more timber for sale than we could sustain. But then the chief was able to put up enough 'passive resistance' to get us through it. Now we have a chief who seems to agree with the people in the White House. He apparently thinks that multiple-use means 'fish and wildlife' and very little else. And we work for the administration, so it makes it tough. If Congress would stand up to the administration a little more, it would help. Trouble is, if we get a change in the next election, we could flip-flop and be back to pressure for overcutting. Too bad politics has to be so extreme. I wish they'd set their policies based on sound science and good inventory data, but that may be too much to ask of politicians." Larry looked at his son and said, "That's probably a lot longer answer than you bargained for, pal, sorry."

"No problem, Dad," Ernie said, "I need to know this stuff, and I'm glad you vent like that once in a while. And I know enough to keep it to myself, don't worry."

When Larry finished lunch and was ready to head back to his office, the phone rang. It was Tom Cordova, and from the sound of his voice, Larry could tell there was something wrong.

"They've struck again, boss!" Tom exclaimed. "Another spiked log went through the bandsaw, apparently just a few minutes after you left the sawmill this morning."

"How bad was it?" Larry asked. "Was anyone hurt?"

"I'm not sure," Tom said. "I'm on my way to the mill right now. Want to meet me there?"

"I'll see you in about ten minutes," Larry said, and he kissed Peggy, grabbed his hat, got in his pickup and drove to the sawmill.

The ambulance and sheriff's department car parked at the mill were indicators that someone or ones had indeed been injured by the lethal flying metal of a broken bandsaw. Tom was there when Larry arrived, and he was relieved to see Clark Brightfeather, apparently unhurt, as they entered the mill. Emergency medical technicians were working on two people, one sitting upright, the other stretched out on a gurney. Deputy Sheriff Virgil Craft was taking pictures of the bloody scene.

"How are they, Bill?" Larry asked the sawmill manager.

"It could'a been worse, a damn sight worse!" Bill Crawford replied with disgust and bitterness in his voice. "It nearly took my bandsaw operator's arm off. The EMTs have the bleeding stopped and he's on his way to the hospital in Centerville, as soon as they can get him in the ambulance. The other guy was sorting boards and just got clipped on the shoulder by a piece of flying metal. He was really lucky! They bandaged him up, and it looks like he'll be okay. But by damn, ranger, this vandalism business has got to stop!"

Virgil Craft had put his camera away and started digging with his pocket knife into the remaining part of the log being cut. "Another ceramic spike," he said. "You'd better figure a way to detect those things before someone gets killed around here, Bill."

"We're working on it, with all the big profits we're making these days," Bill Crawford said sarcastically. "About the best we can do right now is to put up some sort of Plexiglas shield in front of the operator. In the meantime, we'll probably just stay shut down. We're just about out of logs anyway."

When the ambulance left, sirens blaring, Larry and Tom went back to the district office to resume their work on the Bear Hollow timber sale.

Tom Cordova had come to the Elk Creek District five years earlier with a reputation as a malcontent and a troublemaker. Larry had accepted him with this knowledge and had made it a personal objective to salvage an otherwise capable professional employee. They had several run-ins early on, but Tom soon realized that Larry was not only a demanding boss, but an understanding and considerate one as well. Larry had given Tom a choice: perform his assigned tasks and get along with the other district employees or prepare to face adverse personnel action and possibly eventual removal. Tom had seen the light and decided to become a team player and model employee. It had been that way ever since, to Larry's extreme gratification.

Bear Hollow was about a six-million-board-foot* timber sale, mostly salvage (removal of dead or dying trees) and thinning in a relatively flat and accessible part of the three-quarters-million-acre Elk Creek Ranger District. The main haul road was already in place, and only about twelve miles of temporary roads would be needed. Appraised* to the Alliance Sawmill in the town of Elk Creek, this sale should put about $240,000 in the U.S. Treasury with another $90,000 returned to Adams County for use on roads and schools, after allowances for road construction, obliteration, slash disposal* and cleanup. Predominately ponderosa pine, with some Douglas fir and white fir in the canyons and gentle north slopes, this sale was desperately needed by the Alliance Timber Company and sawmill, but the district would surely receive bids from several other timber companies 200 miles or more away. Tom had done a good job in laying-out the sale, providing for wildlife needs and erosion control and minimizing conflicts with dispersed recreation and permitted grazing in the sale area. It shouldn't have been controversial, but it was.

A local environmental group, Wilderness Plus, prompted by state-level preservation groups, had appealed an earlier version of the Bear Hollow sale. Larry, knowing that Rio Verde National Forest Supervisor Frank Johnson wanted to avoid controversy and battles with the well-organized environmental groups in the area, decided it best to withdraw and revise the sale proposal. Wilderness Plus President Duane Selzer and Resources Chair Earl Ashworh had agreed to a field review of the sale area. But each time a review was scheduled in recent weeks they called to cancel, citing conflicts with other urgent business of their organization.

Alliance Timber Company, once the most prominent and thriving business in Elk Creek, had been forced to cut back from an around-the-clock, three-shift operation to one shift, and that was often shortened or canceled for lack of available sawlogs. Financial impact on the community had been devastating, with mill workers as well as woods crews* laid-off and forced to seek other work or go on public welfare. There was bad blood in the community as well, with sawmill-dependent families resenting what they considered frivolous interference by the "tree-huggers" and lack of support by the Forest Service.

Traditionally, the Elk Creek Ranger District had offered at least eight or nine million board feet in timber sales per year, an amount that was sustainable* according to inventory figures and projected long-term sale planning for the district. The recently-completed forest plan had cut the Elk Creek District's average share of the forest's allowable sale quantity* (ASQ) to five-million-board-feet.

A quarter of the district's timber was in inventoried roadless areas* and the "threatened" Goshawk was believed to nest somewhere within the ponderosa pine type of the district.

Larry and Tom had worked hard to make this sale acceptable to all concerned, but Wilderness Plus was unconvinced. Duane Selzer and Earl Ashworth had seemed pleased with the various wildlife provisions and other mitigating measures in the revision. But a few days after each meeting and review of the latest changes, one or the other would call to say that after discussing it with some of their colleagues at the state capital, they thought that more changes were needed. Tom was especially frustrated with their tactics, and he told Larry, "I think their real objective is to put the mill out of business and stop all timber sale activity on the whole damn district."

Tom Cordova's black eyes flashed. At five-feet-eight and slightly built, with dark hair and olive skin, Tom's temper was bigger than his stature. That temper had gotten him in trouble before, but lately it had been under control, thanks largely to Larry's supervision.

Larry couldn't disagree with Tom's analysis, but he knew he had to work with Wilderness Plus, as well as with timber operators of the area to make the district's timber sale program "acceptable."

The session in Principal Matthews' office the next afternoon was almost a non-event. All the parents and boys were there and everyone acted humble. Larry had expected Bill Crawford to say something critical about the Forest Service or about the plight of the sawmill, but it didn't happen. After hearing the boys' stories of what led up to the fight and noting that they appeared contrite, Mr. Matthews decided to give each boy two weeks of detention, staying after class for an hour a day in study hall. And they were put on probation for the rest of the semester. That was only about three weeks away and then summer vacation would start. Ernie felt lucky that was all of it, and his parents reminded him how lucky he was too.

That evening at the Weaver family supper table, Larry asked, "Well, did we learn something from this experience, guys? I know I learned that we can work through these kinds of problems if we stick together as a family and think straight."

"I guess I learned to have patience and not jump to conclusions," said Peggy, "and to have faith."

"Well, maybe I learned something about keeping my temper," added Ernie, "and maybe to take some ribbing about things that are serious to me."

Twelve-year-old Jill, a sixth grader at Elk Creek Elementary spoke up, her blue eyes smiling and her blond ponytail bouncing. "I'll bet that Billy Crawford learned not to mess with my brother!" she said. Larry and Peggy smiled at each other.

Thus concluded the fighting and expulsion incident at Elk Creek Junior High.

Things got better on the Elk Creek Ranger District as summer arrived. By some miracle, the forest supervisor's appeal decision, affirming the Bear Hollow timber sale, was upheld by the regional forester. Apparently Tom's hard work in developing mitigating provisions, especially for fish and wildlife, done with Beth Egan's help, had paid off.

The Alliance Timber Company submitted the successful bid. They offered $125 per thousand board feet for the live ponderosa pine and Douglas fir, $80 per thousand for the white fir and $65 per thousand for the salvage. Their provisions for road maintenance and temporary road construction and later for obliteration were judged acceptable, as were those for slash disposal* and cleanup.

Tom Cordova turned his attention from sale preparation and environmental analysis to sale administration. An engineering crew from the forest supervisor's office was detailed to the Elk Creek Ranger District for three weeks to assist with layout and construction supervision of the temporary roads. They would occupy the crew quarters building, normally used by seasonal firefighters in dry years.

Alliance Timber Company added a second shift at the sawmill, and all was well in the small town of Elk Creek—at least for now.

CHAPTER II

RIDING THE RANGE

"What a great day for a ride in the woods, dad!" Ernie found it hard to suppress his excitement.

"It's not just a ride in the woods, pal," Larry admonished, "It's a work day for me and you get to go along as a volunteer. I guess you're taking a day off from your Boy Scout Eagle project. How's that going?"

Ernie was building a nature trail complete with interpretive signs at Moose Lake Campground. He had help from several younger scouts, but with summer vacation just starting, he wasn't able to get any help this week.

"It's going great, dad! I'm more than half done with it," answered Ernie, enthusiastically. "I just have to harden the slope* where it comes out of the campground and haul up some rocks for the switch-backs. And oh yeah, I need to rout the letters* on the signs and put them up. Beth Egan gave me some help with the wording and suggestions on locations. The project's going great!"

"That's neat," said Larry, "A mile-long, signed loop trail will be a fine addition to Moose Lake Campground. I'm proud of you for the work you're doing there, son."

Ben Foster was district staff for range, watershed, recreation and wilderness. When he came to the job, it was called assistant ranger, and getting used to the new terminology hadn't been easy. Ben was a big man at six-foot-four and 220 pounds, with sandy hair and a cheerful nature. He had been on the Elk Creek District for about four years and was ready for promotion to a district ranger job himself. He and his wife, Jean, were excited about the prospect of his own district. He had applied for several ranger vacancies but had not yet been selected, a fact that puzzled Larry.

Like Larry, Ben Foster was a throwback, an old-style Forest Service employee who believed in hard work and was willing to put in long hours to get the job done, whatever it was. He had come from an impoverished background. His father had died when he was only twelve years old, and Ben had been the "man of the house," helping his mother put his younger brother and two younger sisters through school, including college, by working as a farrier, shoeing horses and mules, beginning when he was just sixteen. Also like Larry, Ben was a Vietnam vet, an infantry rifleman, and had gone to college at Utah State on the GI Bill. Because of their many similarities, Larry and Ben had formed a bond, a friendship, that was more than just a normal ranger-assistant ranger association. Larry knew that he could count on Ben to do any job he was assigned and do it well. And Ben knew that Larry would back him on any controversies in the tough job of getting compliance with grazing allotment plan implementation.

Ben had the range analysis and management planning job up-to-date on the Elk Creek District. He had worked with grazing permittees to get solid, workable plans. He and Larry had also started the process of converting community allotments,* those grazed by several permit holders, to association permits or grazing agreements, where one permit was issued to a grazing association, which then took on more of the responsibility for their own management. It was a selling job. Individual permittees had to be convinced that it was safe and also in their best interest to give up those permits in favor of a grazing agreement, where the association held the permit. Under such an arrangement, the association had the flexibility of stocking the permit for a given year without regard for the numbers of cattle that individual permittees had previously been allowed. That way, if one rancher was short on cattle one year, his neighbor might run more, which wasn't allowed with individual permits. Responsibility for maintenance of range improvements, such as fences and water developments, was with the association under this provision, as well as the requirement for keeping livestock numbers within the permit total and following the management plan as agreed to previously.

The Sandstone Allotment, formerly a community allotment* with twelve permittees and a total of 430 cattle, was one that had converted. It hadn't been an easy task; a unanimous decision by all members was required. After that, the Sandstone Association showed promise of being a real success. Their elected officers seemed to understand the arrangement, and each member was doing his share of assigned fence maintenance. Eartags* had been issued to the Association for 430 cattle. A range rider was hired, actually one of the Association members, Hank Eden, took the job. His main task was to assure good livestock distribution, mainly by moving cattle out of the riparian* meadows and away from water, where livestock tend to congregate.

The Sandstone Allotment had a simple three-pasture rest-rotation grazing plan, with a season from 1 June to 30 September. The three pastures were about equal in size and carrying capacity, so it was a simple matter of starting out in one unit, moving to a second unit about half way through the season, and resting the third unit completely. The following year, the previously-rested unit would be grazed first, the former first-grazed unit would be grazed second. Most importantly, the unit that had been grazed last, after seed ripening the year before, would be rested to allow for establishment of new seedlings.

When it was time to move cattle or to gather at the end of the season, all or nearly all of the members would usually show up to help. It was a good arrangement, as most of the members held other jobs besides ranching, and they enjoyed the chance to get out and work cattle a couple of times each summer.

Ben and Larry had scheduled a ride on the Sandstone Allotment with range rider Hank Eden a week after the move to the second unit. They wanted to see how the plan was working and to check on livestock distribution, fence maintenance and grazing plant utilization. It would be a tough, all-day ride covering twenty five miles or more. If necessary, they could come back a second day to finish. They planned to ride through a corner of the rest pasture, cut through a cross section of the first grazed unit, and spend most of their time in the stocked unit checking distribution and improvement maintenance, including stock-water pipelines.

Larry and Ernie were at the district horse pasture barn and corral promptly at 7:00 A.M. with personal horses in Larry's trailer. Ben had already caught his government horse, had him fed and curried and ready to saddle.

Larry's horses, under an equipment agreement* with the Forest Service, and all of the district's horses were Missouri Foxtrotters. The Elk Creek Ranger District and other districts on the Rio Verde National Forest used Foxtrotters almost exclusively because they afforded a number of advantages. They were gentle; they wouldn't try to buck you off on a cold morning after not having been ridden for a while. They were smooth-gaited with a long stride and able to cover long distances over rocky trails or rough terrain in less time than most other horses. And they were easy to catch, to handle, to shoe and to load in a trailer.

Some people in the regional office had expressed worry that forest officers* riding Foxtrotters might not be able to ride with permittees, but would leave them far behind. That theory had been disproved, however, simply by holding the trotters back to a slower pace. In fact, Foxtrotters were just about the ideal Forest Service horse.

And Larry had long since decided on Foxtrotters as the Weaver family horses as well, for many of the same reasons. An early objector to that decision had been Jill, the most dedicated horse lover in the family. Jill had plans to be a champion barrel racer, and she just didn't think a Foxtrotter could compete with the popular Quarter horses. She was right in general, and when it came to Larry's horse, Gifford. Gifford was a tall, sixteen-hand, six-year-old black gelding, with a gait as smooth as glass, but not a lot of speed outside of his foxtrot. But Cougar was a different matter.

Cougar was an eight-year-old, fifteen-one hands tall, bay gelding that was gentle and smooth gaited too. But Cougar could flat out run! He was a perfect fit for Jill. He was a competitive barrel horse, with a great disposition. With Gifford and Cougar, Larry and his family had a good pair of horses for all their needs. The only problem was that only two of them could ride at one time, but they were normally able to deal with that.

On the way to the district pasture, Ernie told his dad, "It was nice of Jill to let me use 'her horse' today, wasn't it?"

"I think she appreciates you keeping shoes on him, son," Larry replied. "And besides, Cougar is not just Jill's horse, he's one of our family's horses. Both of them can use the work today too. We should have a good day."

Larry and Ernie loaded Gifford and Cougar in the big goose-neck government trailer, along with Decker, the district horse that Ben would ride that day. They drove the fourteen miles to the Sandstone Association corral to meet Hank Eden by 7:30 A.M.. The plan was to ride from the corral in a big circle through the allotment and end up back at the corral that evening, hopefully by dark.

"Morning, Hank," said Ben. "All set to show us some country today?"

"Sure am," was Hank's reply, "and I expect we'd better get started if we're going to cover it all in a day."

"Hank, this is my son, Ernie. He's going along today as a volunteer and to learn something about range management. Hope that's okay with you," Larry said.

"Sure," Hank replied, "That'll be fine. Glad to have you along, young fella."

They shook hands all around, mounted up and started up the trail into the rest pasture; the corral was near the center of the allotment.

It was a brisk pace, and Hank soon realized he would have to keep his big brown Quarter horse in a fast, bone-jarring trot if he wanted to keep up with the Foxtrotters the others were riding. And Hank certainly didn't intend to lag behind.

The rest pasture was in good shape. It had been grazed last the previous year, after seed set, and an abundance of new grass seedlings could be seen, even at the fast pace they were traveling. There were signs that past erosion areas were healing, and the creek bottom "riparian" areas looked good too. Even though there were no cattle in the pasture, or at least there weren't supposed to be, drinkers or stock tanks along the pipeline on the ridges were kept full for wildlife use. All in all, the rest pasture was in highly satisfactory condition. The four riders came to the gate into the first grazed unit after about an hour of riding. Ernie jumped down to open the gate, saying it was the least a "volunteer" could do. It also gave him a chance to fish into his saddlebags for a candy bar and some trail mix, which he offered around, but there were no takers.

Ben had set out some production/utilization cages* before the grazing season had started, and he stopped briefly to clip some grass from each one they saw. He used a little .96-square-foot wire ring to automatically convert grams of vegetation clipped to pounds of forage per acre. He stuffed the clipped grass into carefully-labeled paper bags to dry and weigh later. This was the "production" figure. He also clipped a couple of randomly-selected ring locations outside each cage to compare in determining "utilization." From experience, Ben estimated utilization to be close to 50%, which was quite acceptable under the rest-rotation system in use.

Ben and Larry were feeling good about the way the Sandstone Allotment was looking, and they wondered why the Wilderness Plus group had targeted it to challenge for a reduction in permitted numbers, season of use, or both.

About halfway through the first-grazed pasture, the riders encountered a small bunch of eight cows and calves that were supposed to have been moved a week earlier. "You always miss a few," said Hank. "Let's take them along with us and put them through the gate."

This was fine with Ernie, as it gave him a chance to give "Jill's cowhorse" some work.

Larry said, "Yeah, I can sure understand missing some in the gather, but how come three of them have last year's 'blue' eartags? This year's are orange, aren't they?"

"Yes, they are," said Ben. "Hank, didn't you get them all properly tagged before putting them on in June?"

"We put the new orange tags on all that went through the corral on put-on day," said Hank. "Some of the members were late getting there with their cows and might have gone on a day or so later, still wearing last year's blue tags. Come to think of it, I think we had about fifteen or twenty orange tags left over."

"Well, fine," said Ben, "but you'd better note the brands

on the blue-tag cows, and make sure those owners know that they're in violation with the Forest Service as well as with the Association. To make this new arrangement work, the Association needs to police itself." Ben Foster could look and sound intimidating but not unreasonable on such matters. Larry smiled to himself in approval.

"Yeah, I know," said Hank, "we'll try to do better," and he looked sincere in saying it.

Five more cows and calves, all with proper orange tags, were added to the "drive" before they got to the gate into the grazed unit. Again Ernie opened the gate. This little herd seemed anxious to go onto the "fresh grass" and were easy to move.

As he closed the gate, Ernie said, "Hey, isn't it about lunch time?"

"I think he has a hollow leg," Larry told Ben and Hank. "I recall there's an aspen grove near a big meadow about a half mile from here just over that knoll, isn't there, Hank?"

"Yeah, there is," answered Hank, "and I'm about ready to put on the feed bag too! Now if I can just get this old pony to stay up with your walkin' horses for another half mile. . . He stays in a rough jog so's not to get left in their dust. Where'd you get those horses anyway? I think I could use a couple of'em in my line of work. They even seem to know something about cows."

"Well, if you're really interested, there are several Foxtrotter breeders in the state, Hank," Larry replied. "I can put you in touch with them if you like. They're not cheap, though, but I can tell you it's worth a little extra for this kind of horse."

Two logs were on the ground parallel with each other about ten feet apart at the edge of the aspen grove and enough live trees for shade. "This looks like a ready-made spot for a picnic in the woods," said Ernie, as he pulled the saddle and bridle off Cougar and fitted him with a set of nylon hobbles, unsnapped the lead rope from his halter and turned him loose to graze.

Larry and Ben did the same, but Hank tied his big Quarter horse to an aspen tree, saying, "He's too fat anyway. Besides," he joked, "it looks like those hungry horses of yours are gonna take up all the grass 'utilization' in this pasture if we stay here very long."

The four riders sat on the logs facing each other while they opened paper sacks filled with sandwiches and fruit. Larry also had a big thermos of hot, black coffee, which he offered to Ben and Hank.

Ernie had a can of by-now warm rootbeer, in addition to his water canteen. Saddlebags were a great invention! Not only was the rootbeer warm, it was well shaken by the ride, despite Cougar's gentle gait. As he popped the tab, it hissed and spewed out about half its contents. But Ernie was quick enough to get the can to his mouth to avoid losing more. The others laughed, and Hank said, "Maybe those trotters aren't as smooth as they look." Ernie just smiled.

Lunch was eaten in about twenty minutes, while they discussed range condition and the management plan. "It seems to be working fine," said Larry. "The grass is responding well to the rest and deferment it's been getting, and the meadows look better than I've ever seen them."

"Browse looks good too," said Ben, "and the deer we've seen all look fat and healthy. Yeah, I'd say the plan is working all right."

"I'm hoping to see some elk," Ernie interjected. "This looks like good elk country and a good place to hunt, doesn't it, Dad?"

"We'll keep it in mind if we draw-out this fall, pal," Larry answered.

"What I like about this plan is there's just one move during the season," Hank observed. "And the cattle seem anxious to make it, despite the fact we left some stragglers this time. And yeah, Ernie, there are elk on this allotment all right. I think they account for a good part of the utilization you've been measuring, Ben."

"Probably so," answered Ben, "but that's part of the multiple-use you're involved with here. That's one reason your grazing fees aren't as high as you might pay for a private lease."

"I wish our environmental critics could understand that better," said Larry. "Why Duane Selzer and Wilderness Plus want to challenge the grazing that's permitted on the Sandstone Allotment really puzzles me. Incidentally, I've talked to the folks in the Soil Conservation Service office in Centerville, I guess it's the Natural Resource Conservation Service now, about a coordinated resource management, or CRM, effort here, and they were receptive. Since most of the members also have BLM* permits too, and a good deal of private land, CRM looks like a good way to go to resolve conflicts, real or conjured up."

"They're saying it's wildlife conflicts that concern them," said Ben. "We could also involve Glen Romero, the Sportsmen's Club president, as well as BLM Area Manager Steve Underwood and the NRCS folks. And Wilderness Plus, of course. I've seen the CRM process work well in a lot tougher situations than this one. The Society for Range Management, state section, can make facilitators available if we need them. Since we're both SRM members, it's a good fit. By the way, Hank, you and other association members would get a lot out of SRM membership. They have a great practical magazine, "Rangelands," and good meetings at the state and local levels where you can learn a lot about how to make your operation here more effective. You ought to think about joining."

"The cattlemen's organization takes up most of my spare time and dues money," Hank responded, "but I'll give it some thought. And if you get this CRM process started, we'll damn well be participating in that! Sounds like it would sure be worth trying anyway. We don't need to be at odds with our neighbors, even if some of them are 'environmental wackos.'"

With lunch over, they resaddled, fed apple cores to their horses, and got ready to continue the ride. Gifford especially seemed to enjoy the treat. Ben told Larry what a spoiled horse he had, and they all laughed.

Hank spoke up and said, "You know you've really got me curious about those Foxtrotting horses. Mind if I ride one of them for a mile or two?"

"You can ride Cougar for awhile," Ernie responded. "Jill will never know. Besides, I'd like to ride your cowhorse and try him out."

They agreed on the temporary swap, and Hank was all smiles as he moved out on the smooth-gaited Cougar. But Ernie, mounting the big brown Quarter horse with Hank's saddle, dragged a spur across his flank, and the brown horse spun around and started bucking. A surprised Ernie barely managed to get his foot in the unfamiliar stirrup and gather up the reins to pull the brown horse's head up before losing his seat.

"That was a good ride, kid," Hank said, "Sorry about his manners, but I enjoyed watching the rodeo." After about a quarter mile, he said, "Say, Larry, this is about the most comfortable horse I've ever been on. What'll you take for him?"

"You'd have to talk to my daughter about that, Hank," Larry replied, "and I doubt if there's enough money in the whole Association to buy him." All four of them laughed again.

The rest of the ride was fairly uneventful. They saw a

good part of the 430 permitted cattle and only a handful of blue eartags. Livestock distribution was good, and the water developments and fences were well maintained. They saw a nice herd of about forty elk, calves included, which delighted Ernie.

Hank had conveniently forgotten to switch mounts, and his fat horse, with Ernie still aboard, was about worn out when they finally reached the Association corral just before sunset. Gifford, Cougar and Decker were still dancing and seemingly ready to go another twenty-five miles.

Range management was in good shape on the Elk Creek Ranger District, despite environmental challenges.

That evening at the Weaver family supper table, Ernie was anxious to tell his mother and sister about the day's ride. "Anything exciting happen?" asked Peggy.

"Tell your mother about the rodeo," Larry said.

"Aw, Dad!" Ernie replied."I just got a little careless with a strange horse, and..."

"What's this?" Peggy exclaimed, "You were riding someone else's horse? Just what happened out there today, young man?"

Larry enjoyed the next few minutes as Ernie tried to explain the "rodeo" to his mother and a very interested Jill.

"I'm not sure you're going on any more range rides, young man," Peggy said.

"Aw, mom!" was Ernie's final utterance, thus ending that part of the discussion.

"By the way, Jill," Larry said, "we had a chance to sell Cougar today. Hank Eden really liked him and wanted us to quote a price."

"No way, Dad," Jill replied, her face flushing red, "Just tell him that Cougar is not for sale!"

“That’s about what dad told him,” Ernie said. “but I wonder what he would have given....?” And Ernie ducked as a wadded-up napkin sailed past his head.

CHAPTER III

THE FIELD TOUR

An important item in wildlife biologist Beth Egan's program of work for that summer was organizing and conducting a one-day field tour on the Elk Creek District for the interested public. In addition to her fish and wildlife and endangered species responsibilities, Beth was in charge of the district's public information and involvement efforts. These extra duties had been assigned by Ranger Larry Weaver for a specific purpose, to help Beth better understand and thereby support the multiple-use concept. It may have been an unconventional move from an organizational standpoint, but it was paying dividends.

Beth planned to hire a school bus, maybe two if interest was high enough, with her limited information and education budget. She would also rent a porta-potty or two that would be set on and attached to a small flat-bed trailer and hauled along behind.

Although there was no longer a provision for a general district assistant or GDA in the modern district organization, the incumbent, Chet Wagoner, had been "grandfathered" into the position because of his longevity on the district. Chet had agreed to cook one of his famous Dutch oven meals at the midday lunch stop, with help from fire crew foreman Joe Garza. Beth planned her itinerary carefully to include stops to illustrate a full variety of district activities within the time available—one full day. Ranger Larry Weaver and the other two professional assistants, Tom Cordova and Ben Foster, would go along to discuss programs and activities at each stop. It was going to be an interesting, worthwhile and challenging day, and Beth was looking forward to it.

When her planning was nearly finished, she went into Larry's office and asked, "Got a minute, boss? I'd like to review this field tour plan with you and see what you think."

"Sure," said Larry, who had been reviewing the latest progress report from Tom for the Bear Hollow timber sale, "but I'm sure you have it all covered."

"I hope so," said Beth," but I could use any ideas you might have."

At five-foot-three, Beth wore "packer boots"* with high heels because they were comfortable and functional, but also to appear taller. Her auburn hair was closely cropped and her green eyes sparkled as she prepared to discuss details of the plan.

Beth Egan had been a "wildlifer" first and foremost when she reported for work on the Elk Creek District. A graduate of Cal-Berkeley with a biology degree, she had joined the Forest Service intending to "change the world" by convincing this timber agency that there were more important things than forestry or even multiple-use. She, somehow, had survived her first assignment as an assistant to the range and wildlife staff officer on a west coast forest, but when she came to the Elk Creek Ranger District with that attitude, she very soon discovered the facts of life.

Ben Foster had been the first to challenge her ideas that other resources must yield to wildlife needs and values. As they worked together to update the district's portion of the forest transportation plan, Ben had firmly and forcefully let her know that all resource and user needs must be considered, not just the ones she was responsible for. Tom Cordova had reinforced Ben's ideas, but with less diplomacy. By the time the disagreement was elevated to the ranger, Larry could see the makings of a real inter-personal conflict on his district. He arranged to spend additional time with Beth explaining not only how they did business in "this outfit," but, more importantly, why. His logic, patience and persistence had paid off, and Beth eventually became perhaps the most staunch multiple-use proponent on the district. Her assignment as district information officer had been helpful also, essentially forcing Beth not only to understand but support the other resources. The public field tour would be the "proof of the pudding."

"Well, first," she told Larry, as he turned his attention to her project, "we'll do it on a Saturday to get the turnout we'd like. I'm figuring two weeks from now is enough lead-time; we'll never satisfy everyone with our schedule. I'll send notices to the Lions and Kiwanis Clubs, the League of Women Voters, the County Commissioners, the Sportsmen's Club, the Chamber of Commerce and Wilderness Plus. I'll post notices in the library, the town hall, and in Henry's Market and Barney's Cafe. I'll ask the local radio station and the Elk Creek Weekly Bugle to help with public notices and maybe send reporters. People will need to come in and sign up or at least call by the Wednesday before, so we can make firm plans on transportation and food."

"Sounds like all good ideas," Larry commented. "How many people do you think will respond?"

"Well, two busloads. That's eighty people that would strain our budget for this activity. Do you think Chet and Joe can feed that many?" Beth asked.

"I think so, sure," replied Larry. "We have extra Dutch ovens in the fire cache,* including several of the big-fourteen inchers. Where are you getting the food?"

"Henry Salazar told me he thinks this is a fine idea. He said Henry's Market will give us all the potatoes and onions it takes and let us have the meat, beans and bread at his cost. There are extra paper plates, plastic utensils and charcoal in the fire cache, that we didn't use last year and we'll be replacing because they're 'shop worn,' so except for a few minor details, I think we're okay in feeding up to eighty people."

"I'm figuring on starting promptly at 8:00 A.M.," Beth went on. "I know that's early for a Saturday morning, but we need to get started early if we're going to cover it all. I'm planning stops at the Bear Hollow timber sale, Moose Lake Campground, Powder Bowl Ski Area for a look at those slopes in the summer, the trailhead into the Trappers Cache-Sheep Camp Wilderness, the Sandstone Allotment corral as a lunch stop. Then we'll head for last year's oil and gas drilling site, and finally the Elk Creek stream improvement project. We can mostly follow the main loop road through the district. I hope we'll see some wildlife on the way and have a chance to discuss it. What do you think?"

"I think that's a full agenda," Larry replied. "We'll really have to hustle to get it all done inside of ten hours or so; we shouldn't keep a group like this out any longer than that, should we? You'll have to crack the whip as 'wagon boss'."

"Well, we can cut out or cut short a stop or two if we have to, like the Wilderness trailhead and maybe the ski area, but I'd like to try it this way," Beth said. "And another thing, we can have a certain amount of discussion with loudspeakers on the bus or buses. With two buses, you and Tom can be on one and Ben and I on the other.

"Everyone's set to participate. Mildred said she'd like to come along and help any way she can; she says it's a chance to see some of the things she only hears about in the office, and besides, it's on her training plan. Rita will likely come too, and of course Chet and Joe. So, nearly all of us will be involved in this project. And we all should be wearing Forest Service uniforms, clean and pressed, with badges and nametags, don't you think?"

"Of course I do," Larry replied.

Beth seemed very pleased as she added, "And we'll have stick-on nametags for the participants too."

By the following Wednesday, seventy people had signed up for the tour, including representatives from all the organizations that Beth had contacted, and even a few local politicians. She firmed-up arrangements for two buses and two porta-potties and asked Mildred to just cut it off when it got to eighty. Rita, along with her husband, Ray Vigil, agreed to drive the pickup pulling the porta-potty trailer. Chet and Joe would leave at the crack of dawn for the Sandstone Allotment corral to start cooking. Everything was set. Peggy had even signed up to go along, saying it was the best chance she'd ever have to see first-hand all of those interesting district activities.

At 7:45 Saturday morning, they started loading buses, and remarkably they were full and ready to go just after 8:00. The speakers and discussions on the buses turned out to be a good idea with Larry, Tom, Ben and Beth able to cover many points of interest along the way.

At the first stop, the Bear Hollow timber sale area, Tom explained the timber inventory and sale planning processes and the National Environmental Policy Act or NEPA requirements. He briefly discussed the appeals about the sale that had been made to the forest supervisor and told about the various mitigating measures provided. Beth added that she was very satisfied with the wildlife and fish provisions. Tom showed how the trees to be cut were marked with yellow paint at both the butt and breast height,* and the sale area boundary was marked with blue paint. Bill Crawford, from the Alliance

Timber Company, said he was amazed that everything had been done so fast, but pleased that logging was about ready to start. He added that the needed temporary roads were nearly completed. Then Tom asked if there were any questions or comments.

Duane Selzer, president of Wilderness Plus, raised his hand and took the opportunity to complain about how his organization's concerns had been swept aside in both the planning and appeals processes, and how timber priority and other commercial activities dominated the Forest Service's agenda.

When it became clear that it was more of a filibuster than a question or comment, Larry interjected, "Duane, I have to disagree with you, because you know that's just not true. We worked closely with you folks and listened to your suggestions, especially the wildlife habitat needs and the cleanup provisions, and we fit them in whenever we could. And the forest supervisor bent over backward to address your concerns in his appeal decision. We want this to be an enjoyable tour rather than a running debate, so why don't we move on?" Several in the crowd nodded approval.

A few minutes later, at the Moose Lake Campground, Ben told how the camping reservation system works and explained the fee procedure where campers pay for their recreational use of the forest. He described the campground cleanup and maintenance process as done by concessionaires.* He told about Ernie Weaver's Eagle Scout trail project, and Peggy beamed with pride.

Beth explained the fish-stocking program by the State Fish and Game Department at this popular lake, which was nearly forty acres and in a basin, not on a dammed-up stream as were most of the lakes on the forest. She told about the fine cooperation between that state agency and the Forest Service. State Fish and Game Officer Kent Maluski spoke up to agree with the advantages of this cooperative effort.

Beth apologized that the day's schedule did not allow this to be the lunch stop, with tables and all, and that the group would have to "rough it" at the Sandstone Allotment corral.

Tom took a moment to point out the Granite Peak fire tower lookout, 8,500 feet elevation, in the distance on the neighboring district. He told how a good part of the Elk Creek District was covered by the lookout's viewing area. He explained that time did not permit them to go there as a stop on the tour, and added that the road to the lookout was too steep and rough for a comfortable bus ride. He briefly discussed fire management activities on the district, adding that this had been a light "fire year" so far. (Beth felt like kicking herself, because she hadn't thought of having someone make an appearance in the Smokey Bear costume.)

Beth then made an on-the-spot administrative decision to forgo the uphill trip to the Powder Bowl Ski Area, so Ben briefly discussed the special-use permit held by the Powder Bowl Ski Lift Company. He said he would tell about the graduated-rate fee-system, but that only three people understood it, and that two of them were retired and the other was dead. Larry chuckled at this and nodded his head. When Ben mentioned plans for possible expansion, to get a lift and several runs higher up on the mountain, Earl Ashworth, resources chair for Wilderness Plus, voiced his strong objection, saying that only a few people would benefit.

"We're quite a ways from an actual proposal, Earl," Larry commented, "You can appeal it later." Several people laughed, although Larry had not intended it to be a joke.

"As a matter of fact," Larry added, "I'd like to express my views about ski areas on the National Forests in general. Most of the major ski resorts in the United States operate on National Forest land under special use permit. Most have a small amount of private land at the base where lodging, restaurants and other related facilities are located, but the lifts and runs are mostly on the forest. I know of no activity on public land where so many people have so much fun on such a small area, with so little impact on the land. When you say it's only for a few people, Earl, I think you're wrong!"

"I would certainly agree with that," County Commissioner Sam Turner broke in, "And in addition, the County gets good revenue from this ski lift business. All we have to do is plow some snow off the road occasionally."

Powder Bowl Ski Area manager Roger Jones spoke up to thank Larry for his support for the downhill skiing business. Larry went on to say, "Skiing is a wholesome family activity too. We have bought a family season pass to Powder Bowl every year we've been here, and we all enjoy it. Trouble is, it's getting hard to keep up with the kids, isn't it Peggy?" Peggy nodded agreement as Beth asked the crowd to get back on the buses to head for the next stop.

At the North Fork trailhead into the Trapper's Cache-Sheep Camp Wilderness, Ben pointed out the corrals and hitch racks for pack and saddle stock used in the Wilderness. Then he discussed the Forest Service's pioneering efforts in Wilderness designation and management leading up to the Wilderness Act of 1964. He mentioned how the Gila Wilderness in New Mexico was the first administratively-designated Wilderness in 1924. And he told a little about early Forest Service wilderness champions Aldo Leopold, who had been the driving force for the Gila Wilderness, and Robert Marshall, after whom the big Bob Marshall Wilderness in Montana is named. He also discussed the district's inventoried roadless areas* of nearly 100,000 acres, and how resolution was needed, either by Congressional Wilderness designation or else by release* so that other appropriate multiple-use activities could take place.

At this point, Duane Selzer and Earl Ashworth spoke out simultaneously in objection. Duane said, "Oh, those roadless areas, as well as others that should have been inventoried, need wilderness protection! The Forest Service should stop those destructive commercial activities like timber cutting and mining, and the best way to do it is by putting such areas off-limits as wilderness."

There was a murmur in the crowd as Larry stepped forward. "Let me comment on that a minute, fellows," he said. "I can understand and appreciate your priority for wilderness, but to claim the purpose of the Wilderness Act was to'protect' areas of land from 'use' is just not so! The Act calls for designation of special areas, often remote and poorly accessible, but always with unique scenic and other qualities. These were to be areas where it would not be 'business as usual,' where people could have remote recreational experiences, but they would not stay. The Act talks of areas 'untrammeled by man' and 'where man is a visitor but does not remain.' It certainly didn't envision that routine or common areas be so designated so they might be 'protected' or exempt from appropriate resource management and use. The Forest Service has always been the leader in wilderness advocacy. To say that this agency is biased against wilderness and toward exploitation of natural resources is insulting! I suggest we go on to the next stop, Beth." There was spontaneous applause from the crowd, but the Wilderness Plus representatives did not participate.

When the buses pulled into a flat area to park near the Sandstone Allotment corral, the aroma of Dutch-oven cuisine filled the air. Ben and Beth could see in an instant that a discussion of range management activities would have to wait. Chet Wagoner and Joe Garza had their Dutch ovens stacked high, containing a special dish of beef, chicken and pork in Chet's barbeque sauce, potatoes and onions, baked beans and the

SCHOOL BUS

coup-de-grace, Dutch-oven apple and peach cobbler. Hot coffee and iced tea were in big fire-cache vats. Portable roll-up tables were used for serving, but Chet and Joe also served directly from the Dutch ovens. The "chowline" formed quickly, and Mildred, Rita and Peggy helped by passing out the heavy-duty paper plates, cups, plastic utensils and napkins. The line moved rapidly, and this large crowd sat or reclined on the ground, or some stood to eat, balancing plates on corral poles. A few got back on the buses to eat in greater comfort. Everyone got their fill and enjoyed it all. Beth led a round of applause in appreciation of the cooks. Chet and Joe acknowledged in their best "aw shucks,'twern't nothin'" style.

Sandstone Association range rider, Hank Eden, had ridden in to join the crowd, enjoy the meal, and participate in the next discussion if needed, although he vowed he was not a "public speaker." Ben explained the range management program on the district in general and the management plan for the Sandstone Allotment in particular. He told of the grazing agreement with the Association and the responsibilities that it carried. He also discussed the three-pasture rest-rotation grazing system employed on the Sandstone Allotment. He then asked Hank to comment on how the plan was working.

"It works fine," said Hank, "I like it a lot. At least, I do now. I didn't at first. I especially like how easy it is to move the cattle just once during the grazing season. And I like what I see in the way the range is responding. The grass is getting thicker and better. We even have the flexibility, if we need it, to use the rest pasture in a bad year. But I hope we never have to."

"What about wildlife, deer and elk?" asked Earl Ashworth, by this time making an obvious anti-use pest of himself for all to see. "Your cattle are taking away forage that wildlife need. Who looks out for them?"

"Well, I'll tell you," answered Hank, before Ben could speak up, "them deer and elk do a pretty good job of getting their share of the available feed. They're in each pasture before, during and after grazing by the cattle, and what they take is figured into the utilization measurements that these fellas make. I like to see the wildlife too, and it's for sure that we can get along together."

"I don't think I need to add anything to that," said Ben.

Glen Romero, president of the local Sportsmen's Club, spoke up, "You know, I'm very impressed with the wildlife provisions these Forest Service people are making, both in the timber and range programs. I think we should commend rather than condemn them."

"Well, thank you, Glen," said Larry, "Shall we move on?"

"Wait a minute," said Beth, taking charge of her tour. "We have one more discussion here, which Tom Cordova and I will lead, and that has to do with aspen management. This is a good place to talk about aspen, because of the large grove or clone of aspen on the side hill just south of us."

Tom continued, "Beth says 'clone,' because although it looks like a bunch of separate trees, in all likelihood they're all hooked together underground, and in effect, the same organism. Some people may ask the question, 'what is the earth's largest living organism?' You might think it must be the blue whale or a giant redwood tree. Wrong! Some believe it's the Great Barrier Reef off the coast of Australia, all thought to be a single connected organism. I say no, it's probably an aspen clone in Utah, where the largest grove is located. Or maybe it's in Colorado; there's a continuing argument about which state has the largest aspen grove. In any case, it would weigh many millions of tons and cover several thousand acres. Keep that in your 'trivia file,' folks."

Beth went on to explain that aspen, a tree of low to

moderate importance for timber production, is extremely important for wildlife, both as forage and as cover. Our problem here," Beth related, "is that aspen stands tend to stagnate and become unproductive. We have to find ways to stimulate sprouting."

Ruth Osborne, president of the League of Women Voters, local chapter, asked,"What exactly do you mean by 'forage'?"

Beth explained, "In this case it's a food source for wildlife, although cattle and sheep will certainly eat aspen sprouts too, when available."

Tom went on to say, "One good and relatively inexpensive method to get sprouting is the use of prescribed fire.* When we burn an aspen stand under proper conditions, the fire consumes much of the woody material, but sprouting is profuse. That's why aspen is commonly known as a 'fire subclimax species'."

"So fire is one means of stimulating aspen sprouting," said Beth. "Another is mechanical treatment, which is much more expensive. We can contract for bulldozers actually to push it over and mash it down. It's wasteful, it's costly, it's unsightly, but it generally gets the same result, an abundance of aspen sprouts."

"And a third method available to us," Tom continued, "is a timber sale. Aspen has commercial value for pallets, for doorcores, and for paper pulp and excelsior, among other uses. It can also be used for corral poles and for fuelwood. The best part of this option, in my opinion, is that it costs little or nothing, but it puts money in the Treasury. It's a win-win deal."

"Yeah," said Duane Selzer, "but that way, some timber company makes money out of it!"

"And just what the hell is wrong with that?" Bill Crawford asked, indignantly. "I think you guys have really tipped your hand this time. You're simply against any commercial use of the forest. I think these rangers have laid out the options very clearly, and the obvious best one costs the taxpayer nothing; in fact it makes money. You damn tree-huggin' nuts ought to stick to your dickey bird watching!"

"Let's not get into name calling on this tour," Beth interjected, with a harsh look toward Bill Crawford and before Duane or Earl could respond, likely with a retaliatory insult. "Now it's time for us to move to our next stop."

When the buses were loaded and moving out, Rita started the porta-potty-pulling pickup and moved forward, only to hear a piercing scream coming from the trailer. She stopped immediately and hurried back to investigate. Out of one of the porta-potties came a shaken, red-faced and disheveled Ruth Osborne, who had made a quick 'pit-stop' at the conclusion of the last discussion.

Various questions continued to come from an interested crowd on the buses, and answers came over the loud-speaker from Larry, Tom, Beth and Ben. Several deer were seen along the way, and those on the left side of the first bus were lucky enough to see a young black bear scramble up a hillside through the brush.

The next stop was an abandoned oil and gas well drilling site, a flat area of about two acres on a ridge overlooking a deep canyon, which was part of one of the district's roadless areas. An excellent graveled road into the site had not been obliterated because the district had entered into an agreement with the oil company to leave the site as a trail-head into the canyon. The company had agreed to build some corrals at the edge of the clearing, and to place a pit toilet on the site. The local Back Country Horsemen would install several slip-stalls and hitch racks. They would also build a trail nearly a mile into the canyon, connecting with the existing trail system.

Tom outlined the details of the three-way agreement and

went on to discuss several other cooperative efforts involving oil companies on the district. He explained the energy-mineral leasing provisions as administered by the Bureau of Land Management on public land, including the National Forests, which gave leaseholders the right under the law to drill. He contrasted these provisions, which included payments to the Treasury, to hard-rock mineral exploration under provisions of the 1872 Mining Law, which allows prospectors and mining companies free access to public lands with no compensation to the United States, except for a small transaction fee. He explained that this law even allows prospectors and companies to gain title to the land involved, if certain conditions are met.

"In some cases the mining is a subterfuge. The real objective is to get the land in private ownership for recreational or other purposes. It's really a badly-outdated law!" Tom was adamant in his opinion.

The crowd was nearly unanimous in its support and appreciation for the agreement as outlined. But as usual, the Wilderness Plus representatives grumbled about how the Forest Service allows oil companies to run roughshod over the National Forests.

"What do you expect them to do?" asked George Meredith, president of the Lions Club. "The oil companies have lease rights under the law, but they're going out of their way to cooperate in site restoration, and in this case, with a trailhead and other facilities. The public benefits for sure."

State Representative Fred Graves spoke up, "I sure agree with you, George, and this site looks great! If this is an example of how the oil companies cooperate with local folks, I'm all for it!"

Following more discussion about minerals activities and management, the buses departed for the last scheduled stop of the day, a stream improvement project on Elk Creek, namesake of the town and ranger district. This time Rita made certain the porta-potties were unoccupied before following the buses.

The Elk Creek project involved an eight-mile stretch of the stream where check dams, stream bank gabions,* willow plantings and other measures had been undertaken to improve the stream as a fishery, primarily as a spawning site for the threatened bull trout. State Fish and Game officer Kent Maluski joined Beth in discussing the project. Appropriated money from the Forest Service and the state had gone into the project, but most of the work had been done by volunteers, primarily the Sportsmen's Club and the Boy Scout Troop. Glen Romero was reluctant to accept much credit, but he expressed great pride in the project and its cooperative nature.

Beth talked about the importance of healthy riparian* or streamside areas to both wildlife and fish and to watershed values. She showed how buck-and-pole fencing* had been installed to keep permitted livestock from"camping" on the streambanks for an entire grazing season, allowing them only short-term use and needed access to water. She pointed out that the old streamside road had been relocated to near the foothill, a quarter mile from the creek.

Kent told about additional work that had been done on the East Fork and other tributary streams and drainages leading into the main Elk Creek. He reinforced the value of the cooperative efforts and gave high praise to the Sportsmen's Club, the Boy Scout Troop (of which he was Scoutmaster, by the way) and other volunteers.

At the conclusion of this discussion, Beth again asked if anyone had questions or comments about this or about any previous stop on the tour. Duane Selzer and Earl Ashworth had complimentary words to say about the stream improvement project. They said they had enjoyed the tour even if they did get beaten up some.

Lion's Club President George Meredith said he would like to speak for the entire group in expressing appreciation to the district for taking time to show the interested public what was happening on "their land." Several others in the crowd said, "Hear, hear!" This time it was Beth Egan's turn to receive the applause.

The buses pulled into the ranger station parking lot promptly at 6:30 P.M.. Beth admitted it was a good half hour ahead of her projected schedule. She slept well that night.

There was no supper-time discussion that Saturday evening. The kids went to an early movie with friends, and Larry and Peggy chose to relax and reflect on the day's events, which had been gratifying to Larry and informative to Peggy.

Before breakfast the next morning, Ernie and Jill were anxious to hear about the field tour. Larry was the Sunday morning breakfast cook in the Weaver household. He was busy cutting out a big pan of sourdough biscuits to go with his specialty, scrambled eggs with sausage, green chili and onions, that was bubbling away in a big cast iron skillet.

"Why don't you ask your mother?" Larry advised, "She was the unbiased observer."

"How about it, mom?" Jill asked. "Was it good, or just a dusty bus ride through the woods?"

"Well, I don't know how 'unbiased' I am," Peggy answered. "But it was very interesting and enjoyable, I'd say. And I learned quite a lot about what goes on up on that mountain. Your father is good about telling us about district activities, but there's nothing like seeing them first-hand."

"Like what, mom?" Ernie asked. "What did you learn?"

"Well, for one thing, I learned a little about that Eagle Scout project of yours," Peggy replied. "Ben was very complimentary, and the crowd seemed impressed too. I was the proud mother accepting congratulations from several people on the bus."

"What else, mom?" Jill asked.

"I sure learned what a pain the Wilderness Plus people are," she said."I don't know how your father puts up with them. And I was very impressed with the explanations about the Bear Hollow timber sale and the Sandstone Allotment management plan. And I liked the oil well site that's going to be a trailhead, and the stream improvement project, and I guess just about everything!"

"That's a pretty good rundown," Larry said. "But now breakfast is ready, and if we keep gabbing all morning, we'll be late for 9 o'clock Mass at Saint Agnes, and you know how Father Carlos feels about latecomers."

CHAPTER IV
WILD HORSE ROUNDUP

Steve Underwood, Bureau of Land Management Area Manager, left a message with Elk Creek District Business Management Assistant Mildred Bronson, that if the ranger was free, he'd like to meet him at noon for lunch at Barney's Cafe on Main Street.

"Wonder what Steve wants?" Larry asked Mildred.

"He didn't say," she replied, "but I'll bet it has to do with wild horses. I've been reading a lot about them in the Bugle lately."

Mildred Bronson, a widow in her early sixties, had been the Elk Creek District clerk for over thirty years. The title change to business management assistant was something she was still trying to get used to, and she didn't particularly like, despite the lofty title. Mildred's white hair and friendly smile identified her as the district's mother, or even grandmother, figure. Along with Chet Wagoner, Mildred was an "institutional memory" for the district, as well as its budget officer, personnel officer and overall business manager. She was an essential element in the smooth operation of the district, and very well appreciated by her ranger.

"Yeah, I've been reading about those wild horses too," said Larry. "I'm glad it's BLM's problem and not ours."

"Where did the horses come from?" Mildred asked. "I don't remember hearing anything about them when I was growing up here in Elk Creek. Have they always been around?"

"They're commonly called 'mustangs' and they're not actually 'wild' horses," Larry replied, "not in a true definition of the term anyway. Technically, they're 'feral' horses, that is, domestic animals that have been running wild over a period of years. Ranchers in the area used to just turn their mares loose on the public range and put some stallions out there too. That way, they could 'raise colts' with little or no trouble or expense, and all they had to do was gather the offspring as they needed them, either to use or to sell. Sometimes they would release some pretty good stallions, even pedigreed horses, to upgrade the herd. I understand that was the case in this area."

"Well, what's the big deal?" asked Mildred, "why all the controversy?"

"Several things," Larry replied. "One has to do with range condition. There's no management involved, and sometimes the areas where they run get pretty beat out. But that's a minor problem compared to the emotional public issue of the romantic, wild and free roaming horse. A lot of environmentalists took it up as their 'cause,' to protect wild horses, after some officials started killing-off the surplus."

"They killed them?" asked Mildred.

"They sure did," Larry replied. "When there were too many horses for the range they occupied, along with permitted livestock, the responsible government official could request a 'closing order', which authorized them to shoot any horse they could find. Seems like a drastic solution to the problem, but I guess they thought that was the quickest and easiest way to get rid of the surplus. The 'wild horse lovers' finally got enough of that, and they made it a political issue. Lots of people, including school children, started writing letters to Congress and to the President, until the 'Wild Horse and Burro Act' was passed in the seventies. That's the law that protects these animals and makes it difficult to remove them. Later amendments to the law provided authority to gather surplus horses in a humane manner and allow them to be adopted by willing and qualified individuals. The local BLM area currently has a good many more horses than the range will carry, but there are those who don't want any removal at all. I hear that Wilderness Plus is divided on this issue. Some just want to leave the horses alone, and others are worried about the range. I understand that Duane Selzer and Earl Ashworth are on different sides; it's kinda' funny. Guess I'll go eat lunch with Steve and see if this is what he wants to talk about."

Ranger Larry Weaver and BLM Area Manager Steve Underwood both arrived at the cafe at 12:00 noon sharp. They exchanged warm greetings and shook hands, Larry wearing his light green uniform and Steve his tan one.

Steve was Larry's counterpart and equivalent in the town's other main Federal Governmental agency. His BLM Area was over twice as large in acreage as Larry's Elk Creek Ranger District, but its measured workload was considerably smaller, with no timber and considerably less recreation. Their policies regarding wild horses and range management were similar, although BLM was in the Department of the Interior and the Forest Service was in Agriculture. Steve had been Area Manager for five years, which had given Larry and him time to become good friends as well as professional colleagues.

"Glad you could make it on short notice, Larry," Steve said. "I have something to talk to you about that I think is rather important. Let's grab a booth in the back, so we can have some privacy."

"I'm not so sure there's such a thing as privacy at Barney's," Larry replied. "But you lead the way."

They were no sooner through the door when they ran into Ike Elliot, editor of the Elk Creek Weekly Bugle. "Hey, what a break to find my two favorite Feds together!" Ike said, "I have questions for both of you."

Steve knew from experience that he couldn't put off the persistent editor, so he said, "Sure, Ike, what's on your mind?"

"Let's not just stand here," Ike admonished, "Where are you guys sitting? I already had my lunch, but if you don't mind, I'll sit with you a while and see if I can get some of my questions answered."

Ike Elliot had been editor of the Bugle for three years and was a beat reporter for the Centerville Sentinel for five years before that. In his mid-forties, he was short and stocky with thinning brown hair and intense blue eyes. Ike had a reputation for getting to the bottom of any story he tackled. And he tackled lots of stories. Public land issues were among his favorites.

"Fire away," said Steve as he and Larry slid into a back booth facing each other, while the editor sat down next to Larry.

"Steve," said Ike intently, "tell me about this wild horse situation. Rumor has it you're planning a roundup, despite public objection."

"Well, in the first place," Steve countered, "the 'public objection' you refer to is limited to Wilderness Plus, as far as I can tell, and only from part of the group at that. As far as plans for a roundup are concerned, we've been wanting and needing to do that for quite a while now, but haven't had approval from the State Office—or funding for that matter. In fact, that's just what I want to discuss with Larry. We could use some help from the Forest Service. With all due respect, Ike, it sounds like you're trying to make it into a controversy. Newspaper sales a little slow lately?" he joked.

"Oh, you're no fun at all," Ike shot back. "I was hoping you could give me a scoop about a wild horse roundup, where they are, how many you're after, that sort of thing."

"Well, I'll tell you, Ike," Steve replied, "they're in Rock

Creek Valley, and we're not sure yet how many there are or how many need to be removed. As soon as our plans are firm, with funding in hand, I promise I'll give you a call, how's that?"

"Better than nothing, I guess," Ike answered, and he turned his attention to Larry, "I'd like your comments about the tree spiker they have in jail over at the county seat. I hear it was one of those hard to detect ceramic spikes in a Douglas fir log, or snag log, from somewhere on the forest. What do you think should happen to the guy? Didn't it cause serious injury to the head-rig operator at the mill and to your scaler?"

"Hey, one question at a time, please," answered Larry. "In the first place, I hadn't heard that anyone had been arrested. In the second place, if they have a guy in jail, he has to be convicted or maybe confess to the act, before he's considered guilty, doesn't he? And finally, yes and no, Alliance's bandsaw operator was hurt rather seriously, but our scaler, Clark Brightfeather, was only scratched. Actually, there were two incidents of broken bandsaws at the sawmill. Everyone who was involved is okay now, I understand, or at least on the mend. What's the deal on the guy in jail?"

"As I understand it, and it was Deputy Sheriff Virgil Craft who told me this, another deputy over in Centerville overheard some guys talking in a restaurant booth, about like this one, and one of them was bragging about pounding ceramic spikes in some snags marked for salvage logging near the main road through the Forest. The deputy apparently slapped the cuffs on him right there, read him his rights, and hauled him off to jail." Ike looked intently at Larry for his response.

"Isn't that interesting?" Larry remarked. "I guess my comment would be—if they try the guy and find him guilty, I hope he gets some serious jail time. It's about the same as attempted murder in my book. Did they say who he worked for or what group he represented?"

"I guess I just assumed it was a Wilderness Plus member," Ike said, "but I really don't know. That's something I need to check out. I'll give Duane Selzer a call. Thanks, guys!" And the Bugle editor hurried out of Barney's Cafe.

"Wow, the guy's a whirling dervish!" Steve observed. "Why don't we order lunch and then get down to some serious discussion about horses?"

"Whirling dervish?" Larry laughed, "I hadn't heard that expression in years, but you're right. That's a pretty apt description of our local editor."

Just then a young woman with "June Gomez" on her nametag arrived at their table with menus, water and silverware. She said, "You two seemed to be engrossed in your conversation with Mr. Elliot, so I thought I'd wait until he left. Hope that was okay. Today's special is beef stew. I'll be right back to take your order."

Before she could leave, Steve said, "I'll have the special; how about you, Larry?" The ranger ordered a big bowl of homemade chili with extra onions and jalapino peppers. Both asked for coffee, black. And at last they began their intended conversation.

"We tried trapping horses using one-way gates* on corrals built around stock tanks for several years," Steve said. "We were able to catch a few, but not nearly enough to make a difference. I've asked for approval to gather, but I keep getting turned down. I finally got the okay last week, and the promise of money for a roundup. Helicopters, two of them, already under contract for fighting fire, have been ordered, and I'm hoping that fire standby will pay for most of the air time. We're about ready, except for one thing. We need some additional on-the-ground horseback help, and that's where I hope you'll come in."

"How many do you need, when, and for how long?" Larry asked.

"We need three more riders, Larry," Steve answered, "each with at least two saddle horses. We're set to start five days from now, next Monday morning, and I think it will take about three days to gather them, maybe a little longer. We have two big strong corrals, with wide wings, all ready. They're strategically located about twelve miles apart in Rock Creek Valley in the middle of the mustangs' range. I'm sorry about the short notice; I know you guys have plenty to do. Do you think you might be able to furnish us three riders?"

"Yeah, I think so," said Larry. "I can juggle some schedules for next week, and we can be ready bright and early Monday morning."

"What do you mean, 'we'," Steve asked. "I wasn't expecting you to be part of the operation personally, Larry."

"Oh, I wouldn't miss it for the world," Larry said. "And I suspect that Ben Foster and Chet Wagoner wouldn't either. Why don't I have Ben stop by your office in the morning and get the details on your plans and find out exactly where and when to meet?"

"That would be fine," Steve replied, "and thanks, my friend, I'll owe you one."

"There's one other thing concerning these horses that I need your advice about, Larry," Steve continued. "It has to do with reproduction. Just letting the mustang herds expand to problem levels and then rounding up and removing the surplus, hopefully for adoption, is a losing battle. I'm thinking we need to do something positive, maybe even aggressive, to keep these herds from expanding so fast. I heard about some Forest Service and BLM people in Nevada a few years ago that performed vasectomies on some of the stallions. They learned the technique from a local vet, and then just did it themselves after trapping several bands with one-way gates at water holes. Vasectomy is effective in situations like this, as opposed to gelding them, because they still behave like stallions, they just shoot blanks. And that way, they still run with their bands of mares and drive other stallions away. But there's just no reproduction in that band. I understand it works very well. Also, I've been told there's an experimental injection or implant that can be given to mares to retard reproduction. Seems to me we should be taking advantage of such technology and get proactive with 'prevention' rather than just reacting with periodic removal projects. What do you think?"

"Well, I sure agree that a prevention effort would be desirable," Larry replied. "Trouble is, the 'do-gooders' and horse lovers would probably raise the roof if you did it in secret and they learned of it later—which they undoubtedly would. You'd better be open with the public, especially with something as potentially controversial as this is, however logical. I doubt if you have enough lead-time to do anything like that as part of this gathering. I'd suggest you start laying the groundwork now, and try to get it done the next time you need a roundup."

"That sounds like good advice; thank you," Steve said.

At that point, June arrived with lunch, and they turned their attention to serious eating and discussions on other subjects, including the alleged tree spiker in the county jail.

When Larry told Ben and Chet about the roundup, they were eager to participate.

Chet said he had helped with a wild horse roundup a number of years ago, and he wouldn't mind another go at it.

Chet Wagoner was in his late fifties. He had been general district assistant or GDA on the Elk Creek District for over twenty five years. He had been proud to retain that title even though the modern district organization failed to recognize it as appropriate. Officially, Chet was classified a "non-professional," but that was a real misnomer. He was professional in everything he did, and that was just about anything that needed doing on the district. A lean 5'10" and 160 pounds, Chet was the only black employee on the district's permanent work force. A ring of white hair showed beneath his well-worn Stetson hat, which covered a shiny brown pate. His cheek constantly bulged with "chawin' tobacco," but no one ever saw him spit.

Ben went to the BLM office the next morning, and was briefed on the details of their plan. Then Larry and Ben spent most of Saturday morning putting new shoes on the district's six Foxtrotting horses, who were about due for a change anyway. They knew it was important that no old or wornout shoes be lost on such a ride. Larry had re-shod Gifford the week before. He wouldn't take Cougar, because Jill would be practicing her barrel racing on him nearly every day.

Every other district on the Rio Verde National Forest hired their horseshoeing done. Larry did his own shoeing on the Elk Creek District, with help from Ben, a professional at such work, who usually shod the mules. Occasionally Chet would help too, but his old back couldn't take much of that sort of work anymore. Larry and Ben did it to save money for other needs. Larry had learned long ago from his father and grandfather that shoeing was a "ranger's job."

Ernie and Jill were excited when they learned about the wild horse roundup and wanted to go along. Ernie used his most persuasive argument technique in pointing out how much help he could be; he promised to open every gate.

"Sorry," Larry told them, "this was not an open invitation from the BLM, but very specific for three experienced forest officers.* Besides, it's going to be three long, hard days, and probably it won't be as exciting as you're imagining."

"Aw, Dad," they grumbled, reluctantly accepting his decision.

Rock Creek Valley was a broad, sagebrush-covered drainage about sixty miles south of the town of Elk Creek. Various sagebrush thinning and juniper control projects in recent years had improved forage production, but permitted cattle, up to full range capacity, and a growing herd of mustangs had left the area in less than satisfactory condition.

Larry, Ben and Chet were paired with BLM riders familiar with the country. Two other BLM staff formed a fourth pair of riders. They spent the first two days scouting the area to get an idea about locations of the various mustang stud-bands in a twenty-five-to-thirty-mile stretch of Rock Creek Valley. Each pair of riders carried a two-way radio linked to Steve in his control center at the field station near the center of the area.

Larry rode Gifford in the morning and changed to a district Foxtrotter, Badger, in the afternoon. His BLM partner, Jack Fisher, rode a little roan mustang that had been captured four years before, broke* by a state prison crew and used by BLM as a saddlehorse ever since. Although hard and tough, the mustang, Scooter, had trouble keeping up with the long-striding Gifford. When they changed horses after lunch, and Larry switched to Badger, a fifteen-hands-tall, brown trotter, and Jack rode another mustang, the same problem persisted.

"Steve, you're going to have to break down and buy some Foxtrotters for the BLM one of these times," Larry commented at lunch back at camp. "Or else you could turn out some Foxtrotting stallions and upgrade your wild herds." Those gathered for the lunch stop and change of mounts nodded in good-natured agreement.

Ben rode Decker in the morning and changed to Comet, a big bay trotter, in the afternoon. His BLM partner, Bob Lopez, riding Quarter horses, had the same trouble keeping up as Jack had. Chet, riding Chief in the morning and the gray horse, Major, in the afternoon, had the same experience. They kept Rocket in reserve the first day, then Larry took him as his afternoon horse and let BLM riders use the gentle Badger the next two mornings.

Jack told Steve, after riding Badger, "Ranger Weaver is right. The BLM needs to get up-to-date with their saddle-stock."

They slept in bedrolls on the ground or in horse trailers each night and were fed well by a caterer from Centerville. It was not unlike a fire camp, but without the smoke and black soot. Chet remarked that it was like a vacation, not having to do the cooking. Among the four pairs of riders, in two days of scouting, they were able to locate ten stud bands of about twelve to sixteen mares and colts each, some as high as twenty. Steve plotted the general locations on a big map at control center for the helicopter pilots to use the third day. The riders would then be strategically located for a final hazing into the wide-winged corrals after the helicopters brought the bands in, one at a time. Two helicopters working two different corrals, each with two horseback pairs on the ground, made for an efficient operation. The corrals were partitioned so that they would hold up to ten bands each, following initial capture in a big, open pen.

Another innovation, which made the whole operation work better, was use of a "Judas horse," usually a gentle mare or sometimes an old gelding that had been fed in the corral the past few days. A blind of juniper brush was set up in the approach area about 200 yards from the big corral gate, where a BLM man held the haltered mare in the open but on a short rope. As the helicopter hazed a wild band toward the wings of the corral, the mare was released, and when she ran to the corral, the wild ones followed her on in. This was a great aid in avoiding a last-second reversal and possible loss of a band.

The gathering on the third day went smoothly, with experienced helicopter pilots and BLM crew members on the

ground. The Forest Service "trainees," Larry and Ben, caught on quickly as to techniques effective in hazing each band that the "choppers" brought in, into the big corrals.

"One thing to remember," Jack told Larry as the first band approached, "is that it's not the stallion in charge of the band, but a lead mare, who heads up the band and makes the decisions as to where to go. Get her identified and headed right, and it solves lots of problems. But keep your eye on the stallion. He thinks he's in control, and could decide to make a run at your saddlehorse to protect his harem."

"That sounds like good advice," Larry replied,"I hope that Ben gets the word on that too."

But Ben didn't get the word. As the first band he was hazing approached the wings of the corral, a big black stud made a charge at Decker, with ears back and teeth bared. Ben's heavy bat-winged chaps saved him from a serious bite, as he whirled Decker around into a prompt retreat.

"Sorry about that, pard," Bob Lopez, his BLM counterpart apologized. "I should have warned you about what to expect from the stallion."

"I shoulda' known better, Bob," Ben responded. "Besides, I'm not hurt, just a little shaken."

The remainder of the morning went well, and by the noon-time change of mounts, four bands had been gathered into one corral and five into the other. Only one band had gotten away and had to be "re-gathered" by the helicopter.

"That's exceptional," said Steve, "This is a good crew! And we've been lucky that only one band turned back as the riders took the bands from the choppers. When they start to stampede away from the corral they often scatter, and it's darned hard to get'em headed back. This is where the Judas horse really helps!"

The afternoon gathering went just about as well, and by

then, Larry and Ben were experienced and capable "mustangers." By the end of the day, they had fourteen stud bands in the pens, including four that hadn't been located during the scouting phase. Two bands had been lost and later retrieved with some difficulty, but it was an excellent average, all things considered. Steve was ecstatic. "This is way beyond what I thought we could accomplish in three days," he exclaimed.

In total, 276 head of horses were gathered. This included mares, colts and stallions. In addition, several "bachelor bands" of young stallions without harems of their own were brought in. After gelding, these would be the most desirable individuals in the adoption program.

The next several days would be spent by BLM ground crews sorting out the various categories of horses captured and then releasing the revised bands one at a time. Generally, a released band would have a mature stallion and ten or twelve mares that were healthy and vigorous. Several veterinarians, working under contract, would health-check each animal, draw blood to check for infectious anemia and other diseases. A portable lab allowed them to analyze blood in the field so that decisions could be made on the spot. Most of the colts and nearly all of the bachelor stallions would be loaded into trucks and sent to the adoption center. A few of the older mares and some of the stallions that showed signs of physical incapacitation would be shipped to a special, fenced "retirement range" operated by BLM. There they would live out their days, since they were not "adoptable."

In all, 136 head were removed, and 140 were released back into Rock Creek Valley. It was deemed a highly successful operation, and Steve was lavish in his praise for all involved, with special thanks to the three Forest Service folks for their help.

Larry asked Steve if he had informed editor Ike Elliot about the roundup as he had promised. Steve shrugged his shoulders and slapped his forehead, saying, "You know, Larry, that's one thing that I completely forgot! I'll have to tell him all about it when I get back. I took some photos that he can use. Maybe we can get some favorable publicity."

"You'd better think up some good reason that he wasn't invited along," Larry chuckled. "Otherwise that publicity might not be the kind you want."

Larry, Ben and Chet pulled the big gooseneck trailer with seven mustang-chasing Foxtrotters back to the ranger station the next morning. Larry took Gifford on home and was back to work by early afternoon. He told Ben and Chet to take the rest of the afternoon off as "comp time," but Ben was in the office that afternoon too, saying that he had some catching up to do.

That evening at supper, Larry's family was anxious to hear about the wild horse roundup.

"How did Gifford do, Dad?" Jill wanted to know. "Did he learn to herd the mustangs, and was he able to keep up with the BLM horses?"

"You know better than that, sweetie," Larry said. "He ran them into the ground. Not really, but they did have a tough time keeping up with our gaited horses. And old Gifford was just fine hazing mustangs. I think he has a knack for it."

"Was it exciting, honey?" Peggy asked. "These two were really disappointed that they couldn't go along."

"It was deadly dull," Larry answered. "They would have been bored to death. It was mostly standing around and waiting."

"I'll bet!" Ernie said. "By this time I can tell when you're kidding and when you're shooting straight. How many did you bring in? And were there any nice looking ones, or were they all broomies?"

"We caught 276 total and turned about half of them back out. A few of them were very nice looking," Larry replied. "Most were pretty common. But you know, the mustang saddlehorses that some of the BLM folks were riding were pretty nice, and they were tough as nails. And while they couldn't keep up with Gifford, Badger or Rocket, I had to admire the way they behaved and how long they could keep going."

"Do you suppose they remembered their wild days on the range?" Jill asked.

"I guess we'll never know the answer to that one," Larry admitted.

CHAPTER V

THE PARADE

Staff meetings were not a big priority on the Elk Creek Ranger District. Ranger Larry Weaver believed there were better ways for his staff and him to communicate. But this Monday morning the last week in June was different. There was an important agenda item to discuss.

They gathered in the district conference room. Larry was there, along with Tom Cordova, Ben Foster, Beth Egan, Chet Wagoner and Mildred Bronson. Rita Vigil was at the front desk to greet visitors and answer the phone, but she was also listening as best she could.

"Mayor Braggs has asked us to put an entry in the town parade on the Fourth of July," Larry announced. "We need to decide, first if we're going to do it, and second, if so, what form will our entry take? I'm open to your ideas."

"Oh, let's do it!" Beth said eagerly. "It will give us a chance to show what we do, what the forest is all about. I say yes!"

"Why not?" said Tom. "Besides, it might be fun; give us a project we can all work on together. I vote yes, too."

"Well, it's not a vote, you know," Larry said, "but I appreciate your enthusiasm. How about the rest of you?"

"I agree," Ben said. "We can hardly turn down the mayor's request, not if we're part of the community."

"Okay by me," Chet added. "But I don't think a float is what we want. Everyone has a float, and most of them are not so great."

Mildred chimed in, "You're just spoiled from watching the Tournament of Roses Parade on TV, with their elaborate floats made of flowers. Besides, what else could we do to show what happens on the forest?"

Ben said,"How about this? Why don't we use our pack string to show the various multiple-use products and activities? We have five mules and five decker pack-saddles* that we could hang things on. It works out just right."

"Now that's not a bad idea," Chet said. "I saw a Forest Service pack string in that Rose Parade a couple of years ago, and they looked darned good. It would be different for us anyway. But we'll really have to scratch our heads to figure out just what to tie on those mules."

"Yeah, that's right," Tom said. "To show timber, for instance, we don't have a mule big enough to carry a sawlog." The others chuckled, as Tom thought a minute, then continued, "We could tie on some fenceposts and maybe some fuelwood. That shouldn't be too tough."

"Forage is a little trickier," Ben said. "Maybe we could dig up some grass and display it, roots and all. It would show how much root there is on a grass plant, compared to the top. The tough part would be tying it on."

"I think we can manage that," said Chet. "Just bind it up good and hang one big plant off each side of a mule, as Ben says, 'roots and all.' How about using tall wheatgrass?"

"Good choice," Ben said. "And for watershed, or just water, we could simply hang a bunch of plastic waterjugs on one of the mules, and label them, 'WATER'."

"And for recreation," Tom said. "Maybe a miniature picnic table?"

"There's a lot more to recreation than that," Beth said. "But you know, we have some excellent photos showing various kinds of recreational opportunities on the Forest, like camping, skiing, fishing, hunting, hiking, horseback riding—the full spectrum. And they're enlarged to a size that people could see them okay from the sidewalks along the parade route."

"Fine," Chet said, "so we could pack a kind of bulletin board on each side of a mule, and tack those photos on them."

By this time, Beth was openly showing her enthusiasm and excitement for the project. She said, "Wildlife could be the toughest of all, and that's the one we have left. I guess we could show a couple of mounted heads."

"How about something alive?" Ben asked. "Isn't there something we could trap? Something not too big."

"Now that you mention it, there sure is!" Beth replied. "Some beavers are working in the headwaters of Elk Creek, above our stream improvement project. Their dams are spreading water and it's starting to wash out the road. I've been talking to Kent Maluski about the possibility of trapping them out of there and relocating them to another drainage, where they could be helpful instead of causing damage. We could time it so as to be able to use one of them in the parade."

"Tying on a beaver trap with a live beaver in it could be a real challenge," Chet said. "It would scare the beejeebers out of most mules." He thought a minute. "I think maybe old Molly would be a good candidate for this beaver-in-a-trap assignment."

"And how about our old'mule skinner' to pull the string?" Ben asked. "It's your logical task, Chet."

Before Chet could respond, Larry said, "Then it's all settled. This has been a productive session, and again I appreciate your enthusiasm—all of you. Any questions about assignments?"

"Not really," Ben said. "If Tom will get the posts and fuelwood assembled, and maybe the waterjugs, I'll dig the tall wheatgrass the day before. Beth, could you and Mildred help me put the recreation photo-boards together?"

Mildred nodded, and Beth replied, "Sure can! And I'll make arrangements with Kent so we can get the beaver. I'm confident he'll go along with it. It's not a bad idea to show nongame wildlife while we demonstrate State-Forest Service cooperation."

"And I'll get the mules ready, and old Chief too," Chet said, "maybe even wash'em, paint their hooves black, and put a fresh clip job on their manes and tails. Gotta have those U.S. mules looking real pretty for the big parade."

Mildred spoke up and said, "That reminds me, Mr. Wagoner, I was looking through the property records the other day, and I saw a list of the district's pack and saddle-stock. Tell me, if you would, why is it that we have a mule named 'Mildred'?"

"Well, I'll tell you," Chet replied without hesitation. "It so happens that there's a Forest Service tradition that every ranger district that has mules should name one of them for their district clerk. I figured you knew about that, and I thought you'd be honored."

"Somehow it doesn't seem like that big an honor," Mildred said, "And are you certain there's really such a tradition?"

This discussion was still going on as the special staff meeting adjourned that Monday morning. Larry smiled to himself, remembering that the district's employees had not always been so unified.

There was really no time to "practice" very much before the morning of the parade. So when that day came, Chet, dressed in his Forest Service green uniform and shiny badge, lined up the mules at the start of the parade route on Main Street. The mules were washed and polished as Chet had promised, and Chief looked his best too. The mules, wearing their decker saddles and freshly-washed green saddle blankets, were loaded with such strange cargo that they looked at each other suspiciously. As Chet moved Chief out and the mules started walking, they began to shy and balk, and the unusual packs began to shift. Chet maneuvered his parade horse over, to line the mules up at the edge of the street, so that Larry and Ben could pull the latigos* up a little more snugly and tighten the hitches holding the pack loads. Then Chet resumed leading them in a path that went from the center to the edges of the street. He knew it was important to keep the mules moving and not let them stand around and think up mischief, and probably end up getting tangled in their own lead ropes.

Amos carried the wood, followed by Rufus with water-jugs and Ruby with the grass. Next came Molly carrying the nervous beaver in a live trap, tied on top between the saddle's rings. Mildred, the namesake, with photo-boards secured on both sides, brought up the rear. Chet and his packstring's position in the parade was directly behind the all-school band, where Ernie played the trumpet and Jill the clarinet.

This unique equine entry got lined-out fairly well with Chet's persuasion, and they started down Main Street. But it was evident that the mules were uneasy and about as nervous as the beaver in the livetrap tied on top of Molly. Ruby's tall-wheatgrass load appeared to be swinging back and forth, which didn't help her or those behind her to stay calm.

When the all-school band would stop, because the float in front of them had stopped, and they played their music, Chet would circle his packstring to keep them moving and occupied. On the third such stop, as Chet was circling his mules, it happened that a power pole at the edge of the street became an obstacle for the mules to go around.

And they did go around it, all but Mildred that is. She

decided to head up the sidewalk on the other side of the pole, and that one discrepancy, with the spooky state those mules were in, set off a chain reaction.

The mules' halter ropes were not tied hard and fast to the pack saddles in front of them, but rather to "pigtail ropes," light cords designed to break away under an unusually strong pull. This was standard practice on the trail, so that if a mule fell or pulled unusually hard, the pigtail ropes would break and not pull the next mule off the trail or over a bank.

When the pigtail holding Mildred's halter rope to Molly's pack saddle broke, because the power pole had come between them, Mildred passed the others at high speed, at least faster than usual. The normally-docile Molly, startled by Mildred and her strange cargo of large photo-boards going past her, bolted to the left, and Ruby, with her wheatgrass load swinging freely, bolted strongly to the right, breaking both pigtails in front of them. Rufus, not to be outdone, whirled around and started bucking, thus breaking his pigtail and scattering waterjugs all over Main Street.

When mules stepped on the waterjugs, they broke, and the street was soon wet and just a little slippery. Chet spun Chief around in an attempt to grab Rufus's halter rope, and in the process Chief slipped on the wet pavement and almost went down. As Chet grabbed the saddlehorn to pull himself back onto Chief's middle, he lost Amos, who also began bucking and scattering wood along Main Street. Soon all five of the mules were bucking, and four out of five loads were, for the most part, shaken loose and likewise scattered.

Only Molly's load, the beaver trap, the most unlikely one of all, stayed tied on. But that load slipped, and the trap was soon hanging down under poor Molly's belly, which caused her to be considerably distressed.

Larry was stationed about a block up the street and Ben

about a half block in the other direction, just in case there might be a mishap. Both came running to help. Ernie and Jill, seeing the commotion behind them, handed their instruments to the marching musicians beside them, and they too ran to help, wearing their bright blue band uniforms with gold trim.

Tom and Beth were both some distance down the parade route, several blocks from the action, but they could see that something was dreadfully wrong with the pack-string, and they hurried in that direction.

It was all to no avail, too late to reassemble the pack-string and continue down the parade route. The bucking mules, with scattered loads, then began acting like homing pigeons, and headed back up Main Street in the general direction of the ranger district horse pasture.

Only Molly, with load intact, but shifted to a strange new position, kept bucking, and rather than retreating toward the pasture, bucked right into Mayor Braggs's yard.

Mayor Harriet Braggs and her husband, Hamilton, the local banker, were extremely proud of their house and yard on Main Street. It was a showplace in the town of Elk Creek, with manicured lawn and beautiful flowerbeds. The geraniums and pansies were especially beautiful and well tended. And that is precisely where Molly did her level best to unload the alien, now hanging below like a pendulum. She virtually destroyed both the geranium and pansy beds, and then rounded the house toward the backyard.

Despite the holiday, Mayor Braggs had hung a load of clean, wet laundry on the backyard clothesline earlier that morning. Molly proceeded to tear the clothesline down, not on purpose certainly, but down it came just the same, all five strands. A nightgown adorned Molly's head when she finally came to a stop and stood, straddle-legged, with the trap dangling below.

The beaver, dizzy from his wild ride and harrowing experience, had a bloody nose and red, glazed-over eyes. His big, broad tail appeared to be somewhat bent. No doubt he was thinking about how much nicer his life had been yesterday, chomping trees and splashing in the headwaters of Elk Creek.

Jill was the first to reach Molly in the mayor's back-yard. She got there just as Molly had finished shaking the unwanted nightgown off her head and stomping it into the turf of the mayor's manicured lawn. Jill patted Molly's neck gently, calming her down, as she grabbed the halter rope. Then she reached down and untied the ropes that held the beaver trap suspended under the now, much more peaceful mule. The trap hit the ground with a thud, but by now Molly was back to her old self, calm and quiet.

Ernie, who had been distracted by the mule, Mildred bucking down Main Street and scattering recreation-illustrating photos in every direction, arrived on the scene as Jill was leading Molly out of the backyard. At Jill's suggestion, he set the trap upright, made sure it was latched securely, and then he borrowed the Braggs's wheelbarrow that was leaning against the toolshed. With some difficulty, the gangly youth hoisted the trap and forty-pound beaver into the wheelbarrow and maneuvered it around the house to the street. Kent Maluski, who had witnessed the entire incident, arrived a few minutes later with his State Fish and Game pickup to haul the shaken beaver to his new residence in a more remote part of the district. Kent was laughing all the while.

Larry had managed to grab Rufus's halter rope before the big mule could get more than a half block down the street. Only two waterjugs were still hanging from his decker saddle. Ben likewise caught Ruby, who had no trace of wheatgrass remaining as she hurried past his position on the parade route.

Beth was even luckier. With Ernie's help, she snagged

Mildred (the mule, not the clerk) as she appeared to be heading back to join her pal, Molly, in the mayor's yard. Mildred's photoboards had long since been shed, and photo enlargements were scattered for nearly a block down Main Street.

Chet had been able to recapture the elusive Amos, sanswood, before he left town completely. Chet then made the rounds, retrieving his packstring, retying the pigtail ropes; then he led them back to the ranger district barn and pasture at the edge of town. The packstring seemed almost eager to comply at this point, thankful that their part in the town parade was over. The mules appeared to be none the worse for wear as Chet pulled off their packsaddles and scratched their backs with a currycomb.

As Larry, Ben, Tom and Beth began the monumental task of gathering the debris that the mules had distributed over more than a block and a half of Main Street, Ernie returned the wheelbarrow and surveyed the damage. It was severe. Vandals could not have done more to destroy the Braggs' beautiful landscape. Ernie muttered to himself that he wouldn't want to be around when Mayor Braggs and her husband returned home after the parade. Their official position had been on the review stand at the end of the parade route. At this point they knew nothing of the "mule incident."

Ernie later remarked that the rehabilitation job on the mayor's yard alone could well qualify as an Eagle project for another scout in his troop.

Ben observed that they were lucky to have been placed near the end of the parade, with only three floats behind them. Those three had been able to maneuver through, around and past the wood, grass, waterjugs and photoboards without too much difficulty. If the pack-mule string had been near the front of the parade, as they had hoped to be, it would have been a different matter and could have spoiled the entire parade.

Mildred Bronson had been stationed near the end of the parade route with a video camera, ready to document the multiple-use packstring as they went past. They didn't make it that far. "Just as well," Beth remarked later, "if she had been in the vicinity of that power pole, we would have had some videotape footage that I'm not sure we would have wanted to keep."

"Oh, I think we might have," Ben remarked. "We need a good laugh now and then, and we'll likely forget the embarrassment of this incident in time."

Peggy had been watching the parade from a vantage point near the wreck. She took several "still" photos, and then joined the rest of the crowd in laughter when she realized that no one was hurt and no real harm had been done, except of course to the mayor's poor dismantled yard.

Ernie and Jill caught up with the band near the end of the route. They retrieved their instruments and apologized to the band leader for their absence.

"Well, I still say it was a good idea and a wonderful entry as long as it lasted," Beth said later as they gathered to critique the effort. "How could we know that some dumb old power pole would get in the way?"

"We looked darn good for several blocks," Ben added. "I heard a number of really favorable comments before the whole thing went 'gunny sack'."

"I don't think we have anything to apologize for," Tom said, "except to Mayor Braggs that is. I'm thinking we'd better go to her house as a group on Saturday, and do what we can to repair the damage."

"Good idea," Larry said. "I'll talk to her this afternoon and let her know. Anyway, I was proud of the whole crew for the recovery effort."

"Your kids, too," Beth added. "They were wonderful!"

"I'll say they were, especially little Jill, catching old Molly and calming her right down," Chet added.

The Weaver family had a Fourth of July picnic in their backyard that evening, before walking down the street to the junior high school to watch fireworks.

"What about the prizes and awards for the parade?" Jill asked. "Did you hear who got them?"

"No, I sure didn't," Peggy answered, "but I doubt if the district crew got much of it."

"Maybe the trophy for the most exciting entry," Ernie said. "Dad, are you going to cut that watermelon...?"

CHAPTER VI

THE SPEECH

Larry's parents, retired Ranger and Mrs. Lawrence E. Weaver Jr., had promised a visit for several months, but their busy schedule, including extensive touring with their big, "cab-and-a-half" pickup, with fifth-wheel travel trailer, had kept them from it. They stayed in touch with phone calls and "E-Mail."

Finally, when their itinerary brought them into some proximity to Elk Creek, Grace Weaver told Lawrence, "Let's call the kids tonight and tell them we can be there for a visit starting next week. We haven't seen them since last Christmas, and we probably won't even recognize Ernie and Jill."

"That's fine with me," her husband replied. And so impromptu plans were made for a visit with their son, Ranger Lawrence E. Weaver III, and his family.

"We can just stay in our trailer parked in your driveway," Grace said, when they arrived. "We're self sufficient you know, and there's no use putting you out when it's not necessary."

"You'll do no such thing, Mother," Peggy exclaimed. "We have plenty of room, and we wouldn't think of letting you 'camp' in our yard!"

"Don't argue with her, dear," Lawrence advised. "Haven't you learned that our daughter-in-law can be pretty firm on matters that are important to her?"

Ernie and Jill were excited to see their grandparents and hear about their travel adventures. And those feelings were certainly mutual. A lot of visiting and catching-up took place that afternoon and evening. Lawrence wanted to hear about current happenings on the Elk Creek District, while Grace was more interested in Ernie and Jill's activities.

Jill eagerly told about her barrel racing with a Foxtrotting horse. "Cougar is wonderful!" she told her grandparents. "I'll show him to you tomorrow. Maybe we could have a ride together, grandpa."

"Absolutely," her grandpa responded. "I'm assuming you have something gentle I can ride, and maybe keep up with you."

"You bet we do," Jill said, not recognizing his kidding style. And she began telling him all about Gifford.

Ernie avoided telling about the fighting episode at the junior high, but he enthusiastically described his Eagle Scout nature-trail project at Moose Lake Campground. "It's just about finished and ready to use," he said. His grandparents agreed on what a worthwhile project it must be.

The whole family took turns telling about the Fourth of July parade and mule-wreck incident. Lawrence and Grace, holding their sides and tears rolling down their faces, allowed that they had not heard anything so funny, true or otherwise, for a long, long time.

That evening at supper, Larry said, "Dad, the Lions Club has been after me to give them a talk about the Forest Service and contrast what's happening today with earlier times. You're a lot better qualified to do that than I am. How about it? They meet Wednesday noon at Barney's Cafe. Barney Shultz has added a big banquet room in the back, and there's probably enough room to invite the Kiwanis Club for a joint meeting to hear you. I'm sure that Beth Egan, who handles public information for the district, can make all the arrangements, even on short notice, if you'll agree."

"You're pretty persuasive," his father answered. "I guess I can do it, if you'll furnish a joke or two for me to throw in."

So it was settled, and Beth, in her usual efficient style, made all of the arrangements with both service clubs and with Barney's Cafe. Beth and Ben were both Kiwanis members. Tom, Chet and Mildred wrangled invitations to attend that day. Mildred was to videotape the speech, and also make an audio-tape on cassette. Grace and Peggy were invited also. Ernie and Jill came in later just to hear their grandpa talk.

Barney's banquet room was full to overflowing as Lions Club President George Meredith made the introduction." It gives me great pleasure, at this joint meeting of Elk Creek's two fine service clubs, to introduce a special speaker." Then, reading from notes that Larry had given him, he continued, "Lawrence E. Weaver Jr. grew up in eastern Washington, the son of one of the original forest rangers hired by Chief Forester Gifford Pinchot. He graduated from forestry school at Oregon State and started a career with the Forest Service, U.S. Department of Agriculture, in 1937. He was district ranger on five different districts in three states and two Forest Service regions, retiring in 1977. He also served in the U.S. Navy on a destroyer in the Pacific during World War II and was highly decorated." Then, looking up he said, "Please join me in welcoming the father of our own district ranger, Lawrence Weaver."

The featured speaker moved quickly to the lectern. At seventy eight, he was spry and vigorous, well-tanned and with a shock of white hair and a white mustache that accentuated a winning smile. "Ladies and gentlemen," he began, "about a week ago Grace and I were on a beach in southern California, and the idea of making a speech, anywhere, was the furthest thing from my mind. But I can tell you we're glad to be here and especially happy for the chance to visit our family here in Elk Creek.

"I'm going to start this 'historical resume' back a number of years before I was born, which was in 1915. My grandfather, Ernest Weaver, homesteaded in southeastern Washington in the Palouse country near the Idaho Panhandle in the year 1883. On his small ranch he raised some cattle to scratch out a living, and he did some logging. His portable sawmill furnished lumber used by neighbors for miles around. My father, Lawrence Ernest Weaver, and his two older brothers grew up on that ranch and knew forestry from a hands-on, practical standpoint. At age eighteen right out of school, he was hired by a fledgling agency of the Department of Agriculture called the Forest Service, which was charged with the care and protection of the Forest Reserves. As Mr. Meredith told you, Gifford Pinchot was the Chief Forester, having attended Yale University and later studying Forestry along with other training in Europe. Following his Forest Service career, Pinchot was governor of Pennsylvania, and he also established America's first forestry school offering professional degrees at Yale. He was a remarkable, far-sighted leader.

"My father and my Uncle Harold were both hired as forest guards, and in a short time both were designated 'forest rangers,' because of their practical experience with timber and livestock. Two of Uncle Harold's sons also had careers with the Forest Service. In addition to Larry here, my son Jim is also a forest officer, currently stationed in Montana. You might say, the entire Weaver family wears 'green underwear'." There was laughter and applause at this point, although not everyone fully understood what he meant.

Lawrence Weaver continued, "Pinchot established the principle of multiple-use and sustained yield as Forest Service

bylaws. That meant that the land was to be managed for the best and most appropriate combination of uses, according to the capabilities of the areas involved, and that these areas must be managed so as to continue producing indefinitely.

"And speaking of multiple-use, I understand that you folks had an exciting Fourth of July parade, featuring a multiple-use mule packstring entry by the local ranger district." The entire crowd, except for Mayor Harriet and banker Hamilton Braggs, laughed with the speaker as they recalled that event.

"Early management of the Forest Reserves was mostly custodial; protection from wildfire was a prime objective. My father and Uncle Harold spent a lot of time fighting fire and marking the new forest boundaries. By the time I started my career in 1937 we were well into scientific forest and range management. But there was little public interest in how the Forest Service managed the National Forests, as they were called by this time. Production of timber and livestock was a high priority, and hard-rock minerals were available for the taking by prospectors and mining companies, in accordance with the Mining Law of 1872. If a ranger imposed strict requirements on a rancher, who was called a grazing permittee, or on a miner or a timber company, to take better care of the land, there would often be a Congressional inquiry on behalf of the permittee or the company. It was difficult, even then, to get a good resource management job done because of political interference."

"These political inquiries weren't normally directed to the ranger, you understand, but to levels on up the line, the forest supervisor or regional forester, sometimes even to the chief of the Forest Service. It was probably just as well. I'd have likely just told them to jump in the lake, and then I might have lost my job." This evoked laughter from the crowd at Barney's.

"I was made a ranger in 1939 after two years in the service. It was just before the war. And when I came back from the war, I was a ranger again. I was what was called a 'career ranger'. I never wanted to be anything else.

"On the lighter side, let me tell you an old 'joke' about the ranger job. The old-time ranger used to say he'd had a successful year when he saw the forest supervisor three times and the supervisor only saw him once. That happened to me a time or two." Again, there was laughter throughout the room.

"In 1960, Pinchot's multiple-use principles were made the law of the land with passage of the Multiple-Use Act. Four years later, the wilderness preservation concepts promoted by forest officers such as Aldo Leopold and Robert Marshall were adopted as law in the Wilderness Act. The Forest Service had previously designated wilderness administratively, starting with the Gila Wilderness in southwestern New Mexico in 1924. By the mid-sixties, public interest in the National Forests and indeed in public land management was increasing, and the National Environmental Policy Act, or NEPA, was passed by Congress at the end of the decade. This was significant legislation, requiring that any major projects or actions undertaken on federal land be subject to environmental analysis, done with public involvement.

"It should be noted that the Forest Service had been, in effect, complying with the elements of NEPA well before its passage. Multiple-Use Survey Reports, also with public involvement, were done as a matter of course on projects or actions of any significance for several years before NEPA. In fact, if the truth be known, NEPA was modeled after existing Forest Service requirements and procedures. You might say we were showing them how to 'protect the environment' before it was made the law, or the popular thing to do." Again there was some laughter and a scattering of applause.

"To keep in chronological sequence here, I should mention that the Endangered Species Act was passed in 1973, and that opened up a whole new ballgame, as far as environmental involvement was concerned. I'll have more to say about that later. For now, I'll just mention that, in my opinion, there has never been an environmental law passed with nobler intentions, but resulting in greater abuse.

"The Forest and Rangeland Renewable Resources Planning Act of 1974, called for short the Resources Planning Act, or simply RPA, and subsequently the National Forest Management Act, or NFMA, were passed which mandated that forest plans be written for each National Forest in accordance with NEPA. That meant with full public involvement and also requiring scientific evaluation of economic, social and environmental effects of a proposed action. I ended my active career just a few years later, before it got so confounded complicated, I might add. But I observed that it took a good deal longer to complete the first round of forest planning than Congress intended or the Forest Service anticipated. This was largely because of the difficulty in agreeing on an appropriate or acceptable level of timber harvest, as well as complexities in developing and applying computer models for timber inventory. Forest plans that were completed were routinely appealed, often by both sides of the issues involved. In some areas, perhaps I should say most areas, there was intensive Congressional oversight at the local level.

"With increasing public interest in the National Forests, polarization of the public developed and intensified. The growing environmental movement was met with resentment by commodity-production interests, such as the timber, mining and livestock industries and their supporters. The Forest Service, as usual, was squarely in the middle, trying to make forest resources available for beneficial uses as the law provides, and also insisting that users protect and not over-use those resources. There was a concurrent swing in Congress, with many members, primarily in the East, siding openly with environmental groups who wanted more wilderness designations and less commodity uses of public lands in general and the National Forests in particular. Western Congressional members, for the most part, stayed loyal and supportive to timber, mining and livestock interests, but they also started paying closer attention to environmental concerns."

"The Assistant Secretary of Agriculture, overseeing the Forest Service in the late seventies, had been executive head of a major environmental organization. He made no secret of his priority to work toward an increase in wilderness acreage. The second roadless area review and inventory, called RARE II, was undertaken at his direction. An earlier such review, simply called RARE, had been completed in the early seventies, but was virtually ignored by Congress. Although the Forest Service hoped for Congressional action on the entire, completed RARE II package, Congress instead chose to address each state's situation separately, according to the interest and initiative of individual state delegations. Some acted promptly, largely in connection with forest plan recommendations. In some states a completed Wilderness Act took a good deal longer, and in a few cases, such as Idaho and Montana, the issue of National Forest wilderness has yet to be resolved.

"The next Assistant Secretary of Agriculture, in the early eighties, had been an executive and counsel for a major timber-producing firm. Just as his predecessor had openly promoted wilderness additions, he insisted that the level of timber output from the National Forests could be greatly increased, nearly doubled. As forest plans were developed and timber inventory information was assembled, it became apparent that such increases were unrealistic and unachievable.

"While the 'pendulum' for priorities swung sharply between the two administrations, like about 180 degrees, it was my observation that the 'Forest Service pendulum' swung in a much smaller arc. I credit the Chief for applying some common-sense moderation and a degree of passive resistance to keep the outfit away from extremes in each case.

"But with the directed timber emphasis in the early 80's came a vigorous 'recruitment' by environmental organizations. These groups saw the administration in power as not only a threat to environmental values, but a great opportunity to increase their collective memberships and their influence with the public, the Congress and the courts. That increased membership and influence grew through the eighties and continues to the present. While some groups concentrated on imposing their will on public opinion and court decisions, others took more extreme and strident measures to get their objectives met. This included destruction of property, like cutting of fences or pouring sand or sugar into fuel tanks of road construction equipment. Another highly visible and well publicized act of vandalism was tree-spiking, to halt the cutting and milling of timber, because of the harm done to chainsaws and sawmill equipment, as well as to operators. Larry tells me you had two cases of tree spiking involving the local sawmill. I sure hope there's a successful prosecution in these cases to nip the problem in the bud, and to send a message to the perpetrators that such acts of malicious vandalism won't be tolerated here." Many in the crowd looked at Deputy Sheriff Virgil Craft who nodded his agreement.

"Other strategies by some environmental groups, seeking publicity for their 'cause,' included 'tree sitting,' where these zealots climb to the top of a tree they want 'saved' and sit there in the tree, sometimes for long periods, to prevent it from being cut. They do this on private as well as public property, and the worst part is they often get away with it! I personally think the loggers should just start cutting anyway and see how fast the tree-sitters come down." Again there was laughter and applause from the audience.

"I mentioned the Endangered Species Act earlier. While Congressional intent was to provide for protection of animals and plants that were identified as being in danger of serious decline or, at worst, extinction, environmental extremist organizations have manipulated the process to slow or stop resource management activities. A prime example is the case of the northern spotted owl. Early research indicated that this little raptor needed large tracts of old-growth forest to survive, and such areas were set aside as off-limits to logging, enough so as to do great harm to the timber industry. In fact, many sawmills throughout the owl's habitat range were closed, putting many people out of work. Now perhaps there were too many sawmills there anyway for the amount of timber available under sustained yield, but that's another issue. Later revelations from research findings that spotted owl habitat requirements were not nearly so demanding, that the spotted owl could and did, in fact, live and nest in cut-over stands, have done little to change standards or reverse economic damage done to companies and communities. It has also been revealed that predators, including other species of owls preying on the spotted owl, may be a significant factor in declining populations.

"The same thing has happened or is happening with other species, with several variations on the theme. For example, different kinds of anadromous fish, such as salmon, have been 'used' to modify, that is decrease, timber harvest activities, including road building, in forests with spawning streams, despite the fact that, in recent years especially, provisions have been made in timber sales and road construction standards to avoid putting silt in the streams. Environmentalists have targeted the spawning and rearing habitat of salmon as a 'limiting factor,' even though dams on the major rivers involved, commercial fishing in oceans and rivers and even Indian fishing rights, are far more significant in harming these fish or decreasing their numbers.

"Now I'm sure not saying we should take out the dams, far from it. They are needed and appropriate. I'm saying the dams should be better modified to allow passage of fish, both downstream for the little smolts, that go tail-first with the current downstream, often stalling in the slack waters of reservoirs, and upstream for spawners, that fight all obstacles to return to the areas where they were hatched. I'll say it again, removing the dams sure isn't the answer. And also we could do better in policing the commercial fishing and tying limits to numbers needed for successful spawning.

"I could go on with other examples of 'abuse' of the Endangered Species Act, but I think the point is made.

"But before I move from the subject of wildlife completely, let me just say that the National Forest System, which also includes the National Grasslands, provide habitat for countless populations of wildlife and fish, not just endangered species, which get so much attention. A major share of this country's big game populations, deer, elk, moose, antelope, bighorn sheep, mountain goats, caribou, as well as predators such as bear, mountain lion, bobcat, lynx, fox, and small game and nongame animals and also fish and birds, all reside on the National Forests and Grasslands. The Forest Service enjoys a strong partnership with the various State fish and wildlife agencies, because the animals and their habitat must be considered together.

"As I get ready to wind-down this long-winded oratory, let me just say that I had an interesting and rewarding career with the Forest Service. I certainly don't envy today's forest officers who have to contend with what I'll generously call a misguided administration in Washington DC. Up to now and throughout my career, I've always been 'a-political.' My agency was part of the administration in power, and I had no trouble working within the various emphases and priorities of administrations as they changed. That was because they were working within the law as established by Congress, and they allowed the professional agency in charge of the National Forests to do its work in managing these lands in the public interest, according to sound scientific principles of natural resource management. This is no longer true today. This administration has its own environmental agenda, and they have no qualms in ignoring Congressional intent or even existing laws, such as the Multiple-Use Act of 1960. I might add that the courts have played a strong role too, in stopping or modifying resource management activities needed on the National Forests. All the pity!

"It is insulting to me and to other forest officers, active or retired, to hear environmental extremist organizations say that commodity outputs from the National Forests must be curtailed or even eliminated. They imply, or state flat-out, that forest management, with production and proper use of resources, such as timber and forage, is not achievable. They're saying the things that I spent a career doing cannot be done. In fact, one of the major challenges of my day was to assure environmentally sound use and management of forest resources in the face of Congressional pressures to 'ease up' and allow use beyond safe and proper levels.

"These 'enviros' seem to think they invented wilderness too, when, in fact, the Forest Service originated and fostered the concept of wilderness long before Congress finally decided to make it a law. While the Forest Service concentrates on protection and management of wilderness, these groups agitate for more acres, as many as possible, to be added to the system. They want 'wilderness protection' for common tracts of land, including Public Domain lands managed by the Bureau of Land Management that happen to be roadless or essentially so. Protection from what? From resource use, that's what! Those people simply don't want to allow commercial interests to make money from the use of public resources, even though the result is increased wealth for our Nation and employment for its citizens. If such use actually harmed the resources or the environment, I would be the first to agree with them. But it doesn't, and I don't!" Lawrence Weaver pounded the lectern and shook his fist for emphasis, and the audience responded with enthusiastic applause and nodding of heads.

"Now I'll climb down from my soapbox and maybe field some questions. I hope you'll forgive me for being so opinionated, but hey, I'm retired now, and I guess I can say whatever I want to, as a senior citizen."

At this point those in attendance rose to their feet in applause. It was obvious that the great majority of the two service clubs assembled agreed with the speaker.

"Thank you so much, Mr. Weaver," said George Meredith. "That was an interesting, entertaining and delightfully candid assessment of past and present management of our National Forests. Even though we're running a little long, I think we'll take time for just a couple of questions."

Ike Elliot was the first to leap to his feet and be recognized by the Chair. "My name is Ike Elliot, and I'm editor of the Elk Creek Weekly Bugle," he said. "We keep hearing about consolidations or combinations of forests and districts. We don't want to see the Elk Creek Ranger's office combined and moved to another town. Isn't there a limit to how much Forest Service land one ranger can take care of?"

"Well, Mr. Elliot," Lawrence Weaver responded, "I'm glad you asked that question, because I have some definite ideas on the subject. But first, if I might, let me correct your terminology. As a newspaper man, I know you want to get it right. There's no such thing as 'Forest Service land'. The Forest Service is an organization, an agency within the US Department of Agriculture, that's made up of people who do a variety of tasks. They accomplish scientific research upon which proper land management is based. They offer technical assistance to states and to forest landowners in a program called 'State and Private Forestry.' And they manage publicly-owned lands of the National Forest System, which as I said earlier includes National Forests, National Grasslands and Land Utilization Project areas. The Forest Service doesn't own an acre of this land; you and I, we, the people do. The Forest Service is the agency, the organization. The land it manages has a specific title; it's called the National Forests, and in total it's the National Forest System. So please, Mr. Elliot, in the future be careful to refer to National Forest Land, never Forest Service land, and I'll thank you for it." Ike nodded acknowledgment.

"Sorry to be so picky, but it's an important distinction," he continued. "Now about these consolidations; in a word, I'm against them! When the Forest Reserves were first designated and divided into ranger districts, in the early twentieth century, transportation and communication systems were decidedly more limited than they are today. It was logical that small units be established, so that supervisors and rangers could cover their responsibilities effectively. As transportation and communication capabilities improved, it was also logical to combine units for greater efficiency; many such combinations were made, and properly so. But there is a point of diminishing returns. When units, forests and districts, get so large that they can no longer be effectively covered by their managers, the 'span of control' has been exceeded. The ranger must be in contact with the land and with the people, not just an office executive, a button-pusher or computer jockey. I think, in many cases, we've reached that point, and in some cases, exceeded it. Despite what the 'bean counters' would tell us about efficiency, there's a limit to how large a forest or ranger district should be. Does that answer your question, Mr. Elliot?"

"Yes, it does, and very well," Ike replied, "and now I have another one..."

"Wait a minute," George Meredith interjected, "it's one to the customer, and I said we have time for just two." Ike Elliot sat down reluctantly.

Meredith next recognized Glen Romero, Sportsmen's Club president, who stood up next. He identified himself and his affiliation and said, "Mr. Weaver, I'd like to second Mr. Meredith's observation that you've given us a wonderful talk, and I especially appreciated your remarks about wildlife and fish. My question is this: How do you think the Elk Creek District is doing, in light of all the problems and complexities you've outlined?"

"What a setup!" Lawrence exclaimed. "You've given me the opportunity to brag on my son. I've tried to keep up with the goings-on here, and Larry keeps me posted on a variety of issues, activities and problems. Now and then, if I say so myself, he even asks my advice, which always makes me feel good. Well, to answer your question, Mr. Romero, I think the Elk Creek District is in good hands, and I'm especially pleased to see the level of public interest and support as displayed in this meeting. I'm proud of Larry as a hands-on ranger, who's in touch with the resources and issues, and with the community. I'm impressed with his staff. Tom Cordova, Beth Egan and Ben Foster are strong, loyal and capable professionals. Mildred

Bronson runs a good office from all I can tell, and my old friend Chet Wagoner provides the long-term memory and continuity to hold the whole thing together. Yes sir, I think the town of Elk Creek and the ranger district are mutually beneficial. They're lucky to have each other."

Again, there was warm applause, and most of those attending stopped to shake Lawrence Weaver's hand and thank him for his talk.

Kiwanis member and League of Women Voters President Ruth Osborne said, "Oh, Mr. Weaver, I wish you could have been here earlier for our field tour. It was wonderful!"

"I wish I could have been there too," Lawrence said, "I've heard some good things about the tour. My daughter-in-law attended, you know?"

The eager editor Ike Elliot cornered the speaker for several more questions and took his picture for a Bugle article, until Larry rescued his father, saying he wanted to introduce him to the mayor.

With that, Lawrence Weaver's speaking engagement concluded.

Later that afternoon, Jill and her grandpa took a horseback ride in the woods to allow them some time together, and to let him wind-down following his talk to the service clubs.

There was a good back road from the Weaver barn to a trailhead at the Forest boundary, about a mile and a half from the house. There was an excellent loop trail from there, with two options, a seven-mile loop and an eighteen-mile loop. Jill was ready to take the long ride but agreed that they probably shouldn't be gone that long, so their total ride, from home and back, was about ten miles.

Jill took the lead on Cougar in a fast, flat-foot walk, alternating to a foxtrot on the long level stretches. Her grandpa, followed closely behind on Gifford. They reached a rest stop at the half-way point in less than an hour.

"Grandpa," Jill said, "I have a question for you."

"Go ahead, little girl," he replied.

"Oh, grandpa," Jill said, "You always call me that. In case you haven't noticed, I'm getting to be a pretty big girl."

"Well, you are getting big, and pretty too I'd say," he admitted. "What's the question?"

"First, I really liked your speech, grandpa, and it got me to thinking. Ernie is always talking about how he's going to be a forest ranger, a fourth generation forest ranger. I was wondering, why couldn't I be a forest ranger too some day, or maybe a wildlife biologist like Beth Egan? There's no reason why a girl can't work outdoors, if that's what she likes, is there? I don't want it just because Ernie is doing it. I just think it's something I might like to aim for too. What do you think, grandpa?"

"Well, sweetie," he answered, "I think a girl can do anything she wants to nowadays, and there's no reason you can't shoot for a Forest Service career the same as your brother if you want to. Have you talked to your folks about this?"

"No, I haven't," she said. "Like I said, your speech got me thinking, and I realized that it's what I might like too. Up to now, I've thought I wanted to be a horse trainer, maybe I still do, but this could be even better."

"If you're going to be a forest ranger, little girl," he chided, "you'd better help your dad put shoes on that Cougar horse of yours. That's a ranger's job, you know."

"Well, Ernie shoes Cougar, you know, but I already help with the hoof-trimming in the wintertime," Jill said, as they remounted to start the ride home. "The next step shouldn't be too hard, if Ernie does it."

Lawrence Weaver laughed." And I'll bet you can do about anything your brother can do, can't you?"

At supper that evening, he said to Larry, "Say, that granddaughter of mine is some horsewoman! And those are two fine stepping horses, son. I'm really impressed with their smooth, ground covering gait. But it just dawned on me where you got Gifford's name. You really do have green underwear, don't you?"

They all had a laugh at that. It was a good time for three generations of the Weaver family to be together.

CHAPTER VII

FIRE, TRESPASS and RESEARCH

California was burning up! That's what the newspaper headlines and the TV anchors were saying. After a wet spring and early summer, producing an abundance of annual grasses and other vegetation, the rains had stopped, and it didn't take long for a drought to set in.

Despite the best efforts of the Forest Service and the State Division of Forestry in spreading Smokey Bear's message of fire prevention, despite patrols by air and ground to assure early detection and suppression, fires were started by careless smokers and campers, by faulty mufflers on chainsaws and all-terrain vehicles, and by various other "preventable" means with people being responsible. When a high wind blew down a powerline during the night in the southern part of the State, sparking dry grass beneath it, the big one was started. The "Dry Gulch Fire" spread rapidly, covering some 5,000 acres of chaparral* and annual grasses before daybreak.

The state joint agency fire team, composed of state, BLM and Forest Service fire suppression specialists, was spread thin already, with numerous "project fires" throughout the state. The incident command team that included Ben Foster as a division supervisor (formerly called division boss), was called to handle the Dry Gulch Fire. Beth Egan was called as liaison for an Indian crew, composed of twenty five skilled and experienced firefighters.

Their fire bags* were packed and ready ahead of time, as was customary during fire season, complete with hard-hats, gloves, goggles, headlights, "Nomex"—fire-resistant trousers and shirts, and canteens. They also carried compact fire shelters on their belts, aluminum tents designed for one prostrate person in an extreme emergency, such as, when being over-run by a fire. Ben and Beth were on an airplane headed for California by early afternoon the next day.

It had not been easy for Ranger Larry Weaver to give up his assignment on incident command teams. He had been an active firefighter for more than fifteen years, with a full range of assignments including division supervisor and as incident commander the last four years. But he knew that his staff needed this training and experience too, and he knew his district could not send everyone to off-forest fires and still operate at home. This was the first year that Larry did not have an incident command assignment, and he felt the blood surging through his veins, like an old firehorse, as Ben and Beth left for the fire and he stayed home.

This was also the week that an investigation team was to visit the Elk Creek District to look at and evaluate candidate areas for"Research Natural Area," or RNA classification. On Tuesday afternoon, the team arrived at the district office and sat down in the conference room with Larry and Tom Cordova. Dr. Gene Murphy, research scientist from the Forest and Range Experiment Station, had the primary responsibility for RNAs in his organization, the research arm of the Forest Service. Paula Russell was the regional ecologist, who worked as coordinator with the Experiment Station and the National Forests in the region. Timber staff, Don Hendricks, was RNA coordinator for the Rio Verde National Forest, and those three,

Gene, Paula and Don, formed the team visiting the Elk Creek District.

Gene explained the concept of Research Natural Areas and exactly what they were looking for on this visit. He said they needed an area of sufficient size so outside activities would not influence plant growth and development in the RNA. At least several hundred acres would be desirable. It should be accessible, readily available for study of ecological relationships. It should be protected from grazing, off limits to timber harvest, and withdrawn from mineral entry.*

"An RNA is a field laboratory," Gene said. "It's important to understand what happens to the vegetation in such an area without human interference."

"This is an administrative designation, you know," Paula added. "No Congressional action is required."

Larry and Tom spent the afternoon with the RNA team in the conference room, reviewing criteria and looking at maps and aerial photos. Larry had to concentrate hard on the subject to keep from thinking about Ben and Beth and the Dry Gulch Fire. Gene said they were hoping to establish a Research Natural Area in either the mixed-conifer or the pinyon-juniper vegetation types on the district. He said they needed both, but would not ask for more than one on any ranger district. Several possibilities for each type were on the district, and it was planned to spend the next two days in a carryall,* looking at them and evaluating them on the ground.

That evening, Larry, Peggy, and Tom and his wife, Angie, had dinner with the visitors at Barney's Cafe. The Cordovas dropped off their baby daughter at the Weaver home, where Jill would baby-sit; Ernie would be there for moral support.

Gene Murphy was an interesting guy. As a research scientist, he had traveled extensively worldwide. His job dealing with RNAs was a good compliment for his hobby as a bird-watcher or 'birder.' Much of the evening, during dinner and after, was spent with Gene describing his travels and telling about birds, both common and unusual.

Paula Russell was no less interesting. She was an expert in ecological relationships, and she knew the Region very well, not just the geography, but the plant and animal life throughout the various National Forests, and she could explain their complex relationships. Larry had met Paula before, and was anxious to spend some time with her on the district.

Tom, likewise, looked forward to a visit with Don Hendricks, and during the next two days, he hoped to review with him progress being made by Alliance Timber Company in harvesting the Bear Hollow timber sale. Don was the Forest expert on the subject of timber in all its aspects, and any time Tom could spend with him was always worthwhile.

Peggy and Angie found the dinner conversation interesting, but they also found time to talk together on other subjects. They agreed that a "night out" was always welcome under any circumstances. Barney's Cafe was not only the best in town, it was also just about the only place to have a good dinner in Elk Creek.

Later that evening at home, Larry had a phone call from Deputy Sheriff Virgil Craft, who said he'd had an anonymous telephone call telling about a "marijuana patch" somewhere in a remote area of the forest. Larry arranged to meet with the deputy first thing in the morning. Then he called Tom and told him that something important had come up, and Tom would have to take care of the RNA visitors by himself the next day, possibly the next two.

The anonymous tip had described the area involved as between the Powder Bowl Ski Area and the North Fork trail-head just below the Wilderness boundary. Larry met Virgil

Craft at the district horse pasture and barn. He hooked the small slant-load horse trailer* to his three-quarter-ton Forest Service pickup and loaded the grey horse, Major, and the tall sorrel, Rocket. He put saddles in the trailer tack compartment. They drove to the North Fork trailhead, arriving in an hour and a half. They saddled and rode west along a seldom-used trail below the Wilderness boundary and roughly paralleling it.

A half hour later, as they approached a small clearing in the timber, Larry pulled off the trail and used the halter-rope to tie Rocket to a tree. Virgil followed suit, tying Major, and the two men walked quietly away from the trail and toward the clearing. Both were armed with .357 Magnum revolvers in covered holsters. It was standard procedure for the deputy, of course, and Larry was authorized to "carry" on special occasions, having completed a law enforcement training course several years earlier and a refresher the year before to keep his certification current. Both the initial course and the refresher included firearms training.

They approached the clearing stealthily, not knowing what might be there, but alert to the possibility that it could well be their target. They found nothing but a meadow of about three acres, no garden. They returned to their horses, untied, remounted and proceeded along the trail.

The same routine was repeated with four more clearings. Virgil said, "Maybe it was just a kook call. We get them now and then. If so, I'm sorry to have bothered you, Larry."

"Hey, it's important to check these things out," Larry replied. "Besides, like they say, 'the worst day horseback in the forest beats the best day in the office'. I'm always glad to get out and see part of the district."

As they approached the next clearing, Larry had a feeling that this one might be different. He motioned to Virgil to follow him, and they rode in a wide circle around the clearing to where the trail went out the other end. Still staying some distance from the clearing, they tied the horses and walked cautiously toward the exiting trail. From the obviously greater impact of traffic, it was apparent that someone had been using the trail heavily, coming from the other direction. It looked like mostly ATV tracks, four-wheelers.

"We'd better be damn careful here," Virgil whispered. "If it's what it looks like, we've found our garden, and these guys can be very protective of their investment. There may even be piano wire strung around or some other sort of booby trap or alarm system."

Keeping low and alert to potential danger, they approached the edge of the clearing and looked in.

"Bingo!" Larry whispered.

In a two-acre space, about three dozen rows of Cannabis* plants were spaced about five feet apart. The plants looked to be five or six feet tall and healthy. An elaborate plastic-pipe drip-irrigation system, gravity-fed from a small spring at the upper end of the clearing, completed the picture. It appeared that there was no one around to tend the garden that day.

Larry and Virgil retreated to where the horses were tied, about 150 yards away.

"Let's talk this over," Virgil said. "We have several options. If we want to catch these guys, we can set up surveillance on the road to the ski area to see who's coming and going. We're probably a week or more away from harvest time, because the plants appear to be somewhere between flowering and seed formation. I think we have a good chance of finding out who's involved here, and then nailing their hides to the wall. That would be after they conduct the harvest and are leaving."

"And the other options?" Larry asked.

"Well, we can just come in with some force and conduct

the harvest for them," was Virgil's reply. "It can make an aromatic bonfire. That way, we destroy the product, but probably don't catch the bad guys.

"And a third option is to have our forces ready and follow them in when surveillance tells us they're on the way to the garden and maybe ready to start the harvest. We make the arrest and then have our bonfire. There's more risk with the first and third options, but I sure think it's worth it to catch them. In any case, let's get out of here and go pay a visit to the U.S. Marshal."

They rode a wide circle around the clearing joining the trail back to North Fork nearly a half-mile away. They didn't want to leave horse tracks anywhere near the garden, to avoid alerting the growers that they had been detected.

On the way back, Virgil said, "These guys are really devious. They put their plantation on the National Forest because they know that private land can be confiscated if they are caught growing an illegal crop. And such people have been known to harm or even kill anyone who may stumble onto their activity. There's a great deal of money involved, sometimes millions of dollars. I'm surprised we didn't see any booby traps, but that doesn't mean there weren't any."

"How much of a force will we need to make an arrest and destroy the crop?" Larry asked.

"Depends," Virgil said. "First, we need to try and find out how many of them there are. And it would be nice to know how well-armed. I'm sure the marshal's office in Centerville will cooperate, as well as our whole sheriff's department. We should try for at least a dozen armed officers, I would think."

I'm sure I can get the forest law enforcement officer in the supervisor's office to help," Larry said. "And I'll bet he can get several counterparts from nearby forests too."

"That sounds good, but we sure need to keep this quiet,"

Virgil said. "If word gets out there's something going on here, it could blow the whole deal, as far as catching anyone is concerned."

When they reached the truck and trailer at the trailhead, Virgil said, "Say, that was some smooth ride! With all our looking going out and talking coming back, I hardly noticed I was horseback. That gray horse sure is a nice one! In fact, they both are."

Larry was used to such comments, and he just nodded agreement.

They got back to town after the office was closed, but Larry found Tom inside going through his inbox.

"We got back just after 5:00," Tom said. "Our visitors went back to their motel. We looked at several good candidate areas, but they want to see the others before deciding what to recommend. How'd your day go?"

"Very interesting!" Larry replied. "I'll be able to tell you more about it in a few days."

"What's all the mystery, boss?" Tom asked. "It's not like you to keep secrets."

Larry hesitated. He knew he could trust his staff, but he also realized it was important right now that the fewer who knew about it the better, so he responded, "I'm sorry, Tom, there's some illegal activity going on, and law enforcement is going to be involved. Like I said, I'll tell you more in a few days, but right now it's important to just keep quiet. I hope you understand."

"Sure, boss," Tom said. "Besides, it will be easy to keep quiet, since I don't know anything anyway."

Larry went into his office and telephoned Forest Supervisor Frank Johnson, who as it turned out, was still in his own office at 6:00 P.M..

"We have a little situation here, boss," Larry said. "About

a two-acre plot of Cannabis is growing under irrigation not too far from the ski area. The deputy sheriff and I found it today, based on an anonymous tip. Could you have Phil Ortega call me at home later this evening? We're going to need his help and maybe a few others."

"Sure, I'll be glad to," the supervisor said. "You'll need to involve the U.S. Marshal too before taking any direct action. Do you want me to alert the U.S. Attorney's office here in Capitol City?"

"That would be good," Larry said. "We're thinking along the same lines. Deputy Virgil Craft suggested the same thing. We're on our way to Centerville first thing in the morning to make some contacts in person. I'd like to get Phil over here as soon as he can make it. And by the way, the RNA search team, including Don Hendricks, is here on the district, as I suppose you're aware. Tom Cordova will 'host' them while I'm occupied with this trespass business."

"Okay, that's fine, thanks for keeping me posted," Frank Johnson said. "I'll have Phil call you. Good luck, Larry."

As with his staff, Larry was reluctant to say much to his family at this stage, although he knew they wouldn't say a word if he asked them not to. Still, at this point, he decided to keep the details to himself. He mentioned only that they had a land occupancy trespass case, and he had to go see the U.S. Marshal.

Soon after supper, the phone rang; it was Law Enforcement Special Agent Phil Ortega. Larry took it in the den.

"What's up, Larry?" Phil asked. "The boss said I should call you. He didn't say what it was about."

Larry told him about his ride with Deputy Virgil Craft and their discovery near Powder Bowl Ski Area. He described the Cannabis plants in detail, as well as the irrigation system and the heavily-used trail not far from the Wilderness boundary. He told Phil of his intent to see the U.S. Marshal early the next morning, as soon as his office opened. He also mentioned that the Forest Supervisor would be contacting the U.S. Attorney's Office in Capitol City.

"Very interesting!" Phil said. "If I leave here at about 4:00 in the morning, I could meet you there and then go back to the district with you later. Now tell me some more about what you and the deputy plan to do."

Larry described the options that had been discussed and told about the idea of surveillance on the road to the ski area. He asked if Phil could arrange for one or two more agents from neighboring forests to assist when the time came.

Phil said he thought so and would make some calls when they hung up. "See you in Centerville in the morning, Larry," he said.

Larry then called Mildred Bronson to let her know where he would be the next morning. He gave her no details. Again, the fewer who knew about the Cannabis garden the better.

He picked up Virgil Craft at the sheriff's office at 6:30 A.M. and they drove to Centerville.

"How does the surveillance work?" Larry asked when they got out on the road.

"There are several ways we might do it," the deputy said. "Used to be we'd use time-lapse still cameras mounted in a tree and pointed toward the road. That could help us identify any vehicles passing that point and even show license plates, usually. But we'd have to wait until the pictures were developed to see what we had. Nowadays, a video camera recording on a tape and sending a picture to a remote location, like my office, via satellite, is much more effective. We mount the camera the same way, usually on a tree. That's the system I'd recommend. It can be set up so that it records only when some moving object comes into focus. And we get a good detailed picture. Isn't modern technology amazing?"

"I'll say it is! That sounds great," Larry said enthusiastically. "Does your office have such devices on hand?"

"They have them at the main office in Centerville," Virgil replied. "I can probably pick up the equipment we need before we leave town."

They decided to make a courtesy call at the U.S. Magistrate's office first, since that office was near the Federal Building entrance. The directory said that the Marshal's office opened at 9:00 A.M..

United States Magistrate Horace Enfield was a no-nonsense judge. Larry had dealt with him on several trespass cases, grazing, timber theft and an occupancy case where someone built a cabin on the Forest without a permit. Larry had even taken the judge on a "show-me-trip" of the district a year earlier to familiarize him with their law enforcement problems. If the case was solid, with no ambiguities, Judge Enfield would normally deal harshly with the wrongdoers. Larry felt confident that if and when this case got to him, it would be handled properly.

Special Agent Phil Ortega was waiting in the entrance foyer of the Federal Building when Larry and Deputy Craft arrived just before 8:00 A.M..

"You must have gotten up before breakfast, Phil," Larry joked. "You know Virgil Craft, don't you?"

"Sure do, good to see you, Virgil," Phil said, and they shook hands. "I'm anxious to learn more about your little agricultural enterprise."

They had no appointment, but as they entered the reception area, Judge Enfield opened his door and told them to come in and sit down.

"What's going on, fellows?" he asked.

"We just stopped in to say hello, judge," Larry said, recalling the magistrate's interest in forest activities during the past year. "We're on our way to see the U.S. Marshal about a little occupancy trespass case involving a Cannabis garden on the forest. Apparently some people plan to make a bundle of money selling marijuana by growing it on public land. We're here to ask for the marshal's help in catching them and then bringing them to your court..." As soon as the words left Larry's mouth, he realized he shouldn't have said it at all, at least not in that detail. He knew full well that advanced communication with the magistrate on a pending case was improper.

"Let me interrupt you at this point, young man," Horace Enfield said, shaking his finger in Larry's direction. "I'm not sure you realize that exparte communication on a pending case such as this is strictly forbidden, and you, Ranger Weaver, are out of line to say the least. I would suggest that you hurry right on upstairs to see the marshal and also make early contact with the U.S. Attorney. I'm going to do you a favor and forget I saw you today."

"Thank you, Judge," Larry said sheepishly, and they made a quick exit from his office.

"What in the hell were you thinking about, Larry?" Phil asked abruptly. "Were you trying to get us all in trouble with the magistrate or something?"

"I guess I just wasn't thinking at all," Larry admitted. "I was just so worked up about this case it seemed like the judge would like to know about it too. I realized it right after I said it, but then it was too late. Sorry, fellows."

"Not a very good way to start action on this case...some courtesy call..." grumbled Virgil, under his breath, as they retreated down the hallway.

They walked up the stairs to the Marshal's office, which was open despite the sign that said 9:00 A.M.. After a short wait, they were ushered into the office of Assistant U.S. Marshal Carl

Hess. The clock said 8:15. Introductions were made by Phil, who had met Carl on an earlier occasion.

"What can I do for you?" Carl asked, setting aside papers he was working on.

"We thank you for seeing us," Larry said, having recovered his composure and anxious to move forward on the right track. "I'll get right to the point. Deputy Craft and I, working on an anonymous tip, found a two acre Cannabis garden on the National Forest yesterday. It's an elaborate setup with irrigation, cultivation and everything. Since it's Federal land, we wanted you to know ahead of time that we're starting to work on finding out whose garden it is. We're going to be needing your advice and help."

"I'd say that is right to the point, Ranger Weaver," Carl Hess said, "and I appreciate it. I would think you're going to need some help all right. Have you talked to the U.S. Attorney?"

"Larry's boss is doing that this morning," Virgil said. "But we wanted to let you know about it too, as soon as possible. And we think it best that as few people as possible know about it. If the word gets out somehow it could blow our chances of making an arrest. We plan to set-up a video camera to help us know more about vehicles going in and out. It's near the Powder Bowl Ski Area, but there shouldn't be much traffic up there this time of year."

"Good plan," said the Marshal. "How big a force do you figure you're going to need when it's time to move in? And how soon do you expect that will be?"

"I'm thinking we'll be able to set-up the camera later tonight," Virgil said. "Then if we get good information on who and how many from license numbers, we may be able to follow them in one day early next week. The crop is getting ripe, and I'm sure they're planning to harvest soon, perhaps a matter of days. We'd like to arrest them on the scene, to make it difficult for them to deny ownership or involvement. I'm guessing we'll need at least twelve officers. What do you think?"

"I'd say that sounds about right, give or take a couple," Carl said.

"Can you give us a hand?" Larry asked.

"Assuming you guys set it all up," Carl conjectured, scratching his head, "I can probably provide three marshals plus myself for the arrest. Those marijuana growers can be very difficult to apprehend. They have a big investment, a huge profit opportunity, and they're a crafty bunch. It would be good if we could surprise them. Sure don't want this to be the 'OK Corral'."

"I agree with that," Phil Ortega said. "I'm sure I can get two other Forest Service special agents, maybe more if we need them. And I've been thinking, what if they come in with helicopters for the harvest?"

"That's a good point," Carl said. "If there's a place you could set-up a hidden observation post nearby, well out of sight, and man it around the clock for the next week or so, that could be a big help. That way, even if they plan to move it out by air, we can be there in a short time, before they can harvest and fly out. The outpost guys would need radios with a secure frequency."

"I think we can find such a place," Larry said. "But manning it around the clock could be a challenge. Let me give that some thought. And hey, how about cell phones?"

"Why not," Virgil said, "assuming they'd work in that area. I'll talk to the sheriff and see how much help we can come up with, including radios and other equipment. Our cooperative law enforcement agreement provides for additional assistance for special circumstances."

They made the arrangements to bring in the marshals on

short notice. Carl said he thought they could be at the ski area or vicinity within four hours after receiving a call.

The sheriff was equally cooperative. He authorized four deputies in addition to Virgil Craft, and said that two of them could be available full time for the next week or more if needed. The sheriff was not fond of drug dealers or producers; that was apparent. Virgil picked up the video camera with transmitter and tapes, talked to the other deputies who would be involved, and they returned to Elk Creek early that afternoon. Virgil and Phil spent the rest of the day detailing their plan and going over "what if" possibilities. As soon as it was dark, they set-up the camera in a tree near the road to the ski area.

Larry returned to his office for the more routine work of sitting in on the closeout with the Research Natural Area team and Tom, who had carried the load for the district in his absence. The team had spent the past day and a half on the mountain looking at areas on the ground that had been identified in the office from vegetation-type maps, aerial photos and Tom's knowledge of the areas involved.

Gene Murphy said he was most appreciative of the level of cooperation from the ranger district, particularly Tom Cordova. They had looked at six different areas, three in the mixed-conifer and three in the pinyon-juniper type. Of the six, two met nearly all of the prescribed criteria, including exclusion from grazing. The pinyon-juniper area would require about three miles of fencing in a remote portion of the Diamond Fork Allotment to assure livestock exclusion. The conifer area was sufficiently isolated from livestock use that fencing would not be necessary.

"Both of these are really fine areas for the purpose," said Paula Russell. "I especially liked the mixed-conifer area as typical of the type. It looks like nobody has been through it in years, and it's nearly 400 acres, fairly steep but accessible."

"I agree," Gene said, "but I liked the pinyon-juniper area too. In fact, I could easily recommend either of them for classification."

"We'll be pleased to have an RNA on the district," Larry said. "Which one do you think you'll recommend?"

"Probably the mixed-conifer area," Gene said. "The fact that it's available without any fencing is a big plus."

All three visitors thanked Tom and Larry for their help, cooperation and hospitality. Larry appologized for not being with them the whole time, but they said they understood the obligations a ranger must have. They left town just after 3:00 P.M..

"Has there been any word from our firefighters in California?" Larry asked Mildred as he got ready to return to his office.

"Not a thing," Mildred replied. "We did hear that the Dry Gulch Fire had reached 30,000 acres, and there was a fatality involving a slurry drop. Some crew members were on a ridgetop and were hit by the slurry, apparently dropped short of the main fire front. The report said that one of them was knocked over a cliff and killed."

"Oh man! What a shame!" Larry said. "Sounds like Ben and Beth are going to be gone a while. Let me know if you hear anything, will you?"

Larry briefed Tom and Chet Wagoner about the trespass case and arranged for those two, plus crew foreman Joe Garza, to set-up a round-the-clock observation post at a strategic point above the garden. Tom said he now understood all the secrecy. A study of aerial photos showed that there was a high point along a low ridge about 200 yards north of the clearing. It was well vegetated with spruce trees and low-growing brush to afford a good cover from detection, but with a clear view of the opening below. There was also a small clearing in the timber behind the ridge, where a horse could be staked out while the observation post was manned.

To avoid putting horse tracks on the trail to the garden from the ski area road, which was considerably closer, the plan was to ride in all the way from the North Fork trailhead, although it would take nearly two hours by horseback to get there.

Chet agreed to take the first twelve hour shift starting that night. He would take binoculars, a cell phone and a radio for backup, plus enough food, water and a big thermos of coffee to last the night.

The instructions were clear. Stay in communication while observing the garden below. Stay out of sight, and under no circumstances should they go near the cultivated area or confront the trespassers.

Larry had expressed a concern for the personal safety of the "observers" and told Virgil and Phil that he would feel better if they were armed, considering the possibility that the Cannabis growers would likely be quite protective of their investment. Virgil readily agreed, and Phil reluctantly consented to authorize them to carry a rifle, a saddle carbine, for personal protection. He said he could justify this deviation from standard policy because of the circumstances of this particular case and the fact that all three were experienced with the weapon. Larry told Phil he appreciated it.

The plan was for Tom to relieve Chet shortly after daylight and for Joe to take the next night shift. One possible problem in this stealth operation would be when the incoming horse and the staked-out horse nickered to each other, a noise that could likely be heard from the clearing below and possibly expose the stakeout. It was decided to accept that as a calculated risk. And if there was human activity in the garden at the time for a shift change, the observer could radio his incoming relief not to come in with his horse just then.

Chet called Larry twice during the night, as planned, to report that there was no activity in the garden. Tom rode in on Badger before 8:00 A.M.. As suspected, Badger and the tethered Chief greeted each other, but it caused no problem because there was no one in the garden.

Early that morning, the video remote showed two crew-cab pickup trucks going up the road toward the ski area. A quick check of license plate numbers revealed them to be vehicles belonging to the Powder Bowl Ski Company, and upon checking, it was learned that crews were working on "summer grooming," removing rocks and shrubbery from the ski runs.

An hour later, a stake-side flatbed truck went up the road carrying two four-wheel-drive all-terrain vehicles (ATVs). The license plate was covered with mud and unreadable. Virgil Craft suspected that this was deliberate.

Within a half hour, Tom called to report that two men on ATVs had entered the clearing. One appeared to be adjusting the irrigation system, while the other one walked up and down rows of plants, apparently checking their stage of maturity.

Larry and Phil went to the sheriff's substation to confer with Virgil.

"Looks like we have a choice here," Virgil said. "We could go in right now with a minimum force and arrest those two guys, or we could wait until they start harvesting and likely catch more bad guys. Trouble is, there could well be more resistance on their part with the second option."

"The thing that concerns me," Phil said, "is those two could well be just workers, employees of the ones we want to catch. I'd say we're better off waiting."

Just then Virgil's office phone rang. It was Tom on his cell phone, and he sounded a little bit excited. "It looks like the one guy is disconnecting the irrigation pipes, turning them off," he said. "And the other one was talking on a cell phone for a while. Then he started cutting down plants, looking them over closely, and then stacking them. It sure looks like the harvest is starting."

"Okay, thanks, Tom," Larry said, "I guess that makes the decision for us. It's happening faster than we expected. We have some phone calls to make, and time's a-wasting."

Using all three phone lines available in the sheriff's substation, Virgil called the sheriff in Centerville requesting prompt dispatch of available deputies to Elk Creek. Larry did the same in a call to Assistant U.S. Marshal Carl Hess, and Phil called the two Forest Service agents who were on standby. It was determined that four deputies, including Virgil, three marshals, including Carl, and three Forest Service special agents, including Phil, could be in Elk Creek by noon. In another hour, they could be in place on the ski area road and ready to move in on the trespassers.

Larry called Joe Garza and told him to hold off on relieving Tom at the stakeout and to stand by until further notice.

Tom called a few minutes later with an update. Both men were now chopping and stacking plants. Larry told him of the plan to move-in that afternoon, and he asked him to lay low and keep watching.

By 10:00 A.M., two more stake-side trucks passed the video camera on the ski area road. A half-hour later, Tom reported that three trucks were now in the clearing. Five more men had joined in the harvest.

Shortly after 12:00 noon the strike force assembled at the Elk Creek substation of the Adams County Sheriff's Department. All together there were eleven law enforcement officers. Larry and Virgil had agreed that they should ask Assistant U.S. Marshall Carl Hess to be in charge, with their assistance, since they were familiar with the area and Carl was more experienced in such operations.

Phil Ortega wasn't so sure, saying it was fine to involve the marshals, but not to put them in charge. "What if Hess turns out to be a control freak and we find ourselves committed to actions we really can't justify?" he argued.

"Someone has to be in charge of the operation; it's the only way it can work," Larry said. "It's for certain that Carl has a lot more experience in these cases than any of us. Besides, if it turns out as you speculate, we can overrule him and get things back on track. My instincts say to go with the marshal calling the shots on something as tricky as this could be."

With some additional persuading, Phil reluctantly agreed.

Each participant had brought or was issued bulletproof vests and firearms, including sidearms and either assault rifles or shotguns.

It was 1:30 in the afternoon when they arrived at the point on the ski area road where the trail led northeast toward the clearing containing the Cannabis garden. The trail was well-worn and now had been expanded to a crude two-track road through the Forest, because three stakeside trucks had forced their way through a few hours earlier.

The strike force drove in carryalls along this newly-altered two-track road, to within a quarter mile of the clearing. They parked their three vehicles, effectively blocking the way out. Staying in radio contact with each other and with Tom at the observation point, they walked quietly to within 100 yards of the garden and then spread out to converge on the clearing from four directions.

Tom reported that the seven harvesters were busy chopping and stacking plants, still unaware of any outside activity or intrusion. One of the trucks was loaded and tarped-down, while a second truck was nearly half full.

Soon the strike force, looking very much like the SWAT

teams that Larry had seen on TV, reached the edge of the clearing, effectively surrounding it.

Marshal Carl Hess spoke forcefully in a bullhorn to the surprised harvesters in the garden, "THIS IS THE U.S. MARSHAL SPEAKING! YOU ARE SURROUNDED BY AGENTS WITH FIREARMS. DROP YOUR TOOLS AND PUT YOUR HANDS IN THE AIR. YOU ARE UNDER ARREST. DO NOT MOVE, AND DO NOT RESIST!"

The unsuspecting trespassers were obviously dumbfounded!

The machetes they were using to chop the plants were certainly no match for shotguns and assault rifles. They had guns in the trucks but too far away to be of any help, even if they had been inclined to resist at this point.

Six of them complied with the marshal's order. The seventh, who was working near the north edge of the clearing, dropped his tool like the others, but instead of raising his hands, he ducked into the woods and hurried up the hill. That might have been a good escape opportunity, except for the fact that it happened to be right toward the low ridge that was Tom's observation point.

While marshals, deputies and agents handcuffed the six arrested culprits and read them their Miranda rights, Larry followed the fugitive up the hill. He alerted Tom on the radio, but Tom had seen the escape clearly from his vantage point, and he was ready. When the would-be escapee came within twenty yards of Tom's position, he looked up to see the business end of Tom's .30-.30 carbine. He turned around for an alternative get-away path, but Larry with a twelve-gauge shotgun was just ten yards behind him. He dropped down to all fours and hung his head down in disgust, frustration and probably exhaustion.

Larry placed a pair of Sheriff's Department handcuffs on

the poor fellow's wrists, behind his back, and the three of them walked back down the hill, where Phil Ortega made the formal arrest and read him his rights.

With one two-ton capacity truck fully loaded, and another over half full, and only about a third of the area harvested, Agent Phil Ortega ventured an estimate that the two-acre irrigated garden had produced about eleven tons of Cannabis plant material. With leaves and stems separated in processing for sale, he guessed there would be close to three tons of marijuana, a product that now would never be marketed.

Carl Hess took a cell phone from a holster on his belt and telephoned the U.S. Attorney's office in the State Capital. He had spoken to the Assistant U.S. Attorney earlier, as had the Forest Supervisor, but this time his call was to report a successful arrest operation. His main question concerned what to do with the confiscated Cannabis plants; how much of it would be needed as evidence in a trial?

Assistant U.S. Attorney Katherine Dunlop advised him to keep several plants as a sample and to weigh them as well as count all of the plants. They should photograph the rest, including those harvested and loaded, those stacked and those plants still growing. Then the remaining plants could be chopped down, stacked and burned. There were plenty of law enforcement agents who could serve as witnesses in a trial.

Virgil called the sheriff to tell him about the successful arrests; the sheriff was very pleased.

Tom then called crew foreman Joe Garza and told him of a change in plans concerning manning the observation post. He asked him to come to the area with a ten-man fire crew that were kept on standby. He told Joe to be sure to bring several drip torches.* The harvest could be completed before dark, then the bonfire could take place at night when humidity was up and fire danger was lowest. With the fire in the middle of the clearing, there was really very little danger of it spreading anyway, despite a persistent ten-mile per hour breeze from the west.

Chet Wagoner, having slept a few hours, came with Joe Garza and his crew to have a close-up look at the garden and to ride Badger back to the trailer at the North Fork trailhead.

"I really appreciate it, Chet," Tom told him. "You know that's not my favorite mode of transportation."

"That's what I figured," Chet replied, as he took a chew from his tobacco plug. "Besides, a big hero like you shouldn't have to do such menial chores as transporting horses."

This brought a laugh from Larry and those nearby, but Tom didn't mind at all.

Next, Larry placed a call to editor Ike Elliot of the Elk Creek Weekly Bugle. He told Ike what had taken place on the mountain and the location of the activity. He said if Ike could come up right away, he could witness and photograph the final harvest operation and the bonfire.

Ike said he appreciated the call, but he would have appreciated it more if Larry had called him before the strike force had moved in. Larry's explanation that it simply had not been possible did little to satisfy the eager editor.

Following the needed picture-taking, the two Cannabis-laden trucks were driven to the center of the clearing and unloaded. All three trucks and the two ATVs would be subject to forfeiture in the illegal operation.

Before the strike force dispersed, Larry thanked them all for their tremendous response and the fine job they had done to bring about a successful conclusion.

"Let me just speak for the others and tell you, it's been our pleasure," Carl said. "It's not often that an operation like this goes so smoothly. I credit you, Deputy Crafts, Agent Ortega and all your people for setting it up." Heads nodded among the other officers.

Larry whispered to Phil and Virgil, "The marshal turned out okay after all, didn't he?"

"Yep, he sure did," Phil admitted.

The seven arrested Cannabis growers were loaded into the carryalls and driven to the County jail in Centerville. They were arraigned the next morning in magistrate court. Judge Enfield set bail at $10,000 each.

Larry, Virgil and Phil drove the three trucks, one carrying ATVs, back to town and on to Centerville and the sheriff's fenced compound, where they were impounded. When they reached the ski area road, Virgil and Phil stopped to take down the video camera. Tom rode with Larry, who dropped him off at the ranger station on his way through town.

Word of the arrest had spread throughout the town of Elk Creek before Larry got back. He had called Peggy from Centerville to let her know that he would be a little late getting home, and Peggy had asked just what had happened on the mountain. "I'll tell you all about it when I get home," Larry told her.

It was 8:30 P.M. when he drove into town and dropped Virgil off at his office, where his car was parked. Phil Ortega had stayed in Centerville to participate in the arraignment and return home from there.

A few minutes later at home, Larry was faced with an eager family anxious to learn of the day's events. Peggy and the kids wanted to know every detail of what had taken place that day and the past several days leading up to it as well.

"The phone has been ringing steadily all afternoon and evening," Peggy said. "Mostly just curious people, but several you probably need to call back."

Larry spent the next hour telling his family the whole story and answering their questions.

"Was there any shooting, dad?" Ernie wanted to know.

"Not a shot," Larry answered. "It was a totally-peaceful

operation, although there were guns pointed at people, the bad guys, that is."

"Were you carrying a gun, dad?" Jill asked.

"Just a shotgun, honey, and my pistol in its holster," Larry told her.

"Did you ever feel like you were in real danger?" Peggy asked.

"To tell the truth, not really," Larry said. "But you know, those bulletproof vests are really hot and uncomfortable."

"Bulletproof vests?" Peggy exclaimed, as Larry went to the phone in the den to return a few calls.

One was to Ike Elliot's cell phone. Ike wanted to thank Larry for the hot tip and tell him that a spectacular bonfire was in progress in the clearing. "After Joe Garza torched it and it really got going, it was something to see! I think I got some great photos. This could be the story of the year!" he said, excitedly.

Larry's other calls were to Mayor Harriet Braggs, County Commissioner Sam Turner and State Representative Fred Graves. Each wanted first-hand information about the day's events and assurances that everything was under control. When Larry told them that there were seven suspects in the Adams County jail and a large bonfire burning near the ski area, all three seemed satisfied.

The next morning at the office, Larry and Tom had to tell the whole story again to Mildred and Rita. Larry called his boss, the forest supervisor, to bring him up to date and thank him for Agent Phil Ortega's help.

Joe Garza came in just after 9:00 A.M. to report on the conclusion of the harvest and the bonfire. "It went very well," he said, "it sure took a lot of diesel fuel, because it was so green, I guess, and it took nearly all night to get it all burned up and then put out. The newspaper guy kept wanting us to pose for pictures."

"None of your guys took samples home, did they?" Tom asked, with a wink toward Larry.

"Sure," Joe said. "They all want to join those seven guys in the Centerville jail."

Everyone laughed, but Rita said, "He's kidding, isn't he?"

The national weather report showed rain in southern California. There was also a news item about an airplane crash connected with a forest fire. The day after the reported rain, word was received via the Forest Service computer that the Dry Gulch Fire was contained* at 45,000 acres, and a day later control* was reported.

Beth came home two days later, and Ben the day after that. After a day at home to rest, both were back in the office and ready to resume their regular duties. Larry suggested an impromptu gathering in the conference room so the firefighters could tell of their experiences and learn what had happened at home while they were gone.

"Wow, it sounds like you all have been busy!" Ben said, upon hearing about the law enforcement activity. "I'm sorry to have missed all the excitement."

"Me too," Beth echoed. "All we have to do is leave and things start popping around here."

"What about the fire?" Tom asked. "I'll bet you had your share of excitement too."

Beth led off by telling her experiences as crew liaison. "The hardest part was letting those guys on my crew do all the work and not being able to lift a hand to help out," she said. "I know you impressed on me beforehand that my job was to see after the needs of the crew and relay orders from incident command. Still, there were times when I wanted to grab a shovel or Pulaski* and help build fireline.*"

She went on to tell how her crew and another from the

same tribe built line all the first night, from near the valley floor to a high ridgetop, over two miles through dense chaparral.*

"When we finally reached the top, just at daybreak, and two more crews relieved us to proceed building line along the ridge, I could see that we were in for a long hike back to where the buses would be parked and then a long ride back to fire camp. Just then a helicopter landed on a helispot nearby in the ridge. I hurried over to talk to the pilot and I asked him, 'How's chances for a ride down to fire camp for two tired Indian crews?' The guy made a quick radio call and then said, 'Sure, get'em up here.' Well, I was so excited, not just to get my crew and the other one a ride to fire camp, but hey, it was my first-ever helicopter ride!"

"Good stroke, Beth!" Tom said. "Were the crews excited too?"

"Heck no!" Beth answered. "Everyone of them, all fifty had ridden in helicopters before. It was old stuff to them. I do think they were glad to avoid a long hike and to get back to camp so quickly, five minutes compared to two or three hours. In eleven trips, that pilot took fifty two of us back to camp. It was great!"

"We heard there was a fatality involving a slurry drop," Mildred said. "Did you know about that?"

"I sure did," Beth answered, her expression turning serious. "It was a real 'goof-up.' The third day we were there, five crews, including mine, were building line on a narrow ridge not far from the fire front. I guess incident command ordered a slurry drop, and instead of hitting the fire or just ahead of it like they were supposed to, somehow it hit squarely on the ridge right where one of the crews was working. Several crew members were hit by the slurry and knocked down. Two were hurt badly, and one was thrown over a cliff, about twenty feet down, and into some rocks. A helicopter was there within ten minutes and hauled both of them to the hospital, but I think the one who fell off the cliff was dead at the scene. It was a real shame! I never did hear what the investigation showed, about whose fault it was. I probably never will know. It made me just sick!"

"Did you have a good crew?" Rita asked.

"Oh yes!" Beth said, brightening up again. "They were great! All young guys but with quite a lot of experience. And despite being rather stoic most of the time they all had a real sense of humor, laughed and joked a lot. They had a name for the supervisor of our sector that I'm not sure I can repeat."

"Did they have a name for you too?" Mildred wanted to know.

"As a matter of fact, they did," Beth said. "On the second day of building line, it seemed we just kept getting orders to go up the hill, which they called, 'Yea-ma-coo', and then back down the hill, which was 'Pa-nee-u'. I relayed the orders, of course, as they came over the radio, and by the end of the shift I was known as 'Yea-ma-coo, Pa-nee-u.' That's what they called me the whole time after that. I think they said it affectionately, but I guess I don't know for sure."

"You said they were young guys. How young were they?" Tom asked.

"Most of them were still in high school, eighteen or nineteen years old," Beth answered. "When I picked them up, the dispatcher told me that the governor of the tribe wanted them back as soon as the fire was over; no mopup. School was about to start, and nearly all of the crew were still in high school. It was a reasonable request. As soon as the fire was declared 'contained', I told the regional liaison that, and asked that my crew be among the first released. Well, I think the guy thought that I just wanted to get home myself. He told me that he would decide on the order of crew release, and that my crew was needed for mopup. It would probably take at least three or four more days, maybe longer."

"What did you do?" Larry asked.

"I raised hell with him," Beth said, her green eyes flashing. "Then I decided to go around him, and I went to talk to the incident commander, straight to the top. Actually, I was a little surprised that he agreed to see me, but he was very nice, a regular guy. I explained the whole deal to him. I was about ready to tell him to check with Ben to see if I was credible, but I guess he believed me without that. Anyway, my crew was released right away, among the first."

"Good for you!" Ben said. "I wonder what I would have told him..."

Beth threw a rubber eraser at Ben, and the questions continued.

"Were you two together at all on the fire?" Tom asked.

"Not at all," Ben said. "We never saw each other the whole time. It was a pretty big fire. There were three divisions with three sectors each. I was night division supervisor on the second division. I think Beth's crew was working on the other side of the fire."

"We heard on the news about an airplane crash," Mildred said. "Was that near where you were?"

"I've got to tell you," Ben continued, "I feel very lucky to be here telling you about the fire. Yes indeed, the plane crash was close by, and in more ways than one. I was scheduled to go up for aerial reconnaissance the afternoon before it rained, to get a good look at the fire's progress, hot spots and all, before my night shift. Well, the guy who was supposed to pick me up and drive me to the airport never came. Anyway, we missed connections somehow. They took an aerial observer from the forest to map the fire since I didn't show up. There was another plane, a private one, that intruded into the restricted airspace over the fire, just to see what was going on, a curiosity seeker, I guess. Visibility wasn't the best, with all the smoke, and somehow this intruder collided with our observer plane, clipped off most of his tail section. They didn't have a chance. The crash killed both the pilot and the observer. The other one, the intruder, was damaged, but managed to limp back to the airport and land safely. I understand the pilot and passenger were both charged with trespassing in restricted airspace and with reckless endangerment, maybe even manslaughter."

"Sounds like the good Lord was watching out for you, Ben," Larry said. "That's three fatalities on one fire, not good at all!"

"No, it sure wasn't," Ben said. "And all three were connected with air operations. Only the slurry-drop one was classified as 'preventable.' Investigations were in progress for both accidents when I left. I'll be interested to hear what conclusions they reach."

"How about the fire itself?" Tom asked. "How bad was it?"

"Pretty bad," Ben answered. "It was mostly chaparral and scrub timber with a lot of dried-out annual grass to carry the fire on the ground among the woody stuff. It was all really explosive! There were some strong winds the first couple of days when it made its biggest runs. The wind died down some later, but by then the fire was big enough, at 30,000 acres plus, that it was essentially creating its own weather, wind that is. The steep topography didn't help either. We couldn't get dozers on much of it to build line. The ridges were too steep and narrow. That's why organized crews were so essential. I think there were about fifty Indian crews, maybe more, and at least a dozen hot-shot crews, the seasoned regulars from several different regions. And I think there were ten or twelve prisoner crews from three different states. All the ones I saw were good crews."

"I'm just as glad I had the crew I had," Beth interjected, "even if the prisoner crews were good."

"Oh, they had their own liaison people, the guards I guess," Ben said.

"They've been reluctant in southern California in the past to burn out their fire-lines. Was it a problem this time?" Larry asked.

"It sure was," Ben said. "At the very beginning, the forest supervisor went to the incident commander and told him they couldn't approve our using fire to widen our lines. He said there was just too much private property scattered throughout the National Forest or adjacent to it. If an expensive home was burned by the main fire, that's one thing. But if one of them happened to burn because of our backfires, the liability would just be too great. So we were really handicapped. We lost a lot of line that the crews had worked hard to build, just because we weren't able to burn them out and make the lines wide enough to hold the oncoming fire."

"So, as usual, it took a break in the weather to stop it?" Tom asked.

"That's right," Ben said. "When a cold front moved in and it started raining, we were able to hook it. It was just mopup after that, which I guess is still going on. They released the incident command team and about half the crews."

"Well, we're glad to have you both back home, safe and sound," Larry said. "I hope you considered it a good experience."

"I sure did," Beth said, "and the fire overtime will be nice."

"Jean already has mine spent," Ben said. "Rather than the Dry Gulch Fire, we'll remember this one as the 'microwave oven and new family room furniture fire' at our house."

"This has been some two weeks all around," Mildred commented. "We sent two people off to a fire and nearly got one of them killed; we got a new Research Natural Area proposed; and we put seven people in jail for growing marijuana on the forest."

"Yes," Rita said, "not a dull moment on the Elk Creek District!"

Larry told his family a little about Ben and Beth's fire experiences when he got home that evening but had to save most of the details for later. After a quick supper, he and Tom drove to Centerville for a Society of American Foresters chapter meeting. The speaker was Forest Service Regional Ecologist Paula Russell telling about Research Natural Areas.

CHAPTER VIII

PERFORMANCE RATINGS

Rio Verde National Forest Supervisor Frank Johnson's secretary called Mildred Bronson to schedule Ranger Weaver's annual performance rating. It would be in the supervisor's office, the "SO", the following Wednesday afternoon. She also told Mildred that Granite Peak District Ranger Tony Angelo's performance rating would be the next morning, in case the two rangers wanted to "carpool" into the SO in Capitol City, some 220 miles from Elk Creek. Larry and Tony usually drove into the SO together for rangers' meetings and visits such as this one. They would meet in Centerville and leave one vehicle in the Fish and Game Department's secured parking lot. They also commonly shared a double motel room to save costs, considering limited district budgets.

Larry had already completed performance ratings and training plans for his primary assistants and for Mildred Bronson and Chet Wagoner, the people who reported directly to him in the ranger district organization. Tom handled those for Clark Brightfeather, the district scaler, and for Joe Garza, the crew foreman. Mildred did the rating for the receptionist, Rita. The less than full-time employees were rated by Larry's assistants, according to the functions involved. It was an efficient operation, and Larry made sure this responsibility was accomplished in a thorough and timely manner.

Forester Tom Cordova, who handled timber, fire,

minerals and land-use activities, had been on the district for five years. He was a "timber beast" first and foremost, with no desire for line positions, such as a ranger's job. After a "rocky start" when he first came to the district, Tom had done excellent work in all of his assigned duties, as exemplified by the Bear Hollow timber sale contract and EIS, and most recently by his professional conduct in the Cannabis garden trespass case. Larry rated him highly. For training, Tom had completed most of the appropriate schooling available, so they agreed on a detail to the Supervisor's Office for two weeks to work on timber sale contract reviews from other districts. Larry had arranged this with Forest Timber Staff Don Hendricks, who was pleased to have the help. Tom was also nominated as a division supervisor on a regional incident command team that handled project-type forest fires. Larry and Tom agreed that his next logical career move should be into the regional office or perhaps a forest supervisor's office on a big timber forest, in a timber sale administration or silviculture position. Tom said that he would begin applying for vacancies along that line during the next year, although he wasn't really anxious to move.

Beth Egan, the district wildlife staff, who also handled endangered species and public information duties, was a wildlife biologist, four years out of college. She had been on the district for less than two years, but she also had not started her tenure at Elk Creek very well. But after some initial "battles" with other district staff, Beth had become a model employee and a staunch supporter of multiple-use. During the past year she had done better than average work in all of her assignments, with a real flair for organization. She was an energetic and now a positive employee, and certainly an asset to the district. Larry rated her fairly well, considering her limited experience. Beth said that eventually she would like to have a ranger's job, which they agreed was an attainable goal within the next three to five years. To that end, her training plan called for details during the next year, working under Tom to get timber training in all phases; sale preparation, marking, scaling and cruising. She would also spend some time with Ben working on range allotment analysis and management plans and on recreation administration. She would work with Mildred to learn more about the budget and ranger-district financing.

Larry would recommend that Beth's fire assignments continue to be as a crew liaison for large project fires outside the region and that she train as sector supervisor on any smaller fires on the forest or within the region. She would also continue to act as public information officer on certain large fires as she had during the past year. All of this was in addition to her regular duties on the district in wildlife and information. Beth said she would like to apply for some ranger vacancies during the next year, just to get her name before those who made such selections. Larry agreed that it couldn't hurt, but to be realistic, it wasn't likely that she'd be selected very soon.

Ben Foster, assistant ranger responsible for range, watershed, recreation and wilderness, had been on the district for four years in that capacity, having handled timber and minerals on another district on a different forest for three years before that. It was apparent to Larry that Ben was ready to be a ranger. He had all the training, experience and qualifications necessary for such an assignment. He had outstanding interpersonal and organizational skills, and his work ethic and professionalism were exemplary. There was no reason for Ben not to achieve his goal of a ranger's job within the next year. His training plan was written to provide for acting ranger assignments on other districts as opportunities allowed, and for details to the regional office, or RO, to assist in special projects and gain exposure. Ben was to be a trainee as incident commander on a regional team, having been a division supervisor for two years. Of course he would continue to apply for ranger vacancies.

Mildred Bronson and Chet Wagoner's ratings and training plans were much simpler. Both had been Elk Creek District employees long before Larry came to the district, and would likely be in their current positions a good while after he left, and eventually retire there. Both were competent in their work, but neither was looking for promotion or career advancement. Mildred and Chet represented the stability and continuity of the district, having "trained" five earlier Elk Creek Rangers.

Their ratings were highly satisfactory. Mildred's training plan for the past year had been accomplished when she attended the recent field tour to see district projects and activities first hand. For the next year she would detail to another district to observe how they did business and share ideas. Larry suspected that this assignment would actually be for the benefit of the other district involved.

By assisting with the BLM's wild horse roundup, Chet had achieved the "off-forest" part of his required but really unnecessary training plan. He and Larry would look for another such opportunity during the next year. Mildred and Chet were two district employees often taken for granted by most, but essential to the district's successful operation.

Larry packed a bag for a one night stay in Capitol City, the supervisor's office headquarters town. He met fellow Ranger Tony Angelo in Centerville at 7:00 A.M. on Wednesday, and together they drove in Larry's green Forest Service pickup to Capitol City. They had lots to discuss and catch up on enroute. They talked about the "accidents" at the Alliance Sawmill and the accused tree spiker in the county jail in

Centerville and about the Cannabis garden and raid. Larry asked Tony about the White House phone call to Forest Supervisor Frank Johnson that had stopped a Granite Peak District timber sale that Bill Crawford had complained to him about. Tony said that he and his timber people had tried hard to develop an acceptable sale proposal, but environmental group leaders at the state level had refused to negotiate any mediation measures. Instead, they decided to work through political channels to put a stop to the sale early in the planning process. And yes, the supervisor had indeed received such a call, and he of course had complied.

Larry told him about the district's exciting participation in Elk Creek's town parade, which evoked a hearty chuckle from Tony. He also told about the BLM wild horse roundup, the Cannabis garden arrests, and about his father's speech at the Lions/Kiwanis Clubs joint meeting.

"Wow," Tony exclaimed, "I'd have loved to have heard that one!"

"As a matter of fact, we videotaped it and also have it on an audio cassette; I have it with me," Larry responded. "We can listen to it on the way home if you'd like. I wouldn't mind hearing it again myself." Tony eagerly agreed they should do that.

"Now, neighbor," Larry said, "why don't you tell me all about the Rainbow Family gathering on your district in July. I wanted to come over and observe for myself, but things got busy and I never did get the chance."

"Well, Larry, you wouldn't believe it," Tony responded. "It was about the strangest thing I've ever seen in all my days. As you know, the Rainbow Family's get-together is, in effect, an annual convention of 1960's 'flower children' or 'hippies,' people who mostly lead more or less conventional lives now. But they 'revert' for a week or so every year around the Fourth of July. They meet and camp-out on some National Forest. I guess they decide where the next one will be at their gathering each year."

"Usually there's strongly-voiced community objection, with fear of drug use, public nudity and other disruptions. I suppose the locals are concerned that their young people are going to be corrupted. Well, this year was no exception.

"We got about six months' notice that their encampment was being planned for the Rio Verde National Forest on the Granite Peak District, and we started working with the community, the sheriff's office, and with other local leaders to prepare for the event. It has been going on enough years now so that there's a pretty good file, complete with advice on how to deal with those people and handle the 'problem,' if indeed it is a problem. I think it's more of a challenge."

"Were there leaders you could work with?" Larry asked.

"They seem to go out of their way to avoid designated leadership," Tony answered. "There was really no one leader to talk to throughout the planning phase and even up to and including the event. They seemed to handle everything by committee, and even that fluctuated. As you know, we needed a special-use permit application from them. When it came back, it had an unrecognizable signature on it. They promised to leave their campsite in good shape, like they found it. And you know what? After checking around, they have a pretty good track record on that.

"So anyway, an advance party showed up about the first week in June. They laid out the campsite, more or less, and we agreed on such things as a parking area, sanitation provisions, and drinking water sources. We helped them arrange for porta-potties and tanker trailers for their water. They seemed to have money for advanced payments and deposits. I suppose they collect dues or registration fees or something.

"They started arriving in numbers on the first of July, in

everything from VW vans and old school buses to motorcycles and fairly-new sedans and station wagons. There were hundreds and then thousands of them, and I'll tell you, they were back in their hippie costumes. There was a lot of long hair, even if some of it was thinning on top."

"How many altogether?" Larry asked.

"Between 10,000 and 12,000 we estimated," Tony said. "It was hard to get anything like an accurate count. That includes kids.

"Luckily the weather stayed good all week. They just slept out in the open, although there were a few tents. I suppose a good rain would have had them scurrying back to their vehicles."

"Were you able to inspect the campsite during the event?" Larry wanted to know. "And were you welcome there or looked on as an intruder?"

"Oh, they were all mostly friendly," Tony said. "There was no problem in our visiting the area. Frank even came up and went through the camp with me one day. He was really astounded. Quite a few of them were bare-nude. Most all the kids were, especially the little ones, the toddlers. They had several makeshift playpens, full of these little naked kids.

"Music, I guess it was music, was blaring everywhere, all the time. And dogs, dogs of every shape, size, and breed; there were hundreds of them! And of course there were a few dog fights, nothing too serious.

"There didn't seem to be much organization, no program or anything, at least not that I could see. They seemed to eat in little groups and in big ones, with pots or vats boiling away over open fires. Strange smells were everywhere, including that funny sweet-smelling smoke. I'm telling you, Larry, it was quite a party, late into the night, every night, for nearly a week."

"One surprise though," Tony continued, "they seemed

really concerned about their trash. I guess they were environmentally conscious, or at least wanted to appear to be. They had bins set-up at several locations where people brought their refuse to dispose of. The bins separated trash into several categories, like aluminum, glass, plastic, paper—all separate. They had made arrangements with Waste Disposal Inc. of Centerville to come in, as the group was leaving, to haul the stuff off. Funny thing was, the company just emptied all those bins together in their big trucks and hauled it off."

"Amazing!" Larry commented.

Rangers Larry Weaver and Tony Angelo drove into the motel parking lot, two blocks from the supervisor's office, at 11:30 A.M. and checked in. They put their bags in the room and started down the street. "Lunch time, partner," said Larry. "How about Mexican?"

"What else, knowing you?" Tony replied. "Let's make a deal; we go Mexican for lunch and Italian tonight, okay?"

"Deal," said Larry, and they headed for Pancho's Restaurante, just down the street. Both ordered chili verde burritos, enchilada style, with black coffee.

When the chips and salsa arrived, Tony said, "Wonder what kind of mood the 'old man' will be in this time? He was really on a tear last year at rating time. I guess the 'enviros' were getting to him, and nowadays, they're running the outfit at the top level. Also, he'd just got a new lady boss, younger than he is too by quite a bit. First time in his career for both categories. That was probably hard for him to accept."

"I suppose it all adds up," Larry replied. "Frank has had a long and distinguished career, even though with some ups and downs. Remember how we heard what a terror he was when he was supervisor of the Blue Mountain? And his earlier years as a ranger, dealing with the militant Hispanic group, the

Alianza, in northern New Mexico must have really been a challenge for him. But I've got to say, he's been a straight shooter with me, always backed me up on the tough issues, and I've always known where he stood. Frank's really a pretty good communicator, and that's darned important in his job."

"Yeah, I agree," Tony said, "but I wonder when he's going to pull the plug. There's been talk of him retiring for several years now. I'm wondering if he's just wanting to outlive the current administration, and then try to help get the outfit back on the right track."

"That could be it," Larry pondered. "If so, it's a good objective, and I'm with him. You mentioned his new lady boss, the Regional Forester. She's been on board for about a year now. Have you met her?"

"Yes, I have," Tony replied, "when I went into the regional office for advice on how to handle the Rainbows. Karen Harrison, she says call her Karen, seems like a nice young woman. I guess she's in her late thirties or early forties. She's tall and slender, sorta' athletic-looking. But my gosh, Larry, she sure hasn't had much experience for the job she's in. I understand she was a fisheries biologist with the Fish and Wildlife Service and then the Bureau of Reclamation. She's had no line experience before this assignment. It's no wonder Frank had a hard time accepting it. But he would never admit it. Frank's a traditionalist, and this sure isn't traditional!"

"It's sure a different outfit nowadays," said Larry. "We never used to get political appointments outside of a few now and then in the Washington Office. I wonder where it's all heading?"

The waitress brought their burritos, and the two rangers turned their attention to eating.

"This isn't bad," Tony said, "but you just wait until tonight, when we go for pasta at Luigi's!"

They finished, paid the bill and walked to the supervisor's office, where they ran into South Fork District Ranger Barbara Williams, who was just coming out.

"Just getting finished with your rating, Barb?" Tony asked.

"Yes," Barbara replied, "We were in there all morning, and I was afraid it might take all day."

"How's his humor?" Larry asked. "My turn's this afternoon, but I guess it will be delayed a while if the boss hasn't had lunch yet."

"We're on our way to Pancho's now," Barbara answered, "and he's in a pretty good mood, just spent a lot of time asking about South Fork activities and philosophizing on a variety of subjects. I have to stay overnight, because I'm trying to get a timber sale reviewed this afternoon and probably tomorrow morning. What are you guys doing for dinner?"

"Luigi's, of course," Tony said. "Care to join us?"

"I'd love to," said Barbara. "See you this evening. About six o'clock?"

"That'd be fine," Larry said. "See you then."

Tony started making his afternoon rounds with the supervisor's staff while Larry waited for Supervisor Frank Johnson to have lunch before his afternoon performance review session. Larry reviewed his paperwork and thought about what his boss might have in mind to talk about. He knew he had been in place as Elk Creek Ranger for a long-enough time, seven years, so the supervisor would likely be urging him to start applying for vacancies. There was no set rule on this, but it was common knowledge that rangers were expected to move after so long a time on a district, usually seven or eight years, ten maximum. This was not only to give the ranger new experience, but to allow for new leadership on the district.

Larry was certainly a team player; he would not resist a move if his boss encouraged it, even though he was quite content with the Elk Creek job. In addition, he knew his family liked it there and would not be anxious to move. There was a lot to think about.

When the supervisor returned, he greeted Larry warmly and said, “We’d better get to it, Larry. As you can see, I’m running behind. I seem to be in a talkative mood today.”

Forest Supervisor Frank Johnson was sixty years old, squarely built at 5 feet 10 inches and 200 pounds, a little heavier than he’d like, but it wasn’t easy getting the pounds off at his age. He had a full head of graying hair and a small mustache. Frank was a no-nonsense supervisor, but well-liked and respected by his employees as well as his superiors and peers.

The Supervisor’s Office of the Rio Verde National Forest was in the federal building in downtown Capitol City. Also in the building were other federal agencies like the state office of BLM, the FBI, the U.S. Attorney and offices for both of the state’s U.S. Senators.

Not only was Frank Johnson forest supervisor of the Rio Verde, he had the additional responsibilities as “Capital City Forest Supervisor.” This meant he was to be in communication with the other three forest supervisors in the state, one of which happened to be in a different region, and let them know about pending legislation or issues that could affect them and their forests. He also relayed messages from the other forests to state agencies or the legislature, as necessary, appropriate and convenient. He acted as sort of a “clearing house” for the national forests in the state in addition to the one he was directly responsible for. It was a duty that Frank enjoyed, and he worked hard at it. For instance, he maintained a personal relationship with Governor Clyde Winston and his key staff, which often proved beneficial to all the state’s national forests.

Frank and Larry reviewed the Elk Creek District work plan accomplishments and discussed the district employees, their career potential and their aspirations.

"Tom Cordova wants to stay in timber," Larry said. "He's an outstanding forester and could be a real asset to any forest. You may recall that Tom was a bit of a problem a while back. It was a matter of attitude. He turned that around and has been an excellent employee ever since. He has good fire experience too.

"Ben Foster is ready for a ranger job now, and that's what he'd like. He's had all the experience required and he works well with people; there are really no 'flat spots' with Ben. I'm blessed with an excellent staff," Larry continued.

"Beth Egan, our wildlife biologist, has good potential. She's competent and well-organized, good at public relations too. She'd also like to be a ranger as a long-term goal. And I think she can do it, once she's had more experience. I'd rather not push her too fast. She's learned about multiple-use in the past couple of years, and in fact, she's still learning."

"Thanks for that rundown," Frank said. "I agree you have good people, and I also realize that they have a good leader. I'm glad to see you working so hard on their development, and also pushing them with me. I'm especially pleased with what you've done with Tom Cordova, to put him on the right track, and with Beth Egan, to give her a balanced perspective."

"Oh, Tom and Beth have done that themselves," Larry said, "I just encouraged them a little."

"I understand how that goes too," the supervisor commented.

Following an indepth discussion of the district's accomplishments during the past year, Larry's own rating was the best he had ever had.

"Now let's talk about your future, young man," Frank

said. "Although I couldn't be happier with your work at Elk Creek, I think it's time for you to be moving on—and up."

"I was expecting you might be thinking that way," Larry replied. "And you know I'm not going to drag my feet. I haven't applied for any vacancies, but I'll start looking closely for a good fit for my family and me. Anything else, boss?"

"Yes, a couple of things," Frank answered. "I mentioned to you a while back that this year it's our turn to host the regional forester's pack trip with the governor, and I would like it to be on your district, on the Elk Creek portion of the Trapper's Cache-Sheep Camp Wilderness. You have the staff and equipment, not to mention the capability, to outfit such an undertaking, and I'd appreciate it if you'd just handle all the details. It's on the calendar for the week of September 10, three days and two nights. That's all the time the governor can spare, but I think it's enough to make an enjoyable and worthwhile trip. He'll probably have about four staffers with him, and Ms. Harrison may want to bring one or two of her staff along, very likely the information director, and who knows who else. You can probably figure on about eight or nine 'guests,' including me, although I'll sure help too, as you know.

"We can handle it with no trouble. I may ask Tony Angelo to help too, if you don't mind, and bring along some extra horses. I sure hate to rent horses for something like this. You never know what you'll get. By the way, does the regional forester know how to ride?"

"We have to assume so," Frank answered. "She knows about this traditional event and has it on her calendar. I guess we'll see what kind of a rider she is. You probably should make sure she's assigned a good, gentle horse, just in case. And Tony helping out would be just fine. I appreciate your taking this on, Larry."

"No problem," Larry said. "Maybe I'll just put her on my

personal horse. All of our District horses are Foxtrotters, good and gentle but some have quite a bit of 'go' in them. Old Gifford will take good care of her. My kids ride him all the time. I'd put her on our other horse, Cougar, which would be even better, but Jill is training him and practicing in running the barrels."

"That's fine. You work it out any way you think best. The other thing," Frank continued, "is a 'political' outing for you, I'm afraid. The Vice President is going to float the Middle Fork of the Salmon River in Idaho, and the forest there is short of qualified sweepboat operators right now. They've name-requested you for a detail to help them out, because of your past experience in that area. Altogether it could take a full week of your time. It's in the latter part of September. What do you say?"

"Well sure," Larry replied. "How could I turn down a request like that? I just hope I don't get in a big argument with the Vice President. I sure don't agree with his extreme environmentalist point of view."

"Not much chance of that," Frank said. "I doubt if you'll even get close to him. The trip will be commercially outfitted, except for support for the Secret Service and maybe some of the media. That's where the Forest Service comes in. I hadn't realized you were an old 'river-rat.' For my part, I've never tried it and I'm too old to start now."

"Yeah, when I was an assistant ranger on that forest, I ran the river every chance I got, spent a lot of time on the sweepboats. That's where you stand in the middle of a big, rubber raft, with long-handled oars fore and aft. It's not hard to do once you get the hang of it. And I have to admit it's a lot of fun."

"Okay," said Frank, "Having a little fun won't hurt you, I guess. I'll tell them they can count on you. They'll likely contact you direct. Have fun!"

They spent another hour elaborating about recent district activities, including the field tour, the RNA candidate area search, the Cannabis raid, the parade, and the wild horse roundup. Frank was pleased that the district could help their BLM counterparts.

"How many did you gather?" Frank asked, "and how did you pay for time and mileage involved?"

"We just charged it to 'training,' because it was valuable experience for Ben and me and such an activity was on Chet Wagoner's required training plan," Larry answered. "We brought in a total of 276 head, but they turned 140 back out. They're thinking about a prevention program..." and he went on to describe how the BLM might slow growth of their horse population with some innovative techniques, following some preparatory public involvement.

Frank was especially impressed with the district's efforts to convert individual permits to grazing agreements and with progress on the Bear Hollow timber sale. He complimented Larry on the cooperative effort with the oil and gas company in converting a dry hole into a developed trailhead.

"That was mostly Tom Cordova's work," Larry said. "I didn't get involved until Tom had the agreement all but finished."

"Anyway, it was a good accomplishment by your district," Frank said.

"I've got to tell you one thing, boss, concerning the Cannabis incident," Larry said. "I nearly goofed myself up with the magistrate. We paid him a courtesy call before contacting the marshal, and I forgot where I was and mentioned the case we were to talk about with the marshal. Judge Enfield let me know then and there that I was out of line. I was ready to crawl into a hole, with Phil Ortega helping to push me in."

"I doubt if the judge will remember it; no harm done," Frank said, in an understanding tone.

"Well, I sure will," Larry replied. "I guess it was a good lesson after all."

They finished up just about 5:00 P.M.. Frank asked Larry if he would be around tomorrow.

"Yes," Larry said. "I'll be making contacts with several of your staff in the morning, like Tony's doing this afternoon. Then we'll drive back to Centerville tomorrow afternoon. I should be home by suppertime. I'm supposed to go with Ernie to his Scout meeting if I'm back in time. They're going to review his Eagle project..." And Larry went on to describe the interpretive trail at Moose Lake Campground.

"Well, you'd better be home in time for that," Frank admonished. "I'll try not to be too long with Tony's rating in the morning. It sounds like your future forest ranger is off to a good start." And with that they concluded Ranger Larry Weaver's annual performance review.

That evening at Luigi's Italian Restaurant, Larry asked, "Barbara, why don't we just let Tony order for all of us? He's the expert in Italian cuisine, isn't he?"

"Fine with me," Barbara replied, "and that includes the wine. I suspect we're in for a real treat."

And a treat it was! Tony Angelo ordered minestrone soup for openers, followed by Fettucine Alfredo all around, along with a California burgundy and Spumoni ice cream for dessert.

The three rangers swapped stories and experiences during the evening and their enjoyable meal. Barb and Larry tried to convince Tony that he was in for a rough morning, as the supervisor had already handed out all the good ratings. Tony wasn't buying their story, but he accepted their compliments on his dinner selections and his expertise in Italian cuisine.

The next morning, while Tony took his turn in the front

office, Larry made his rounds in the supervisor's office, updating staff officers who happened to be in their offices, about district activities and seeking their advice on various matters.

He asked Range and Wildlife Staff Ed Donahue about his experience with coordinated resource management. He was encouraged when Ed recommended it highly, saying it should work well with the Sandstone Grazing Association.

Then Larry found Recreation, Wilderness, Lands and Minerals Staff Georgia Kenley in her office. They talked about several subjects, including the trailhead at the oil and gas well dry hole, the proposed ski area expansion, and the coming regional forester/governor pack trip into the Trapper's Cache-Sheep Camp Wilderness. Georgia told him there should be no real problem in getting approval for the Powder Bowl Ski area work, as long as the company had the required funding assured to do the complete job. A bigger problem would likely be getting through the inevitable environmental appeals. She was complimentary about the amount of volunteer work done on trails projects on the district and encouraged Larry to look for more opportunities using volunteers to get his poorly-financed recreation work done. She also told Larry she would like to visit the district soon and see some of these activities first hand and spend some time with Ben and Tom reviewing their recreation and minerals work.

Larry said, "That would be fine, Georgia. Why don't you give Mildred a call and schedule a trip?"

He stopped in to say "hi" to Phil Ortega and talk about follow-up needed for the Cannabis trial coming up, but Phil was attending, in fact conducting, a law enforcement training session on another forest.

He next updated Timber Staff Don Hendricks on progress with the Bear Hollow timber sale, and they discussed the deputy sheriff's arrest of the alleged tree spiker.

"You want to hear something funny?" Larry asked Don. "There was a bald eagle's nest in a tree near the surveyed route of one of the temporary access roads in the timber sale area, so we had the road built about a mile away from the nest. Well, Beth Egan told me last week that the pair of eagles moved their nest to a tree right next to the newly-built road. It's like they enjoy watching the log trucks go by or maybe they're expecting to benefit from some roadkill. Isn't that wild?'

With a chuckle, Don admitted that it was.

Larry asked Don if he had heard anything about approval of the new research natural area. Don told him that it was too early for that, but he said again that he really appreciated the district's cooperation in identifying RNA candidate areas and especially Tom Cordova's help when Larry had to tend to trespass problems.

Tony's session with the boss was finished at 11:30 A.M., so they grabbed a couple of burgers to go, having already checked out of the motel, and headed for home. They listened to the tape of Lawrence Weaver's speech and Tony remarked, "That was just outstanding! I'm glad I got to hear it. He doesn't pull any punches, does he?"

"That's not Dad's style," Larry admitted.

Larry asked Tony if he could help with the regional forester's packtrip with the governor and bring an extra horse or two. Tony said he'd be glad to. So it was settled. Larry, Tony, Ben, and Chet would outfit the trip and perhaps learn something about state-level politics.

They were in Centerville before 4:00 P.M. and Larry was home at 5:30 after a brief stop at the office.

At supper, Peggy and the kids wanted to know how the performance rating went, and Larry told them that they should start thinking about a move.

"New places are always exciting," Peggy said, trying to

head off any adverse reaction by Ernie and Jill. “We’ve really never had a bad move, and the best part is we can talk together as a family about possible places where dad might apply.”

“It’s really a pretty good time for me,” Ernie said. “I’m just starting high school, and maybe I can finish all four years in one place. Then on to college and forestry school...”

Jill wasn’t quite as enthusiastic. Her main concern had to do with Cougar and making sure they could find a place where they could keep their horses at home.

“We’ll just make sure that’s the case,” Larry reassured her.

The following Saturday morning Larry and Peggy took a little horseback ride together, on the same forest trail that Jill and her grandpa had taken, to talk in some detail about what kinds of jobs and locations they might want to consider. They talked some more with Ernie and Jill later. Peggy enjoyed riding Cougar and said she hadn’t had enough time lately to ride.

Thus the Weaver family was forewarned and prepared for a move to another Forest Service assignment. Larry knew that too many times such matters weren’t discussed in advance; then families resisted or were resentful of moves to new locations. Such problems had damaged many a promising Forest Service career.

The Scout meeting went well also. Ernie explained his Eagle project to the troop leaders and reported on progress.

“I should be finished this weekend,” he said, “when I hang the interpretive signs on the posts that are already in place.”

Ernie also explained that he’d had good help from all three patrols in putting up the signposts and hauling rocks to place below the trail switchbacks. That way he was able to fulfill the requirement that he manage or supervise work of others on his project as well as working on it himself.

"We should have the whole troop come out for a dedication ceremony," said scoutmaster Kent Maluski. "This sounds like one of the best Eagle projects we've had."

"That would be neat," said Ernie enthusiastically. And it was settled.

CHAPTER IX
THE PACK TRIP

A tradition had been established some ten years earlier for the regional forester to host the governor each summer on a horse pack-trip into a Wilderness somewhere in the state. Three different governors had participated during that time, and Karen Harrison would be the second regional forester. The principal value of this outing was communication, the chance for frank discussions on topics of mutual interest and importance in a relaxed atmosphere. The beautiful scenery and "outdoor adventure" aspects of the trip were added benefits. Originally, outside contact in case of emergency was limited to Forest Service radios, but in the past few years cell phones were available to spoil the feeling of solitude.

The former regional forester had hosted a previous governor in the Trappers Cache-Sheep Camp Wilderness several years before, but neither Karen Harrison nor Governor Clyde Winston had been there. Governor Winston decided to take just three of his staff along, Communications Director Betty Jameson, State Fish and Game Director Bert Edwards, and his personal assistant, Jimmy Small. The regional forester was bringing Information Director Joyce Barker with her, so with Forest Supervisor Frank Johnson, that added up to seven guests on the ride.

Ranger Tony Angelo was set to bring his own horse and an extra, plus four saddles from his district. Larry had asked that he make certain his horses were freshly shod, as were the Elk Creek pack-and-saddle stock.

When Larry, Ben Foster and Chet Wagoner sat down to plan the trip's details, they realized they were two horses short. Tony had said that two were all he had available at that time; his trail crew was using the other district horses . The Elk Creek District had six Foxtrotters and five pack mules. Larry had Gifford available for the regional forester to ride, and Jill had said to go ahead and take Cougar, but her dad declined, saying, "You'll be getting him ready for the 4-H Rodeo in a few weeks, so let's not take him to the Wilderness and risk getting him skinned-up or worse." He had thanked his daughter for her unselfish offer, which was so typical of Jill.

"Why don't we borrow a couple of those "mustang" saddlehorses from the BLM?" Ben suggested. "Steve Underwood told us after the roundup that he would be glad to return the favor anytime he could. Let's just take him up on it."

"Good idea," Larry said. "I'll give him a call. But we sure don't want to put any of our guests on them, not knowing just how gentle or reliable they might be, and what sort of riders we'll have along."

"I'll tell you what," Chet said, "I'll ride one of the mustangs and we can pack the other one and put the governor on old Molly. She's our one mule that's been ridden a lot, as well as packed, and she's gentle as they come. Besides, the governor is a Democrat, isn't he?"

"Yeah, he sure is," Larry answered, "and he just might enjoy the symbolism of it, not to mention the ride on Molly. Let's plan it that way. But I wouldn't mind riding the mustang myself, Chet. You'll likely be pulling the packstring, so you'll need to be on Chief to make sure there are no foul-ups. When I call Steve, I'll make sure we get a mustang we can pack. And I think I'll ask for Scooter, the tough little roan horse that Jack Fisher rode on the roundup."

"Okay, if you insist," Chet agreed. "Sounds like a good plan all around. We know our horses are gentle enough for the dudes, and Tony's probably are too. If there's a question about it, we can put the forest supervisor on Tony's extra horse. We know he's a good hand."

Chet went on to say, "You know we're going to have to pack in the camp the day before and get it set up. No telling how much 'luggage' our guests will bring, but I'm sure we can't get it all in there, plus the kitchen and all, with just five pack animals, in just one trip."

"Yeah, that's good thinking," Ben chimed in. "I'll help pack-in the camp and get it set up. Then we can bring the mules on out and be ready to load our visitors' gear the first morning of the trip."

Larry agreed, and they mapped out the travel route. The pack-trip would depart from the North Fork trailhead and camp at the edge of Big Meadow, about fourteen miles in. With the camp all set-up the day before, that would be a reasonable first day's ride. The second day would be a "day ride" of eighteen miles, more or less, looping around No-Name Peak and back to the same camp that night. There would be plenty of horse feed in Big Meadow, and by using a portable electric fence to allow the animals to graze in several different areas, the impact on the meadow would be minimal. And to make sure the animals were well-fed and content, they would pack in some oats, along with the kitchen and their own personal gear, the day before.

The third day's ride out, by another route, would be just 12 miles to Smith's Fork trailhead. Other district staff, Beth, Tom, Joe and Rita, would shuttle the vehicles and trailers to the "take-out" point. Since the mules and two horses would already be at the North Fork trailhead from the day before, the other horses could be hauled in using just two big goose-neck trailers, and the people in two carry-alls.* Logistics weren't all that complicated.

Steve Underwood readily agreed to furnish two BLM mustangs for the packtrip, more if they needed them. Scooter was available for Larry to ride. Flintstone, a nine-year-old grulla, or mouse colored, gelding that had been packed numerous times, would be the fifth pack animal. Steve had them delivered to the ranger district barn and corral the day before the ride.

Chet and Ben packed in the kitchen, tents, horse feed and most of Larry, Ben and Chet's personal gear the day before as planned, going in from Smith's Fork. They used the district's five pack mules, including Molly, who would be a saddle-mule for the governor the next day. They set up the kitchen in a broad, flat area in the edge of the timber adjacent to the meadow. There was a portable two-burner stove with propane bottles, four rollup pack tables and eleven folding camp stools.

They hoisted the food in coolers and pannier boxes* as well as the horse feed in burlap bags at least ten feet off the ground using lash ropes tossed over big tree limbs. This was standard procedure in grizzly country, but it was also a good idea in any case to prevent black bears and other varmints in the area from helping themselves to a free meal. Besides, they realized how inappropriate it would be to habituate wild animals to a human-provided food source.

They set up four tents not far from the kitchen. Two of them were two-man tents, one intended for the governor and his aide and the other for the supervisor and the fish and game director. There was a larger one to accommodate the three women, and the fourth was about the same size, maybe slightly larger, intended to house four men, the outfitter crew.

They also rigged a wilderness porta-potty, consisting of a five-gallon plastic bucket, with garbage bags as liners and a conventional toilet seat with lid. A canvas tarp screen completed the arrangement, not fancy certainly, but adequate for the purpose. (Later they would dig a deep hole in the soil of the meadow and bury the sewage, an acceptable method of disposal in such cases.)

While Chet and Ben set-up the camp, their horses and mules, mostly wearing nylon hobbles, grazed in the meadow. The three mare mules were left unhobbled because they simply wouldn't leave anyway and they were easy to catch. An electric fence, batteries and wire tape with short fiberglass posts, were stashed next to the kitchen.

When the camp was set-up and ready for use, Chet and Ben headed back to the North Fork trailhead, where there were corrals and water for the stock to stay the night. They had gone in from Smith's Fork trailhead, in effect reversing the route of the coming trip. Joe Garza took the truck and trailer back to the North Fork trailhead where the group would start from the next day. This way, Chet and Ben were able to check out the trail both in and out. It was nearly a twenty-six-mile ride for them that day, but covered quickly by Comet and Chief and five mules that were "empty" on the way out. But it was a long day, dawn to dusk.

They put out some hay for the animals and returned to town. Everything was set for a three-day packtrip in the Wilderness.

Three impromptu social events took place in the town of Elk Creek the evening before the packtrip. Larry had let Mayor Harriet Braggs, County Commissioner Sam Turner and State Representative Fred Graves know that Governor Winston and his party would be in town that night, and the three politicians had made arrangements for a reception at the town hall to welcome the governor to Elk Creek. It wasn't every day that the state's chief executive came to their little town, and they weren't about to let this opportunity slip by.

Local Fish and Game Officer Kent Maluski, working with Glen Romero, had scheduled a special meeting of the Sportsmen's Club, so that Director Bert Edwards could visit with local members, discuss department activities and socialize. It was another opportunity that would not be missed.

And there was a potluck supper at the Weaver residence for district employees and their families to meet Regional Forester Karen Harrison and Information Director Joyce Barker and also to visit with Forest Supervisor Frank Johnson.

Jean Foster brought a big tray of veggies, carrots, celery, olives, broccoli, cauliflower, and bell peppers with ranch dressing dip. She also made a guacamole dip and brought tortilla chips and salsa.

Peggy baked a big ham and a small turkey and also provided coffee and other drinks, although several couples also brought bottles of wine.

Gladys Wagoner brought a big pan of "easy bake" potatoes with onions, but she apologized because she was afraid they were a lot like the Dutch-oven spuds that Chet would probably be feeding them the next night in camp. Chet said that hers would be better.

Rita and Ray Vigil brought home-made tamales, which were a big hit.

Beth and Richard Egan brought a big kettle of baked beans, another likely duplicate for the camp, but always good.

Cleo and Clark Brightfeather brought a tub of corn-on-the-cob, and Yolanda and Joe Garza brought two big pans of cornbread with green chili and onions layered in.

Angie Cordova made a great tossed green salad with avocados and a special Dijon dressing. Mildred made her famous deep dish peach cobbler.

Frank Johnson commented, "What a fantastic dinner! This wasn't really potluck was it? No one could be that lucky."

He suspected that the whole thing had been prearranged; Peggy had to admit that a certain amount of coordination had taken place.

Jill and Ernie were there to help with the serving and passing around bowls and platters for seconds. Jill also helped take care of the Fosters' three- and five-year-old boys and the Cordovas' baby girl. It was something she looked forward to.

The new regional forester was greatly impressed and perhaps a little surprised with the "family" atmosphere that evening, involving the district employees and their spouses. It was her first exposure to the Forest Service at the ranger district level, at least on a social basis, and she really hadn't known what to expect. But she was pleasant and cordial, and everyone seemed to like her. When Beth addressed her as "Ms. Harrison," she said, "Oh, I wish everyone would just call me Karen." And from that point on, nearly everyone did.

Frank, of course, knew exactly what to expect, and he was delighted. He was pleased to see his new boss being exposed to a real, down-to-earth Forest Service family gathering.

When Frank got a chance to talk to Peggy in the kitchen just before the eating started, he asked, "How do you and the kids feel about a possible move? I'm presuming that Larry has talked it over with you."

"Of course he has," Peggy replied, "and we're ready to go wherever and whenever. We're a Forest Service family, Frank, and we believe that new assignments are an exciting part of the job."

"Somehow I expected that's what you might say," Frank admitted. "We'll see what happens, but I'm sure it will be good."

The evening went well. Everyone enjoyed the wonderful meal and the good company. Beth hit it off with Joyce Barker, whom she was meeting for the first time. Joyce told her that she had heard good things about her public involvement accomplishments on the district, as well as her fish and wildlife skills.

Karen Harrison managed to have a personal visit with everyone there and seemed to enjoy the evening and the people.

Tony Angelo had sent his regrets that he couldn't make it to the potluck because his son was in a Little League all-star game that night, and Tony was one of the coaches. This was a post-season, all-star game following the "finals" that had been held in August. It was scheduled so as to dedicate Centerville's new Little League field that unfortunately had been completed after the season. Tony said that he would be there with his horses first thing in the morning.

The "riders" had breakfast the next morning at Barney's Cafe and also got sack lunches for the trail, as Ben had advised. They were picked up in district carryalls by Tom and Beth and driven to the North Fork trailhead, where Larry, Ben, Chet and Tony were already saddling up. It was 7:00 A.M..

Tony was bragging that young Dominic had two hits last night, including a triple, and he played errorless ball at short-stop.

"That's great," Larry said, "but did your team win?"

"It's not about winning or losing in Little League," Tony protested.

"This is all-stars," Larry reminded him. "Did your team win?"

"No, as a matter of fact, we lost, six to five," Tony replied reluctantly, "but it was a great game and a good experience for all of us, especially Dominic."

When they started unloading the vehicles, Chet said under his breath to Larry, "Now you can see why I wanted to pack-in the kitchen ahead of time."

The "advice list" sent out earlier clearly stated they should bring only one large or two small duffels each, including a sleeping bag and cot if they desired. But the gear coming out of the carryalls looked like the carousel at an international airport. The governor had one large and two small duffels, and most of the others, except Frank Johnson and Bert Edwards, weren't far behind. The four packers, with help from Frank and Bert, started mantying-up* the gear, that is, wrapping it in canvas bundles to be tied onto the mules and old Flintstone. After carefully weighing each pack to assure that both sides were balanced, whatever they weighed up to a limit of about 75 pounds each, the packs were tied securely to the decker pack-saddles. When they were finished fastening fishing rod cylinders to the packs, every mule and poor Flintstone looked very much loaded down, although it was actually more bulk than weight.

At that point, Joyce Barker went back to a carryall and brought out a large watermelon that she had bought at Henry's market the afternoon before. "I thought this would make a nice addition to our trip," she said.

The quick-thinking Ben took the melon from her, forced a smile and said, "Thanks!" With that he handed it to Beth saying, "Here, Beth, would you please put this in the creek at Smith's Fork? It'll taste great when we come out, day after tomorrow."

Joyce, not quite understanding Ben's assertive action, just smiled and nodded her concurrence.

The next few minutes were spent matching riders to horses and adjusting stirrups. When Chet introduced Governor Winston to Molly, the governor's face lit up. "Finally I get to associate with a true Democrat," he said. Chet shot a knowing glance at Ben, but Larry avoided eye contact for fear of inappropiate laughter.

When the governor climbed aboard Molly to have his stirrups adjusted, he spread out a big map to look at the travel route. This might have spooked some horses, but old Molly just stood there unconcerned. Chet winked at Larry, and he nodded back in approval.

Larry offered Gifford to the Regional Forester and adjusted her stirrups. Even though he was about sixteen hands, she had no trouble mounting, since she was five-foot-ten and athletic. “Oh, he’s beautiful,” she said. “I know I’ll have a great ride. Thank you, Larry.”

“You’re certainly welcome, ma’am,” Larry answered. “I’m sure you two will get along just fine. Just nudge him a little and he’ll move right out. He’s a good traveler. His name is Gifford.”

“Gifford?” she said. “Wasn’t that the name of...”

“Yes ma’am, it was,” Larry answered politely before she could finish the question.

“Please call me Karen,” she said.

“Yes ma’am,” he said.

Joyce Barker was assigned the gentle Decker and Betty Jameson the equally-gentle Badger. Both were about fifteen-hands, which was not quite as tall as the others. Jimmy Small was given the grey horse, Major, and Bert Edwards, the tall sorrel Rocket. Frank Johnson rode Silky, a big bay trotter from the Granite Peak District. Tony rode his other Granite Peak horse, Arrow, another bay with a stripe in his face that resembled his name.

Both Frank and Bert brought their own saddles, so only two of Tony’s were needed. This also meant there were fewer stirrups to adjust.

This distribution of saddlestock left Chief, the parade horse, for Chet, and the lively Comet for Ben. Larry stepped up on Scooter and said to himself, “After lining up all these smooth-riding Foxtrotters for our guests, I’m in for three days of bouncing on this tough little guy.”

"Before we get started, folks," Larry announced, when everyone was mounted, "we need to take a few minutes for a 'safety meeting.' I've asked our muleskinner, Chet Wagoner, to provide us with some pointers on how to prevent the kinds of wrecks that are common with this many animals from several different sources. (He made no mention of this many riders of varied or unknown capabilities.) Chet..."

Chet rode Chief to the front of the group. The packed mules and horse were still tied to the trailers. "With a mixed bunch of horses and mules like this," he said, "the main thing is to keep pretty good spacing and not crowd each other. I doubt if any of these would kick, but you just never know. We'll stop after a mile or so and check cinches. We don't want any saddles slipping. And we'll also make sure the stirrups are okay; no use anyone getting sore, with stirrups too short or too long. The trail is good. Ben and I were over it yesterday. It's a little steep in spots, but overall not bad. If there are any places you don't feel comfortable, just get off and lead your horse a while. No one will think a thing about it.

"I see that several of you are bareheaded, including all three of the ladies. We have some riding helmets in the trailers' tack compartments, and it might be a good idea to wear them, if you'd like to. Lots of folks are doing that nowadays, and it sure makes sense. It's a good safety feature for horse riders, especially those less experienced. Anyone have questions?"

There were no questions, but Governor Clyde Winston removed his ballcap and put on a helmet. Jimmy Small, following his boss's lead, put one on also. So did Karen Harrison, Joyce Barker and Betty Jameson. Everyone looked quite stylish, as well as safety-conscious. All three women took time, while they were dismounted, to inspect themselves in the carryall mirrors.

So, just before 8:00 A.M., the group comprising "the

Regional Forester's pack trip with the Governor," started up the trail into the Trapper's Cache-Sheep Camp Wilderness. Ben was in the lead, followed by Governor Winston on Molly. Chet, led the pack mules, Rufus, Amos, Ruby and Mildred, following the riders while Larry, with packed mustang Flintstone in tow, brought up the rear.

About half a mile up the trail, at a steep switchback, Jimmy Small fell off. He was gawking at the riders behind him and at the same time looking through his saddlebags for a camera. When Major made a sharp turn and scrambled up the slope, Jimmy just slipped off. Luckily it was on the uphill side and he wasn't hurt at all, just a little shaken and embarrassed. Tony, who was two horses behind, jumped down quickly to help.

Major just stopped and stood there, as if to say, "Let me know when you're ready to start again."

Tony helped Jimmy back on, and the procession resumed its ascent up the steep trail. It was a minor incident, but a good warning to the others to pay attention to the trail and to their mounts.

A few minutes later, when the trail leveled and became wider, the group stopped as Chet had suggested. Ben, Tony, Frank, and Bert made the rounds checking cinches and stirrups. Everyone seemed to be doing well.

Larry mentioned to Chet that one of the packs on Mildred, the last mule in line, seemed to be "listing to starboard." This meant that, despite the weighing and attempt to balance as precisely as possible, the right pack was slightly heavier. Chet picked up a rock about the size of a softball, only flatter, and tucked it under the ropes of the left-side pack.

"You're adding weight?" Betty exclaimed, looking puzzled.

"Standard procedure," Chet said. "We can't take weight

off the heavy side, so we need to add a little on the light side."

As they crossed a cold mountain stream at mid-morning, Ben stopped and dismounted. He then pulled out a mesh bag filled with cans of soda pop from a small pool behind a large rock, that he and Chet had "cashed" the day before, and offered them all around. It was a refreshing break on a warm morning. "Just crush the cans and stuff them in your saddlebags when you're through," Ben said.

And so, after this brief stop, they continued up the trail at a moderate pace. There was no big hurry.

Bert Edwards, always on the alert for wildlife, spotted several mule deer on the opposite hillside and pointed them out to those nearby. Jimmy Small snapped some pictures from his moving horse, but it seemed certain the deer would be indiscernible at that distance.

"My wildlife shots never seem to come out very well," Jimmy lamented.

As they topped out after about seven miles on the trail, the terrain leveled and a nice clearing came into view, providing an ideal lunch stop. There were plenty of suitable trees to tie to, and again the more experienced riders made the rounds, removing bridles and hooking them over saddlehorns. Each animal wore a stout nylon halter under the bridle with a lead rope secured to the saddle. These were used to tie-up to trees, well-spaced from each other. Chet explained to Jimmy, when asked, that "We just don't tie-up with bridle reins. It's a near sure way to get the reins broke."

"It's lunch time," Larry called out. "But first, the rule is, 'ladies to the right and gentlemen to the left,' for a rest stop."

Lunch sacks and canteens were removed from saddlebags, and the trail ride party sat on downed logs or reclined on the ground and ate a leisurely midday meal.

Governor Winston asked why the Trappers Cache-Sheep

Camp Wilderness was so named. Supervisor Johnson said it was because the early-day fur trappers had "cached" their furs in pits in the area to return for them later to carry out and sell at trading posts or at mountain-man gatherings. "The sheep camp part," he said, "was because the high country was grazed by sheep rather than cattle. Basque sheepherders made camp in various locations on the mountain. They often carved a historical picture account of their lives and activities on aspen trees. We'll likely see some of them in the next day or so," he added.

"Why did sheep graze here instead of cattle?" Joyce asked.

"Cattle really can't graze this high country," Frank said. "They often get 'big-brisket' disease at these elevations."

Frank then asked State Fish and Game Director Bert Edwards to comment on the wildlife situation in the Wilderness, including habitat conditions, as he saw them.

Bert was enthusiastic about what he had seen. "There's an abundance of desirable browse on this mountain," he said. "The deer we saw were in fine shape; fawns were big and healthy. There was elk sign in the trail too, plenty of it. And I suspect we'll see some moose before long." He went on to say, "This Wilderness is probably the best wildlife habitat of any in the state. The fishing is good too, both lake and stream, native cutthroat in abundance. We should have a great time trying to outwit them in the next couple of days."

"Are you saying that because it's Wilderness, it's automatically good wildlife habitat?" Frank asked.

"Not at all," Bert answered. "In fact, there are cases where Wilderness designation has actually been a detriment to wildlife. When habitat manipulation is needed, plant control projects for instance, and it can't be allowed because it's Wilderness, the habitat condition declines."

"It's a shame that some of those preservation groups can't or don't want to understand that," Frank said. "With a lot of them, it's acreage they're after, despite what might be happening on the ground."

"I agree with that," Bert said. "Their objectives are too often not very well thought-out."

"This is very interesting," the governor said. "I've been led to believe that we simply have to have more Wilderness classified if we want to protect wildlife values. Now I learn that's not necessarily true."

"I'd say the whole trip is worthwhile already, if we never have any more discussion," Frank said. "Don't you agree, Karen?"

The regional forester nodded her head. "Maybe so," she answered. "I know I'm enjoying the discussion and learning from it, I might add."

It was a leisurely lunch with discussions and visiting, mostly one on one, but occasionally the whole group would turn their attention to something that the governor or Bert or Frank was saying.

One example of this was when Frank mentioned to Bert, "It's sure nice to see our relationships with your department improved. We had a tough time working with your predecessor, as you may have heard. When he first came on board, he made a general announcement to department employees that any future Forest Service decision that did not maximize wildlife values would be challenged. As you know, Bert, we just can't do business that way. Multiple-use management implies some give-and-take, and while we're working to improve wildlife habitat all the time, there's just no way that every decision will maximize wildlife values."

"Yeah, I heard about that statement," Bert said. "I agree that's not how to maintain a cooperative relationship. You can't draw lines in the sand."

"I'm glad to know about this and to see a cooperative attitude on the part of both agencies," Governor Winston remarked. "I take it we're getting along well on all counts now?"

"Well, not necessarily," Bert admitted. "I'm not very happy with some of the Forest Service road policies. I'd like them to close more of their roads after timber sales, for instance."

"We close them when they're not needed for other purposes, like fire access or public recreation," Frank replied. "But I guess not enough to make you happy, Bert. And speaking of disagreements, I'd like to see your department recommend that the game commission authorize more doe hunts in areas where we have too many deer. There are places where the habitat is really suffering. You seem to think that just because doe hunting is unpopular with many of the public, you can't recommend it, even though it's good wildlife management."

"There's a lot more to it than that, Frank," Bert responded. "And if your people would get their recommendations in to us in a more timely and better-coordinated way, maybe we could..."

At this point, the governor interrupted and said, "Well, I see it's not all total harmony after all. I didn't mean to stir up a hornet's nest here. I'm sure these problems can be worked out if both sides will get together and talk them through. Don't you agree, Karen?"

"Of course," Karen replied, a little bewildered at the turn the conversation had just taken.

Joyce Barker and Betty Jameson listened with interest and they each jotted notes in their day planners. These two information specialists seemed to have a lot in common, and they spent most of the lunch period sharing experiences and techniques used in public relations. Their conversation also included nonjob-related topics such as families, fashions, and even politics.

There were about seven more miles left to get to the campsite after lunch. Chet and Larry finished eating ahead of the rest. They excused themselves and proceeded up the trail with the pack animals so that packs could be taken off, supper could be started, and the electric fence enclosures could be set up. By this time Larry was comfortable with the fact that Frank and Bert would be able to help Ben and Tony with any problems that the less-experienced riders might have. Molly brayed in mild protest as the other mules left, but Ben fed her an apple core to divert her attention, and there was really no problem.

Just after 4:00 P.M. the group rode into camp. The four mules and one packhorse, along with Chief and Scooter, were grazing in a small, one-acre enclosure in the meadow. The electric fence of wire ribbon and five-volt battery was ample to hold them. A brief introduction to the fence for the two mustangs was all that was needed to acquaint them with this new barrier. They stayed at least ten feet away from the wire as long as they were in the enclosure. Still, as a precaution, Larry had hobbled them both, but halters had been removed to prevent a shod hoof from hanging up in strong nylon halter straps when an ear was scratched by a hindfoot.

Another such enclosure was ready for the newly-arrived eight horses. Molly would be put in with the rest of the mules and Chief. Mules were funny that way. They were content being together and also with at least one familiar horse, but Chet knew that it simply wouldn't work to split up the mules, or to put them in with mostly strange horses.

A meandering stream in Big Meadow cut through a portion of each enclosure, providing drinking water for the pack-and-saddle stock.

"What a beautiful campsite!" Karen remarked. "What is the altitude here, Larry?"

Larry resisted the urge to correct the regional forester's terminology and point out that altitude normally refers to height above the ground or sea level, as in an airplane, so he simply answered, "We're at about 8,500 feet elevation here. It will be cold tonight, I expect, maybe below freezing. I hope your sleeping bag is warm."

"Yes it is," she said, "and I have an extra blanket and a sweatsuit to sleep in. I should be fine. Thanks for your concern."

Ben got ready to explain the camp layout as Larry, Tony, Frank, and Bert unsaddled the horses and turned them into the second enclosure, also without halters. Tony hobbled his two horses that were not familiar with the area. Chet took a minute from his cooking to strap a bell around Molly's neck when Larry turned her in with the other mules.

"Camp music," Chet said. "It helps an old wrangler sleep at night. I wake up when I don't hear the bell."

"I think you're kidding us," Joyce commented. But Chet insisted emphatically that it was true, amid some muffled laughter.

"We have a makeshift toilet behind the screen over there," Ben said. "The toilet paper is in a Crisco can with a plastic lid. When the can is on the path to the screened-in toilet, like it is now, that means the toilet is vacant. When the can is not on the path, that means someone is using the facility. Everyone needs to remember, don't leave the TP can at the toilet. That gives us a false signal that it's in use, when it's not. Leave the can on the path when you're finished, got it?" Everyone nodded. (It was the first time that the governor, or any of the visitors for that matter, had been told how to use a toilet by an assistant ranger.)

"The washing area is that plastic pan and bucket of water on the flat log near the path to the toilet," Ben continued. "A 'community towel' is hanging there, or you can bring your own. If you want warm water, it will be in a kettle on the propane stove in the kitchen. Please remember to put the kettle back. We can wash with streamwater, but you shouldn't drink it. The drinking water will be in a large plastic jug with a spigot, on a table in the kitchen. We'll haul water from the stream, above the enclosures, in canvas buckets and run it through a filter. Anyone wanting to help operate the filter is welcome to it. If you happen to go fill the canvas buckets, remember to take it from the stream above the stock enclosures. There's an old joke about checking upstream before you drink, but we'll save that for later.

"As you see, we have four tents set-up," Ben continued, "two large and two small. One of the large tents is for the ladies, I hope it's suitable, and the other is for the wranglers..."

"That small tent will be just fine for me," Governor Winston interrupted, and headed for it with his luggage.

Ben, quick-thinking as usual, made a prompt adjustment. "Fine," he said, "and the other one can house Bert and Jimmy, if you don't mind. Supervisor Johnson can move in with the crew, since the other big tent will hold five without too much crowding."

Thus Governor Winston assumed control of the single accommodation that he was used to and expected, while the Forest Service made the necessary adjustments.

Just below Big Meadow, about a quarter mile from camp, the meandering stream ran into the North Fork in the headwaters of Elk Creek, which eventually ran into the Rio Verde some thirty miles east of the town of Elk Creek in Centerville. After putting bags in tents, setting-up cots, and rolling-out sleeping bags, several of the group grabbed fishing rods and headed for the creek below the meadow. Bert Edwards was in the lead, followed by the governor and the regional forester. Jimmy Small and Frank Johnson followed along behind.

Tony said, "If everything is under control, supper started and all, and if you don't mind, I think I'll just tag along and see if they're biting."

Larry waved him on without objection.

Joyce and Betty went along too, not to fish, just for the exercise, after the unfamiliar horseback-riding that day.

Chet had scrubbed the potatoes ahead of time, so all that remained was to slice them, skins and all, and start them cooking along with sliced onions and a bell pepper in a quarter inch of cooking oil in a big, aluminum Dutch oven.

"They're nowhere as good as the cast-iron kind," Chet said, "but they're sure nice to pack." He added a couple of envelopes of dry onion soup mix and put the oven on a bed of charcoal that had been placed on an old aluminum fire shelter to protect the ground. He also put several charcoal briquettes on the Dutch-oven lid to help the potatoes cook evenly.

Larry got out the store-ready tossed salad from a cooler, with three dressing choices in plastic bottles, and put them on the table. He also removed eleven nice sirloin steaks from the cooler, while Chet opened packages of frozen peas and put them in a pot ready to cook on the propane stove. A big, wire grill for the steaks was ready to go over the charcoal as soon as the anglers returned, so there was not much more to do for now.

Larry and Ben took currycombs and circulated through the enclosures to scratch the backs of their pack-and saddle-stock and remove the crusted sweat that had accumulated from the trip up the trail. They also hung nosebags of oats on each eager horse and mule, one enclosure at a time.

"The grass is good here," Larry said. "These oats are as much to make them want to stay in camp as to give them 'nutrition' or energy for the work they're doing."

Just after supper they would be haltered again and tied

for the night to picket lines secured with canvas straps or "tree savers" and suspended tightly between large trees near the edge of the meadow. The animals were thus well cared for, with a minimum of impact on the land. They didn't need to be out all night. Chet commented that that would just be "recreational grazing."

As they were tending the animals, Ben noticed a loose shoe on the left hindhoof of Flintstone, the BLM pack horse. He grabbed his pack-in farrier's kit and quickly reset both hind shoes and checked the front ones which were okay.

Joyce and Betty returned after about an hour to watch Ben's shoeing procedure, and then they observed the cooking operation. They marveled at Chet's efficiency and commented on how good the food smelled.

Just before 6:00 P.M., Ben went down the trail to let the fisher-people know that supper was nearly ready. They had kept two nice foot-long cutthroats and released a dozen or so more. Ben took those two back to the grill to cook in aluminum foil with butter, to serve as hors d'oeuvres before supper. Bert was the winner of the "fishing derby" with five, and everyone except poor Jimmy had caught at least one. Jimmy had fallen in the creek as soon as they got there, and spent most of the time trying to dry out in the late afternoon sun.

"You refer to this as supper," Clyde Winston remarked as they gathered around the kitchen area and unfolded canvas stools. "It looks more like a banquet to me!" And the others agreed.

"I'm taking orders for steaks," Chet said. "They've been on about seven minutes now, so the rare ones can come off anytime now. The mediums and more well-done can stay awhile longer. But the fire is hot and it won't take long in any case. Everything else is ready."

And indeed it was a banquet. Everyone sampled the fish

and then filled their plates, as much as they wanted. Some wanted more than others, but Chet advised, "Save room for dessert," as he produced another Dutch oven of apple cobbler.

"This is simply marvelous," Karen said, and heads nodded all around, as Larry poured coffee and Ben offered hot water for tea and cocoa.

When everyone had eaten their fill or at least all they wanted, water was heated and poured into two large pans, one with dish soap and a splash of bleach.

"I'm the dishwasher," Frank proclaimed, but Joyce argued that it was the one job on the trip that she could handle, as she grabbed the dishcloth.

"Then I'll dry," Frank said.

"No, I will," said Betty, "I'm really good at it. You'll see."

So both Betty and Frank dried dishes while Larry, Ben and Tony haltered the horses and mules and tied them to high-lines for the night.

Chet cleaned his Dutch ovens with a nylon "chore-girl" and a little water, then some salt, and dried them with paper towels and rubbed on a dab of cooking oil.

Later, the cooking fires were combined into one small campfire, and everyone gathered around for an evening discussion, which Frank proclaimed to be the most valuable part of the whole trip. "The scenery, fishing and good eating are just bonuses," he said.

They talked about cooperative relations between the state and the Forest Service, avoiding a continuation of the bit of contention that had surfaced at the lunch stop. Both Frank and Bert seemed to go out of their way to identify opportunities to improve relations. Betty and Joyce joined eagerly in the conversation. This was their specialty and they were anxious to contribute.

Karen asked Frank to tell about other activities on the

Rio Verde National Forest, with emphasis on how the public benefits. That took several minutes, close to a half-hour, as it was Frank's favorite topic. He elaborated at length, especially about the forest's outstanding recreational facilities.

Tony told them about the recent Rainbow Family gathering on his district, which amazed and amused everyone.

"I had heard rumbling of that event," Governor Winston said, "mostly from local and county officials in the form of complaints or concerns. I'm glad to hear it was handled with a minimum of impact on the community."

At Frank's request, Larry told about the Bear Hollow timber sale and how the local economy benefited. He explained how the resulting "thinned" forest would be growing with more vigor and therefore would be healthier and more resistant to insects and disease. He also mentioned the tree-spiking incidents, which were, as yet, unresolved, despite the arrest in Centerville. He told about the Cannabis garden and raid and about the BLM wildhorse roundup.

"You certainly have a variety of activities on the Elk Creek District," Karen commented.

To conclude the evening, Tony brought out his harmonica, and the trail riders participated in a community sing. Governor Winston was in especially good voice.

At 9:30, Larry proclaimed it was bedtime for early risers, and the party adjourned.

Everyone slept well in the cool mountain air. The next morning at breakfast Chet said at that he had been restless, because he had taken the bell off of Molly after she was tied up, and there was no "camp music." He said he could have simply turned her loose with the bell, and then he'd have slept well, while the bell kept everyone else awake.

It had rained gently for an hour or more just after midnight.

The crew was out at 6:00 A.M., moving animals to relocated enclosures, while Chet put on the coffee and started the Dutch-oven sourdough biscuits. When they were nearly done, he had bacon sizzling on the grill and eggs ready to fry. He rang Molly's bell to wake the guests.

"If I keep eating like this," Betty said, "I'm not sure I'll be able to get on my horse when it's time to start back. Chet, you're a marvel! Would you like to come home with me?"

"I expect Gladys would be agreeable," Chet replied, not even looking up, "if you have something decent to trade."

Lunch-making materials were set out on the camp tables, and everyone packed what they wanted and filled their saddlebags. There was a good variety of lunch meats and cheese, white and whole wheat bread, lettuce, onions, pickles, mustard and mayo for sandwiches, along with fruit, cookies, and small candy bars. Larry and Ben carried the "chips in a can" in their saddlebags to pass around at lunchtime. Jimmy offered to make the governor's lunch, but was turned down.

Bert pumped the filter for drinking water so canteens could be filled, after Frank hauled water from the creek in canvas buckets. A good camp routine was getting started early.

Joyce offered to wash dishes again, but Chet told her, "Thanks anyway," but he was staying in camp that day, and he had plenty of time to clean-up, care for the mules and horses staying in camp, and get supper started.

The day's ride, an eighteen-mile loop around No-Name Peak on a good trail, offered the riders a chance to see more beautiful scenery and lots of wildlife. Most had not seen the meadow full of deer at daylight when the horses and mules were put out to graze. An exception was Bert, who never missed a chance to see a sunrise and the wildlife that normally goes with it.

"You want to give your rear-end a rest today and ride old

Chief?" Chet asked Larry as they prepared to saddle-up. "I'll be staying in camp as we agreed, and he's sure available."

"I'd like to," Larry said, "but I'd better not. Those mules aren't used to the mustangs yet, and I expect they'll need Chief here for security."

A cow moose and her calf were working-over the willows north of camp in Big Meadow, as the group headed west down the trail at 8:30. Several more, and some bulls too, were seen during the course of the day, but the moose paid little attention to the curious riders. A nice herd of thirty or more elk moved out ahead of them just before noon.

"I wonder if we might see a mountain lion?" Karen asked. "I've heard there are quite a few of them in these mountains, and the population is growing."

"I'd sure be surprised," Frank said. "In all the time I've spent in the woods, I've never seen one."

"I've only seen a couple," Bert added, "and I felt really lucky. But you're right, Karen, their population is on the increase."

The day's ride went well, no mishaps. The lunch stop was at a deep blue lake, and a few fish were rising, even though it was midday. Bert, Frank, Karen, and the governor pulled out a few nice cutthroats, using barbless hooks, and then released them.

On the ride back to camp, they passed a band of domestic sheep scattered out and grazing on a well-vegetated hillside. Ben rode over to talk to the herder while the others proceeded on the trail. Larry explained that this many strangers could be an intimidating sight for a solitary sheep herder, who was likely from some other country.

"How many are there, Larry?" Joyce asked. "It looks like there must be a thousand of them."

"That's a good guess," Larry replied. "The normal size of

a permitted band of sheep is a thousand head. The herders and their dogs do a good job of keeping them dispersed and covering the range 'once over lightly.' It's a fully compatible and appropriate use of the Wilderness, although we have quite a few critics who think otherwise."

"I've heard such objections," Governor Winston chimed in, "but I don't see a thing wrong with it. In fact, it's really kind of nice to see such a traditional use in this remote area."

When Ben caught up with the group, he reported that the herder was Peruvian. They'd had a nice conversation, although Ben admitted his Spanish was limited.

"He's on his way out with this band," Ben said. "Expects to meet the owner at the North Fork trail head in seven days. He's a nice fellow. Wanted to know who all the people were."

"What did you tell him?" Karen asked.

"I told him it was the governor of the state and some other high-level officials," Ben replied, "but I don't think he believed me."

The governor threw his head back and laughed. "If he was a voter, I just might ride old Molly back there and show him some ID," he joked.

When they got back to camp, it was nearly 5:00 P.M.. Chet had moved the enclosures again and had supper ready. It was chicken breasts with wild and brown rice cooked with a rich cream sauce in the Dutch ovens. There was another store-bought salad, green beans and a Dutch-oven pineapple upside-down cake.

"You've done it again!" Clyde Winston said to Chet. "I may have to jog around this meadow a couple of times if I want to get my belt buckle fastened in the morning."

Betty insisted on washing dishes this time, and Jimmy took a turn at drying, while Frank and Bert made drinking water and the wranglers tied up the stock for the night.

The camp discussion was shorter that night; the riders had had a long day in the saddle and morning would come early for the ride out on the third day. But it was lively and thought-provoking to say the least.

The governor told about his idea to re-name the Wilderness where they were in honor of Senator Cecil Pendleton, an environmental champion and wilderness proponent who had died two years before. “I think it would be a wonderful tribute to a great man and a legend in this state,” he said.

There was some uncomfortable foot-shuffling by the Forest Service people and some hemming and hawing. Then Chet, of all people, spoke up.

“With all due respect, Governor,” he said, “I’d sure rather you’d think up some other way to honor the senator. The ‘Cecil Pendleton-Trapper’s Cache-Sheep Camp Wilderness’ would be a real jaw-breaker. It’s too long a name as it is, and we’d never be able to get it all on the signs, without doubling the lumber in them.”

“I’ll tell you what,” Chet continued, to the surprise of Larry, Ben and Frank (especially Frank). “Why don’t we christen No-Name Peak ‘Pendleton Peak?’ It’s one of the highest in the state and stands out well on the horizon. You can see it for miles around, even from town. You folks got a good look at it today; what do you think?”

Jimmy Small unexpectedly chimed in, “Why is it called No-Name Peak anyway? That’s darned strange, I think.” Without intending to, Jimmy had helped break the tension of the moment.

“Funny you should ask,” Chet replied, before anyone else had a chance to reply. (Chet was on a roll). “It used to be called ‘Molly’s Nipple,’ before the politically-correct crowd raised a stink and we had to change it. I don’t believe it’s even included in the geographic place names list anymore. And in case you're wondering, it wasn't our mule it was named after."

"Well that's an interesting alternative," Clyde Winston said. "We'll have to think about it some more. I'm not sure but what I like the idea."

Frank breathed a sigh of relief, but Karen looked a little uncomfortable. And Larry turned his head away to hide a broad smile.

As the campfire conversation was winding down, the governor's cellphone rang. It was the head of the State Office of Emergency Preparedness, who said there had been a fire in the State Capitol building, and the governor needed to be back there as soon as possible to make decisions about file records and other material that needed to be saved. He was told his office had been trying all evening to get approval to land a helicopter in the Wilderness to fly him out the next morning, but the authority for that was "Rio Verde One," who apparently was the Forest Supervisor, and he seemed to be unavailable.

When the Governor told about the problem, Supervisor Johnson and his boss, the regional forester, huddled immediately. "It's not the kind of 'emergency' that normally justifies approval for a helicopter landing in designated Wilderness," Frank said quietly.

"But can't this be considered a special circumstance?" Karen asked, groping for a way to accommodate the state's senior executive.

"It would be stretching a point. It's Wilderness, Karen, and it's really not an emergency."

"We'd sure better call it that!" Karen whispered. "Let's do it!"

Frank reluctantly took the phone from the governor, identified himself as the forest supervisor and responsible authority, and gave verbal authorization to make the flight "legal."

"We're camped on the southwest edge of Big Meadow," Frank told the caller. "It won't be hard to find... Yes, we can rig a windsock and hang it on a pole... There's all kinds of room, no obstructions... Okay, we'll look for the chopper at 9:00 in the morning..." And he handed the phone back, so the governor could get more details and information concerning the fire and the flight.

"Jimmy, there's room for you to fly out with me," Clyde said. "You'd better figure on coming too. I'm sure there will be details you will need to handle."

Jimmy Small seemed very pleased. "I hate to leave early," he said to those assembled, "but of course I'll do whatever is needed."

As the group dispersed and headed for their tents, Frank drew Chet and Larry aside for a brief and confidential discussion.

"Although I really didn't disagree with what you said, Chet," Frank admonished, "it was inappropriate for you to argue with the governor about renaming the Wilderness. It was a little embarrassing for the regional forester and for me."

"Gosh, I'm sorry, Mr. Johnson," Chet responded. "I never meant to embarrass anyone." He shifted his tobacco chaw from one cheek to the other. "Do you think this will hurt my chances for promotion?"

Frank stammered an inaudible reply, while Larry walked away to hide a smile and a chuckle.

As they moved toward their tent, Tony motioned Larry over and said confidentially, "Looks like new Wilderness policy was made tonight. I wonder what our environmental critics might say if they should learn that our boss permitted a helicopter flight in here to fly the governor out and called it a 'emergency'?"

Larry shook his head and replied, "You're absolutely

right, partner. I guess that shows what happens when politics takes priority over resource management. Frank was just following orders, I'm sure, but that doesn't make it right. Anyway, he didn't consult with us, did he?."

Molly's bell rang a little earlier the next morning, since it was "pack-out day," and for the governor, "fly-out day." Hotcakes with heated syrup and sausage patties were on the menu, along with coffee and a variety of juices. The same lunch-making materials were set out, and lunches were packed by everyone except the governor and Jimmy.

Betty remarked that there had been another rainshower last night. "This reminds me of Camelot," she said, "where it never rains 'till after sundown. We've been lucky, haven't we? We haven't had to use those yellow raincoats tied to our saddles."

"Those are called 'slickers'," Bert told her. "And yes, I guess we've been lucky, although these guys set up the tents for us, rather than taking a chance and having us all sleep under the stars, and that wasn't luck. I'd say that was good planning."

The tethered horses and mules had again been moved to fresh enclosures. Tents were taken down and sleeping bags rolled up.

Jimmy approached Larry and said in a confidential tone, "As you know, I'll be flying out with the governor in a few minutes. I've had a great time and I really do thank you and your crew for all you've done to make it a memorable trip. And the ride was especially enjoyable, the smoothest I've ever experienced, not that I'm an experienced rider, as you know. Larry, I'd like to say good-by to my horse. Which one is it?"

Once more, Larry turned his head to hide a smile. "It's the gray one, Jimmy, the only gray one in the bunch. And Major has a blazed face and all four black feet. He's in the north enclosure."

"Oh, I hadn't noticed that," Jimmy said. "Thanks."

Ben fashioned a wind-sock from a burlap feed-sack and a bucket bale and fastened it to a pole that he set up about 200 yards away in the meadow. The helicopter came into sight just after 9:00 A.M., circled once and landed between the sock and camp. Governor Winston expressed his thanks to Karen, Frank and the crew, and stepped aboard, along with a smiling Jimmy Small. The helicopter pilot lifted his machine about twenty feet above the meadow, flattening the grass below, slanted southward and they were gone.

"This gives us two extra pack animals," Chet observed, "and with less luggage to pack-out and the food eaten, we just might make it out in one trip without coming back."

"Let's give it a try," Ben said. And they packed up with that objective in mind.

"My goodness," Betty Jameson exclaimed, when the camp was removed and the animals were being packed. "You can hardly see that anyone has even been here. There are eight spaces in the meadow where the grass is a little shorter and some matted-down grass where the tents were, but nothing else I can see to show that we camped here. I can't even tell where the cooking and campfires were. This is amazing!"

"Well, that's our objective," Larry said. "It's called 'leave-no- trace' camping. If the Forest Service doesn't practice it, we can hardly expect the public to."

"Very impressive," Karen said, having overheard the conversation. "I hope that idea is in practice throughout the region."

"Yes, Ma'am, I think it is," Larry replied.

"Please call me Karen," she said.

"I've been intending to, Ma'am," he said.

Larry switched to Major for a smooth ride out. Molly got her decker packsaddle back, and the two mustangs were loaded with "mantied" luggage on riding saddles. Scooter learned quickly to be a packhorse, bumping his bulky pack against a tree just one time. After that he seemed to gauge his new width and give obstacles near the trail a wide enough berth.

The riders and packstring were on the trail just before 10:00 A.M. and headed toward the Smith's Fork trailhead. Larry had done a quick, last-minute check of the campsite, and proclaimed it acceptable. Everything was packed out, or so he thought. The mules were loaded heavier than usual, but it would be a slightly shorter trip out than it had been coming in. It was necessary to stop and reset the makeshift packs on the mustangs after about two miles. The packs had been weighed and were well-balanced, but they were unwieldy, and the riding saddles weren't made for packloads.

"We're lucky they're staying on as well as they are," Chet remarked, as he tucked a rock under a pack rope.

Tony took the lead for the ride out with Larry, now riding Major, behind him. Ben took a turn at leading the mustang packhorses at the rear of the procession.

After two hours on the trail, they rounded a bend and found themselves face to face with four hikers leading four packed llamas. Arrow had never seen anything quite so menacing before. He went straight in the air and came down headed the other way. Tony hung in the air for an instant, and then tumbled down a steep embankment and rolled fifteen feet to the creek bottom.

Larry grabbed the loose reins of the frightened Arrow as the wild-eyed horse started his stampede back up the trail. Bert dismounted quickly and hurried to check on Tony. When Frank rounded the bend in the trail on Silky, the other Granite horse, a near-repeat of the original wreck took place. Silky spun around, but Frank was able to hang on and stay aboard as his frightened mount tried to escape. Karen, on the steady Gifford, blocked his retreat and Frank got his horse stopped before anymore mischief could take place.

Tony was okay, no broken bones or open wounds, just slightly shaken-up and a little bruised. Larry took his place in the lead.

Gifford and the Elk Creek horses and mules did not appear to notice the "monsters" that had scared the Granite Peak horses. They calmly went past the llamas, now pulled off the trail by their cooperative and somewhat apologetic handlers. The two mustangs that Ben was leading seemed a little nervous but stayed in line.

When they reached a flat level area in a few minutes they stopped to check cinches.

Larry said, "Tony, it appears your horses haven't seen any llamas before. I hope you're okay."

"Yeah, I'm fine," Tony replied. "I don't guess they have. Poor old Arrow must have thought he was going to be eaten up; Silky too, from what I heard. Yours didn't seem the least concerned."

"When we first started seeing llamas on the trail we figured it could cause problems," Larry said. "We rented a couple of them and put'em in our horse pasture for about a week until everyone got used to each other."

"I guess we'd better do that too," Tony said.

"Yeah, I think that'd be a good idea, Tony," Frank agreed. "I thought old gentle Silky was coming undone."

The lunch stop was a small clearing in the trees before the trail started to become a steep downhill grade. As they were tying up, Karen told Frank in a confidential tone, "This Gifford horse is amazing! He's smooth to ride and gentle as a lamb. I swear he's even affectionate. I'd love to have him for my regular mount as I visit different forests and have occasion to ride. I could have him transferred to the ranger district nearest the regional office, and that way I could ride him on weekends, too. I do have that authority, don't I, Frank? And do you think Larry would mind terribly?"

"Yes, I'm afraid he would," Frank answered. "You notice that Gifford has a 'Flying W' brand on his left hip, instead of the 'US' that the others have? That's Larry's personal horse that he let you ride on this trip, just because he's such a good horse. Larry wanted you to ride the best one available."

Karen Harrison blushed noticeably and then said, "Oh, I had no idea. How embarrassing!"

"I won't tell him," Frank said.

The lunch-time conversation centered mostly on wildlife. Bert announced that he had been impressed with both the numbers and the variety they had seen in the past three days, as well as the good condition of the habitat. He also remarked at how good the fishing had been.

"I'm glad to hear you say that," Frank said. "It has been an objective on the Rio Verde to give some emphasis to fish and wildlife. When I came to the forest, there was considerable room for improvement."

"Hell, Frank, there still is!" Bert joked.

"You want to hear something funny?" Ben said. "After our thorough check out of our campsite and our 'leave-no-trace' objectives, I think we left the windsock on the pole in the meadow."

Larry slapped his forehead with an open palm. "I'm afraid you're right," he said, "and it's too far to go back now. It will probably blow down in a few days. Ben, why don't you let the Wilderness patrolman know about it so she can take care of it on her next pass through the area?"

The group stayed nearly an hour at the lunch stop, proceeded down the trail without further incident, and enjoyed another liquid refreshment break from a second stream "cache" provided by Ben and Chet. They arrived at the Smith's Fork trailhead just after 4:00 P.M.. Tom, Beth, Rita and Joe were waiting, and Beth had Joyce's chilled watermelon. They all enjoyed a slice or two, then cut up the rinds for the horses and mules.

As they were unloading the packstock and sorting the gear that needed to go back with the passengers, Bert said, "Larry, you need to tell us what our food bill is so we can settle-up before we leave. We were fed like royalty, and I know the ranger district doesn't have a budget to cover this sort of thing."

"Well, you're right about that," Larry replied. "We can cover everything but the groceries, and Ben bought those at the local market. What's the tally, Ben?"

Ben said, "Split eleven ways, it comes to $28.00 each. I hope that sounds okay with all of you."

"It's a real bargain," Betty exclaimed. "If it's okay, I'll write one check for my share, plus the governor's and Jimmy's. I can collect from them later."

There was a good deal of thanking and complimenting in the next few minutes, while Ben collected payments for the groceries. Regional Forester Karen Harrison said she was glad to have been here for her first horseback outing in the region. Bert Edwards remarked that he was pleased to be part of an improved State-Forest Service relationship. Joyce and Betty both marveled at the beauty of the area and how well-cared-for it appeared. They also gave rave reviews to Chet's culinary skills.

Larry thanked everyone for coming and said they had enjoyed hosting this important annual event. He thanked Tony for coming to help and for bringing extra horses and saddles. He said he hoped Tony wouldn't be too sore tomorrow.

"Yes, thank you," Frank said to Tony. "That Silky horse is really well-named. Now he needs some llama familiarization training. And Larry, we thank you, Ben and Chet, as well as the other support folks for all your good work and hospitality."

Karen made one last stop at the hitch rail to hug Gifford's neck before getting in the carryall for the ride back to town.

Thus the regional forester's pack trip with the governor on the Rio Verde National Forest was successfully completed.

Discussion at the Weaver family supper table that evening was lively. Peggy and the kids wanted to know everything that took place on the packtrip. Larry did his best to recount the various experiences.

"How was your mustang ride, dad?" Jill asked. "Are you ready to switch over?"

"You know better than that, honey," he said. "I didn't hesitate to ride Major as soon as he became available. And you know, the regional forester really fell in love with Gifford. I got the feeling she would have taken him home with her if she could have."

CHAPTER X
THE FLOAT TRIP

Forest Supervisor Frank Johnson had forewarned Larry about the Vice President's pending float trip on the Middle Fork of the Salmon River. The supervisor there had contacted Frank, requesting that Larry be detailed for a week to assist them by operating a sweepboat.*

The call came from Forest Supervisor Ralph Hanson, asking Larry to be there early the following Thursday morning. He said the job would be to provide river transportation and assistance to the Secret Service assigned to protect the Vice President and perhaps to assist some of the media also. He asked if Larry's security clearance was up-to-date. Larry told him that it was.

There would be two Forest Service sweepboats, one ahead of the Vice President's sweep, which would be furnished by a local outfitter, and the other immediately behind. There was a new ranger on the district, Elaine Morris, who was not yet qualified to operate a boat, so she would be with the river manager, Ted Anderson, in the first sweep. Larry would operate the following sweep with Supervisor Hanson aboard. Each boat would carry two or three Secret Service agents; two others would be on the Vice President's raft. In addition, three Forest Service kayaks would be on the river in case anyone fell overboard, or to provide other assistance as might be needed. The outfitter would also have rafts for the Vice President's support staff behind the second Forest Service sweep, and a Forest Service oarboat would carry the chief and regional forester.

Ralph also said that a Secret Service detail had spent the previous week checking out the area with Forest Service support. Ted Anderson had taken several agents down the river to assure them that it would be a safe trip for the Vice President.

The two Forest Service rafts on this trip would put in at Boundary Creek, just below Dagger Falls, and for two days float down to Indian Creek, where the Vice President and his entourage would be flown in by National Guard helicopters. The party would float for three days and take-out at the Flying B Ranch, where the helicopters would pick up the Vice President and his party. The rafts, Forest Service and outfitter, would then float on down to the take-out point at Cache Bar, about 100 river miles from Boundary Creek. Support personnel would be on the river for seven days, but only three days would be with the Vice President and his party.

Larry packed his "seabag*" and traveled by pickup, commercial airliner and finally by carryall to Boundary Creek with Forest Supervisor Ralph Hanson, Ranger Elaine Morris and River Manager Ted Anderson.

The boots, spurs, chaps, and broad brimmed hat of two weeks earlier had been replaced with T-shirt, cutoffs, strap-on sandals, and ballcap. At Indian Creek, the T-shirt and cutoffs would change to a Forest Service uniform short sleeved-shirt, with badge and nametag, and green shorts. A lifejacket with front zipper completed Larry's attire.

The sweeps were supplied with food and provisions for the support staff. The outfitter would fly-in their rafts and provisions by fixed-wing aircraft to the Indian Creek airstrip.

There would also be a Forest Service flight into the

Indian Creek airstrip with the chief and regional forester, who would accompany the entourage in an oarboat operated by the forest recreation staff officer.

There were no other rafting parties at the Forest Service check station at Boundary Creek because the Vice President's trip and security requirements were involved. Reservations had been canceled for those scheduled the entire week. Larry suspected that there might be some disgruntled river-floaters staying home.

The two-day float from the Boundary Creek put-in to Indian Creek would give Larry a chance to brush up on his sweep-operating skills, which didn't take very long. There were two easy and two moderately-difficult rapids before the Lincoln Creek confluence, and by that time Larry was comfortable and ready to take on the river. Ted led the way, making it easy for Larry to find the best routes through the various rapids. The more moderate-level rapids were navigated easily before they reached Sulfur Slide, a type three rapid considered "dangerous," three miles downstream. Larry followed Ted through a mid-stream "V-slick" with little difficulty. Ram's Horn rapid, another type three was somewhat tougher, and Larry bumped hard against a boulder, nearly dislodging his unsuspecting passenger. "Stay left!" Ted called back, motioning as he shouted.

"I'd better pay closer attention," Larry told the supervisor, as they straightened out and proceeded downstream. "Sorry about that, Ralph."

"No problem," Ralph said, as he crawled back into his seat on the raft. "I shoulda' been paying closer attention myself."

By the time they went through Velvet Falls, a type four rapid at mile five which was listed as "very dangerous," Larry was back in the groove. He followed Ted through, hugging the

left bank after they had pulled over to scout the rapid from the river's edge.

At six-and-a-half miles, they pulled into Big Bend camp on the right side of the river, for lunch. Ted set up a roll-up table* and put out the "makings" for sandwiches. He complimented Larry for his fast refresher course, the one "goof-up" not withstanding. Then he asked Elaine if she was ready to take the helm of his sweep. She said she was, if Ted would stay close and be ready to bale her out if she got into trouble. Ted told her he certainly would, and he'd take it completely at Chutes rapid, a type three at the seven-mile mark.

Elaine handled the lead sweep for the two-and-a-half mile stretch early that afternoon, before reaching type three Upper Powderhouse rapid, and type four Lower Powderhouse. Then Ted took over and Larry followed without incident.

By the time they reached Fire Island camp on the left at mile fourteen, the less-experienced members of the crew were ready to stop for the night. Ted allowed that it was his plan all along.

Fire Island was a campsite suitable for a large group, and it seemed a shame that just four people would be using it. They pulled in, tied-up and unloaded what they would need for the night from the rafts.

Ted cooked steaks on a grill over charcoal in a firepan. Afterward, the ashes were dumped in an ammo can to be packed out. Instant rice, a store-ready tossed salad, and a small pound cake completed the simple meal on the river. Ralph washed the plastic dishes and strained the dishwater through a fine sieve. The wet crumbs went into the ammo can with the ashes.

They set-up four small nylon tents and slept on the soft sand of the riverbank. The murmuring river and tired rafters made for good sleeping.

Daylight found Ted cooking sausage and eggs on a propane stove, while the others packed tents and gear into the rafts. Elaine took her turn at washing the dishes and strained the dishwater. They were packed and on the river at 7:00 A.M.. Elaine handled the lead sweep up to and including Artillery rapid, a tough type two She was gaining experience and confidence. Ralph took the long-handled oars of the second sweep during much of the same period to work on improving his own novice skills. He had been on the forest for less than a year, with several trips down the Middle Fork, but was still an apprentice boatman.

Wildlife could be seen from the rafts if the floaters looked at the right times and in the right places. Bighorn sheep, deer, and elk all saw the rafts go by, but those on the sweeps observed only a few. They were lucky enough to see a family of playful river otters shortly after the morning launch.

They ate lunch at Quick Stop camp, above Pistol Creek rapid, and just four miles from Indian Creek, where the Vice President's party was to assemble the next morning. They pulled into Guard Station camp, near Indian Creek airstrip, before 3:00 P.M. and set up camp. The three Forest Service kayakers joined them for supper. Ted had time to cook spaghetti and meatballs and a Dutch-oven peach cobbler.

"I'd almost forgotten how good we eat on the river," Larry commented.

Just after sunup the next morning, a Forest Service Twin Otter, a short take off and landing (STOL) aircraft, well-suited for back country airstrips, but used primarily for smoke jumpers* in fighting forest fires, landed at Indian Creek. It carried the Chief of the Forest Service, and the regional forester plus the forest recreation staff officer, who would be their oarsman. The Twin Otter also carried a medium-sized rubber-raft and river floating gear for the party.

A few minutes later, two large Air National Guard helicopters circled the airstrip and then landed with the Vice President, his family, staff and several Secret Service agents. Others were already onsite, as were the outfitter crews and their rubber rafts.

The chief presented the Vice President with a Forest Service ballcap and lifejacket in a symbolic ceremony. A sort of reverse receiving line formed, and the Vice President and chief made the rounds shaking hands with everyone present. That turned out to be the closest Larry would get to either of them for the rest of the trip.

The regional forester explained to the group that they were not only within a designated Wilderness, but that the river itself was designated Wild and Scenic in a quarter-mile corridor, with scenic easements on the private land parcels such as Pistol Creek, the Flying B, which would be the takeout point, and the Middle Fork Lodge at Thomas Creek.

Ted Anderson, the river manager and the one responsible for everything that happened on the Middle Fork, then conducted a brief but forceful safety meeting at the edge of the river. He explained the classes or types of rapids, from type one "easy," to type six, "foolish to attempt." He said there would be no 6's on this river. Most would be type two "medium difficulty," and type three, "dangerous."

Some of the Secret Service agents who had not been involved with the advance party the week before raised eyebrows at this, but Ted assured them that this was relative terminology, intended to assure caution. He emphasized the need to wear lifejackets at all times and to hold on tight in the rough spots. He said if anyone should happen to fall overboard, to stay calm and keep feet downstream; a pickup-raft or kayak would be nearby to fish them out.

"Stay seated in the rafts," Ted said, "only the sweepboat

operators will be standing up, and that's how we run them."

The Vice President and his wife and daughter would ride in a large sweepboat supplied by the outfitter, along with two agents and an extra operator, in case, by chance, something might happen to the primary operator. This boat, with seven people aboard, would carry only a minimum of gear. The bulk of gear and supplies would be in the other outfitter rafts further back in the procession.

Elaine and Ted's sweep in the lead carried two agents and two media types, one a video camera operator. When asked, they explained that they were actually freelancers with a contract to film the float trip for a major TV Network. The raft was well-loaded and rode low in the water.

Immediately behind the Vice President's raft, Ralph and Larry's sweep had another two agents and a pair of reporters, including a second camera. The three Forest Service kayakers were to be positioned in front of, adjacent to and behind the Vice President's raft.

Three other outfitter-supplied rubber oarboats, carrying staff and gear, followed behind, along with the Forest Service raft with the chief and regional forester. In all, seven rubber rafts made up the floating party.

This elaborate flotilla launched on schedule at 9:00 A.M. amid cheers and shouting. The river was fairly calm for nearly the first four miles, giving the floaters a false sense of security. When they reached the first type three rapid just below Orelano Creek entering from the right, Ted positioned his raft some twenty feet from the right bank, as the river rounded a bend to the left. Then he pulled hard to midstream to avoid several large boulders and stayed midstream through the next several type two rapids.

The Vice President's sweep operator did likewise without incident, as did Larry. The cameramen, holding on with their feet and one hand, managed to get some shaky footage of this first rough ride.

The large oarboat behind Larry's raft failed to move quickly enough to midstream. It bumped a boulder and a Vice Presidential staffer, who had not taken seriously the instructions to hold on tight, fell overboard. To his credit, he managed to keep his feet downstream, and an alert kayaker maneuvered to him and grabbed hold of the back of his life jacket, taking him to shore. The raft behind the one he had fallen from stopped to pick him up, and the wet and embarrassed staffer climbed aboard, shaking his head.

"You just missed some excitement behind us," Ralph Hanson told the camera operator, who was focusing on the celebrity in the raft ahead. "Guy fell out and was rescued while we went through this last series of rapids."

"Damn!" the camera man said. "That would have been great footage. Alert me next time, will you?"

"Well, I'll try," Ralph replied, "but you never know when something like that is going to happen. Maybe we could stage another 'man-overboard' so you could get some action footage."

"Hey, could you?" the guy said and then realized that Ralph was kidding.

It stayed relatively calm for a while until they reached Marble Creek rapid, another type three and Ted pulled to the left bank to scout it out. The others did likewise.

Ted told the other operators, "There are two reversals* in this one, the first is at the entry about ten feet off the left bank. The second is about twenty five yards below in midstream. We need to stay as close to the right bank as possible, but don't hit the boulders there. Stay right through the entire rapid."

The other operators nodded, and returned to their rafts with those passengers who had gone along to see what a scouting trip was all about. That included the Vice President, his daughter, two Secret Service agents and several staffers.

All rafts made it through Marble Creek rapid as advised, and all passengers stayed onboard. Ted pulled into Sunflower Hot Springs camp on the right, announcing the lunch stop as the others followed.

There were three separate lunch groups. The Vice President's party, including his family, higher staffers, Secret Service agents and outfitter/servers formed one group. Theirs was an elaborate lunch, complete with tablecloths and silverware. The Chief was invited to join this group. Some of the media were also included.

The remainder of the staff, media, and outfitter personnel had a less-elaborate lunch nearby. It was a sandwich spread similar to the Forest Service group; the regional forester and Recreation Staff Dave Aldrich joined Supervisor Ralph Hanson's group for lunch. The same separate arrangements remained constant throughout the next three days.

Sunflower Hot Springs was a wonderful cascade of hot water flowing down over rocks and creating a natural shower with pools available for an invigorating soak. Several of the Vice President's party, including his adventuresome teenage daughter, enjoyed a few minutes of unexpected luxury after lunch.

The afternoon's float, until they reached type three Jackass rapid, was relatively calm. Fishing gear appeared on several of the rafts, including the main one. When a nice, twelve-inch Dolly Varden trout was reeled in by the Vice President, with cameras grinding away, there was great excitement.

Exuberantly, the fish catcher proclaimed that their dinner was now on board!

"Sorry sir," the raft operator said, "nice as it is, that's a bull trout, and they're off limits. That's why you're using a barbless hook. You'll have to just get your picture taken, if you like, and then release it."

The disappointed fisherman complied reluctantly, knowing that his image as an environmentalist was at stake.

The same scene was replicated on several other rafts, but a few whitefish were also caught, which were legal to keep. They would be roasted in foil and served as hors d'oeuvres during the cocktail hour that evening at the main table.

Fishing rods were put away as they approached Jackass rapid, which was scouted from the right bank. Then the rafts proceeded, staying midstream, avoiding boulders on the left that created strong hydraulics.* They pulled into Lower Jackass camp for the night. Larry smiled to himself at the significance of this name.

Again, three distinct camps were formed with the main one in the choice center area, and the others flanking on the outskirts. Two wall tents were set up for the Vice President and his family, with low, metal-frame canvas cots and down sleeping bags.

Screened river porta-potties, similar but a good deal fancier than the one used on the Wilderness packtrip two weeks before, were strategically placed on the low bench above the sandy beach. In this case, the sewage would be hauled out in sealed plastic buckets.

A bar was set up for cocktails, while Dutch ovens were placed over charcoal in firepans, for a typical outfitted river meal, albeit a good deal fancier than usual.

For the Forest Service people, Ted cooked fajitas and refried beans, with chips with hot and mild salsa.

"Good eating!" Larry said as he washed dishes afterward. "I'll bet we're doing better than the main camp."

Just before dark, a vice-presidential staffer strolled into

the Forest Service camp and was invited to sit down, drink some coffee and visit. He identified himself as Vince Brill and said he was responsible for Federal agency coordination. He said he was really impressed with the cleanliness of the river and how well the Forest Service was organized for the trip.

"The bulk of the credit for how good the river looks goes to Ted Anderson here," Ralph Hanson said. "Ted has been river manager for a long time. In fact, Ted's father was the first officially-permitted outfitter on the Middle Fork; Ted has run rafts here since he was about fourteen years old. He's respected by all of the permitted outfitters and individual floaters and they all know what he expects of them. There are serious rules requiring that everything be packed out. That includes trash, ashes and human waste—everything. Ted will pull his raft over to a bank to pick up a gum wrapper. The river users know this and they abide by what they call 'Ted's Rules'."

"I think that's super," Vince said. "Recreation is the name of the game, you know. In fact, in my opinion, it's the only game in town, except for environmental protection and ecological diversity, that is."

"Well, you're right that recreation is important on the National Forests," Ralph replied. "That's why they're called 'America's Playgrounds.' But you know, there's a lot more than just recreation going on. We manage for multiple-use, and I'm proud to say that these forests contribute in many ways to the country's welfare and its economy."

"We feel that the whole multiple-use concept is outdated," Vince said. "Commercial interests really have no place on our public lands. They're for the people and they're also for wildlife; that's what's important."

"With all due respect," Larry said, trying not to sound combative, "these lands are capable of providing recreation and wildlife habitat and a whole lot more. And that's with environmental protection. We can make timber, forage and minerals available to those 'commercial interests,' and do it without harming the forest or its capability to produce on a sustained-yield basis. This puts money in the Treasury and it helps local economies. Multiple-use with proper resource management and protection is a win-win situation."

"That's really old fashioned thinking," Vince said as he finished his coffee and got up to leave, obviously studying Larry's nametag. "It's been nice exchanging ideas with you people. Thanks for the coffee, and thanks, on behalf of the Vice President, for the help you're providing on this trip." And with that, staffer Vince Brill ambled back toward the other secondary camp at Lower Jackass.

"Wow!" Elaine exclaimed. "It's pretty apparent where his priorities are, and I suppose his boss feels exactly the same way."

"You'd better believe it," Ralph said. "That's what we have to contend with as long as this administration is in office, I'm afraid."

"That's probably as close as we'll come to a conversation with the Vice President, or the chief for that matter," Larry said. "And for my part, it's probably just as well. I have some career left."

"I'm not so sure about that," Ted chided, "the way the guy was looking at your nametag..."

Breakfast at the Forest Service camp was French toast and bacon with hot coffee. Ted's reputation for good meals on the river was well-deserved. Dave Aldrich took his turn at washing dishes and straining the dishwater. They were packed and ready to go before 8:00 A.M..

Larry was surprised to see the other camps loading-up so soon and getting ready to launch just after 9:00 A.M..

The morning float was without incident with no difficult

rapids. More fishing took place from the guests' rafts, and several whitefish were caught and kept. They stopped for lunch at Middle Fork Lodge, a private inholding on the river, available to floaters for meals and overnight accommodations. The Vice President's party was hosted in style. Tables were set-up on the lawn for a leisurely lunch for the staff and support personnel.

The regional forester pointed out the remnants of the Morter Creek Fire that had charred some 64,000 acres over a decade earlier. The burned area was still visible below them down to the river. After an hour and a half of eating and discussion, the flotilla was on the river again.

Mid-afternoon, Ted pulled over at White Creek pack bridge. The outfitters explained the river tradition that called for first-time floaters to jump off the bridge, some twenty five feet above a deep pool in the river, into the cold water below. The Vice President made a bold move in the direction of the bridge, knowing full well that the Secret Service would never allow him to participate in the ritual. Several staffers looked at the ground and kicked at rocks.

Although certainly not the first time down the river, Elaine, Dave, and Larry climbed up the bank to the trail, stepped out to the middle of the bridge, and without hesitation climbed over the railing and jumped off. The staffer who had fallen in the river the first morning and several others, seeing the need to uphold the honor of the office, climbed to the trail and reluctantly followed suit. Vince Brill was among those who did not. The video cameras captured the moment.

The afternoon sun was warm and the jumpers dried off quickly. Some eight miles later, after relatively-smooth water with more fishing, Ted pulled into Upper Grouse camp on the right side. He pointed out the site and explained the arrangement. The Vice President and his party, including agents and staff, would camp at Upper Grouse, while the Forest Service rafts and kayaks proceeded a short distance downstream to camp at Lower Grouse. Neither camp was big enough to hold everyone comfortably, but they were close by. It would be a simple matter to get together the next morning to start the day's run.

Steak was on the menu at Upper Grouse; hamburgers at Lower Grouse; which suited everyone just fine. The "party" at Upper Grouse lasted until nearly midnight, with music and singing. Those in Lower Grouse were thankful for the distance between camps. They turned-in early.

Ted had time for Dutch-oven sourdough biscuits the next morning, to go with scrambled eggs with ham chunks and onions. Again they were ready to launch at 8:00 A.M., but this time it was 10:00 AM when one of the kayakers pulled in to report that the party upstream was about ready.

After just over a mile on the river, Ted pulled to the right bank, followed by the others, to scout Tappen Falls. A young, black bear scurried up the hill and out of sight as they approached.

The river at Tappen Falls made a sharp right turn and seemed to drop out of sight. Boulders extending all the way across created a waterfall that was labeled a type four or "very dangerous." With moderately-high water, the drop was close to eight feet. Ted said to position close to the right bank to avoid a huge reversal nearer midstream. He said that once past the major drop, to pull to midstream to avoid a boulder some 10 feet off the right bank about 100 feet below.

"Tappen Falls has claimed more boats than any other rapid on the river," Ted said. "Let's make certain that none of ours fall victim this morning. It's not too bad if you hit it right. It can be bad news if you miss it."

At this point, the lead Secret Service agent, who had

joined the scouting party, stepped forward to question the advisability of allowing the Vice President go over a "very dangerous" waterfall.

The outfitter boatman in charge of the main raft told him, "We run this river all the time; we never have trouble with Tappen Falls. That's because we're careful."

When the boatman next asked if they wanted the cameras to film the Vice President walking around the falls, the agent admitted that wouldn't be good.

"Just make damn sure you're extra careful!" he said, and to Ted he said, "Be sure your kayaks are there and ready, okay?" Ted nodded, and they returned to their rafts to prepare for Tappen Falls.

The camera operator on Ted's sweep said he would like to record the falls-crossing from the bank, since he would probably be too busy holding on in the raft to operate his camera. Ted told him to go ahead, and he could film all the boats going over the falls if he wanted to. They would wait for him just downstream. It was agreed that all would pull-over after the falls and watch the rest. Both camera operators took up strategic positions over and just below the falls.

Ted maneuvered his sweep to within five feet of the right bank, dropped off and pulled hard left to clear the lower boulder. It was a clear demonstration of how to navigate the river's most dangerous rapid.

The camera above the falls could not see the Vice President's face, smiling bravely as his raft approached Tappen Falls, nor could its sound sensor record the whoop he made as it fell to the swirling pool below.

One by one, each rubber raft swirled into this foreboding type four rapid, and each one made it through without capsizing or losing a passenger overboard. There was a general celebration as they pulled over to wait for the camera operators to reboard.

The next several rapids, including Tappen II and Tappen III, both type threes and Tappen IV, a tough type two seemed tame by comparison. Those were navigated without incident.

After passing Camas Creek, a large drainage entering the Middle Fork from the right, just past Johnny Walker camp on the left, Ted pulled to the right bank and announced that Kaufman's Cave was just a short distance up the bank. The outfitter guide explained that Clarence Kaufman was a miner who had crafted a door to cover the entrance and made the cave his home for several years. A curious Vice President and his party scrambled up the hill for this historical stop, which took nearly an hour. Since the third day's float to the Flying B was a short one, less than twelve miles, there was plenty of time for stops such as this.

Lunch at Broken Oar camp, just above Aparejo Creek, was leisurely as well, lasting close to two hours. The Vice President made a speech, expounding on his views about environmental protection, expressing his strong support for back-country recreation opportunities like this river-floating experience. He thanked all the outfitter and support personnel for making the past three days so enjoyable. He said all the right things, but somehow Larry thought that it was more political than genuine. He kept these thoughts to himself.

Lunch at the main camp was more elaborate than ever, with a large variety of delicacies, including caviar and paté, laid-out on linen-covered buffet tables.

Bologna and cheese sandwiches at the Forest Service roll-up table were more than adequate, Larry thought, and he said so. The others agreed.

Shortly after the afternoon launch, Ted pulled to the right bank to scout Aparejo Point rapid, where boulders extended across the river for a tough type three rapid, with high rock walls on each side.

"Stay left until the major drop, then pull to midstream and ride the crest of the standing waves," Ted advised the other boat operators. "Then you can have your passengers look for Indian pictographs on the rock bluffs on the left side."

After Aparejo Point, only type one, "easy" rapids remained for the rest of the distance to the takeout point, but the last chance for fishing brought no tangible results.

They pulled left at the Flying B and saw three large Air National Guard helicopters waiting on the airstrip. A little further downstream, the Forest Service Twin Otter had landed at Bernard airstrip, also on the left. It was 3:30 in the afternoon.

As they grabbed their gear and climbed out of the lead sweepboat, one of the Secret Service agents who had ridden with Ted and Elaine the past three days, said to Ted, "Thanks a lot for all your help. This was a great trip, and I'm sure our boss enjoyed it immensely. You know, I'm really impressed with the job you Park Service people do in managing this river."

"Well, thank you," Ted replied, without changing expression or missing a beat, "I've always been impressed with you FBI people too."

The agent's mouth dropped open, but before he could speak again his partner pulled him aside and whispered something in his ear.

Larry and Elaine turned away to hide their smiles and suppress the laughter.

It was with a great deal of ceremony that the Vice President and his party said their good-byes as they proceeded up the embankment to the airstrip and the waiting helicopters. The outfitter rafts, with operators and support staff, put in again without delay and headed down the river, no doubt greatly relieved that the VIP part of their float trip was over.

The Forest Service rafts launched too, maneuvered

through Haystack rapid, another type three and pulled over again below Bernard airstrip. While the chief and regional forester took their gear up the hill to the Twin Otter, the others deflated the oarboat. Larry and Dave carried the frame up the hill, then came back with a cart to help pack the heavy rubber raft to the airplane.

Supervisor Ralph Hanson had decided to fly out and have Dave finish the river float to the Cache Bar takeout. He asked Larry if he wanted to come too, since Dave was a qualified sweep operator.

"No, but thanks anyway," Larry said. "I signed on for the whole trip, and I'll enjoy these last two days, without the high-powered visitors. It will be more like old times."

"Well, thanks for the help, Larry," Ralph said. "It was good having you along. If we can ever return the favor, let us know."

"I just might do that," were Larry's parting words to the supervisor.

And with that, the two sweeps, now carrying considerably less gear and fewer people, riding higher in the water, headed on down the river at a leisurely pace.

They saw Bighorn sheep and several mule deer on the hillsides above the river and two bald eagles perched on the branches of a big Douglas fir near the river's edge. It seemed the wildlife had now decided to make an appearance. Larry found himself whistling a tune and smiling.

Elaine took the lead sweep through type three Jack Creek rapid with Ted's coaching, and on to Survey Creek camp on the left, at mile seventy five from Boundary Creek. Ted said they could camp there that night and make it to Otter Bar camp the next night, leaving just a short run to Cache Bar the next and final day.

Ted took some steaks from the cooler, amazingly still

partially-frozen, and prepared to grill them over the charcoal firepan. Elaine exerted her authority as district ranger, and told Ted to relax that evening; he had earned a vacation from cooking duties. She donned a denim apron and cooked supper. They celebrated their successful VIP tour and the fact that they hadn't drowned any politicians.

The next day, Larry and Dave alternated turns at the helm of the second sweep; Elaine handled all of the rapids in the first one, type threes included.

Otter Bar camp had an ideal sandy beach for a swim, and although the water was hardly warm, they decided it appropriate to complete their celebration with a refreshing dip. Larry had not anticipated this ritual and had not packed swimming trunks, but he determined that a pair of red-and-yellow-striped boxer shorts would suffice for this occasion.

"Nice shorts!" Elaine told him, in a kidding tone, while Larry blushed and headed toward the river.

The four rafters lined up on the sandy beach for a run at the chilly water. They grabbed each other's hands, so that no one would balk and turn back, and ran into the frigid waves, whooping and hollering like kids.

Ted decorated the beef stew that evening so that it was hard to tell it was from a can. After supper and cleanup, Elaine took a deck of cards and some poker chips from her "seabag" and proposed a game of "family poker." After an hour, with chips stacked heavily on her side of the table, the other three better understood why she had suggested this "little card game." Larry said he guessed a lesson like that was worth the little bit of perdiem money it had cost.

The next day, Elaine completed her proficiency course of river helmsman ship by taking the oars for the entire course, through all of the tough rapids, including type four Rubber rapid, type three Hancock rapid, type three Devil's Tooth rapid, and type three House Rock rapid. By the time they reached the confluence, where the clear waters of the Middle Fork joined the turbid waters of the main Salmon, Ted declared Elaine "qualified."

They reached Cache Bar at 1:00 P.M., where carryalls and trailers were waiting. They had floated just over 100 miles. They deflated the rubber rafts, loaded them on the trailer with frames and gear, and headed up the road following the main river to town.

When Larry left for the airport, he congratulated Ranger Elaine Morris on her accomplishment as a sweep operator and said how much he had enjoyed the trip. Then he turned to Ted Anderson and said, "Ted, you're a legend on the Middle Fork. You've set standards in river management that will be difficult to duplicate anywhere else. When you decide to retire, as I hear rumors you might, there will be no way to replace you and what you do here. Congratulations, and my very best wishes!"

"Thank you, Larry. Come back and see us," Ted said.

Back in Elk Creek, as expected, the Weaver family was anxious to hear about the week-long river experience.

"Did you meet the Vice President, dad?" Ernie asked, "and the chief?"

"Well, I shook hands with both of them," Larry answered, "but that was about all. Never had a conversation with either of them."

"Did anyone fall into the river?" Jill wanted to know.

"One guy did, a staff member," Larry said, "but he got fished-out right away. We were lucky that was all. I was surprised the two video camera operators stayed on the rafts. They were holding on by tucking their feet under the straps on the boat deck, but some of those rapids were rough. The Secret Service agents really worried about the Vice President, but then I guess that's their job." Then he told them about Ted's FBI reference, and they broke up laughing.

More questions were asked about the fishing, wildlife seen and the food. "With Ted cooking," Larry said, "you knew we were well fed, better than the VIPs, if the truth be told."

"I'm glad you've had your vacation," Peggy said, trying to sound sarcastic, but somehow falling short. "The kids and I were thinking about going to Palm Springs next week..."

CHAPTER XI
THE ELK HUNT

The Adams County 4-H Rodeo was the following weekend in Centerville. Jill had Cougar well-tuned, and she won a red ribbon for second place. Ernie rode a steer and also got a red ribbon.

"Cougar was wonderful, dad!" Jill said, "but do you think I need a faster horse to win?"

"It wasn't his speed, or lack of it, that cost you the blue ribbon, honey," Larry told her. "You made a great ride, but going a little wide around the third barrel lost you about a second. That could have been enough to win it. Just keep practicing, and I'll bet you and old Cougar will win the next one."

"I'm proud of you both," Peggy said. "And to celebrate, I suggest we all have dinner at a good restaurant here in Centerville, before going home."

"Mexican?" Larry asked, and all heads nodded.

"Mexican it is," they said in unison.

At home later that evening, Ernie and Jill telephoned their grandparents to tell about the rodeo.

"We should have won it," Jill said. "I let Cougar go wide around the last barrel, and it cost us this time. We'll win it next year for sure. And next year I'm going to tie goats too! Do you think Cougar can be a good roping horse, grandpa?" Jill bubbled with enthusiasm.

"I sure don't see why not," Lawrence Weaver said. "We're

proud of you kids, and how hard you've worked to win those ribbons."

When Ernie got on the phone, he told his grandpa that they'd drawn-out for a party-of-four elk hunt in the unit that included the Sandstone Allotment. "Dad and I will have it all scouted-out, grandpa," Ernie said. "We'll see you and Uncle Jim a month from now. And grandma too, and Aunt Vicki, for a visit," he hastened to add.

On Monday morning, Tom Cordova told Larry about the District Court trial for the accused tree-spiker, held in Centerville the week Larry was away on the float trip.

"Clark testified very effectively about seeing the bandsaw break and about the extent of the damage in the sawmill," Tom said. "And the deputy sheriff, who overheard the conversation in the cafe and made the arrest, was the main witness.

"So what happened?" Larry asked eagerly. "Did they convict the guy?"

"They found him not guilty," Tom said. "Without an eye witness to the actual spiking, or indisputable evidence placing the guy at the scene, the jury must have concluded that there was no good case. Apparently, what the deputy heard in the restaurant didn't fit the definition of a confession. The defense lawyer argued that the guy was commenting on the spiking, not admitting to it, and I guess the jury bought it. The defense also said something about what the deputy had heard being 'an invasion of privacy.' The judge ruled otherwise, but the jury must have believed it anyway. So they didn't convict him, and I thought Bill Crawford was going to blow a gasket!"

"I probably would have too if I'd been there," Larry said, shaking his head. "Sometimes it seems a jury leans over backward to give criminals the benefit of the doubt. That's a real disappointment."

Larry walked down the hall to ask Ben Foster how the

coordinated resource management project with the Sandstone Grazing Association was going.

"Really well," Ben said. "The state section of the range society found us a facilitator who really knows his stuff. He has been able to get everyone thinking about their needs and interests rather than their predetermined 'positions.' Even the Wilderness Plus people have had to start thinking about how to improve the range, not just how to get the livestock off. The association representatives have participated in a reasonable and very positive way."

"How about the Sportsmen's Club?" Larry asked. "Have they been active participants? And how about the BLM?"

"The sportsmen, they sure have been active," Ben replied. "Glen Romero has been pushing for improving wildlife habitat, but he thinks it can be done under the management plan in effect on the allotment now, without reducing livestock numbers on the forest. And that goes for the BLM winter range too, for the most part. Steve Underwood has been a strong participant too. He realizes there's some improvement needed, but growing-season rest has really been helping the BLM portion. In fact, Larry, I think we can probably finish in another session or two, and in a positive way. Next session is Wednesday. Will you be there to sit in, boss?"

"Yeah, I'm through traveling for a while, and I'd sure like to be there," Larry said.

And they did resolve it in a positive way. The association agreed to several provisions for range improvement, including some riparian-area fencing to shorten the period of grazing use there. The Sportsmen's Club offered to help with willow plantings to provide shade for stream improvement and also moose forage eventually. At the end, Wilderness Plus had their concerns resolved, and they dropped their objections. The CRM effort was declared a success.

Larry and Ernie spent the next two Saturdays riding the Sandstone Allotment, scouting where the elk were ranging. They knew it could all change before the season opened, but it was helpful to know how they were moving, or staying in certain areas.

The plan was to camp not far from the main corral near the center of the allotment, since the livestock would already be gone. This way they could put Gifford and Cougar in one of the pens at night. Water was available in the pens, and they could be fed hay and some grain with little trouble. They knew there would be other campers/hunters nearby, but there should be plenty of room. They would sleep in the horse trailer or in a big tent, and rig a tent-fly to shelter their kitchen.

They would take both riding and packsaddles for the hunt, and if successful, to pack out. The plan was for two to go horseback in a wide circle, while the other two walked in a smaller circle. The horsebackers could also move out to areas further away if necessary. Then they would alternate the next day, and the next, as needed.

Lawrence and Grace Weaver, not needing to take annual leave, arrived two days early. Jim and Vicki and their two little boys, Kevin, five and Kyle, three, drove in the day before elk season started. It was a good chance for all three families to have a visit, although the four hunters would be missing part of the time.

James Herbert Weaver was two-and-a-half years younger than his brother. At six feet and 180 pounds, he was slightly smaller, but otherwise there was a strong resemblance. He had been assistant ranger on two districts, and was currently responsible for range allotment management planning on two forests in Montana. He had been applying for ranger jobs for about a year and a half.

Jim and Larry had experienced the normal sibling rivalry as youngsters growing up on their father's ranger stations. Both had determined to follow their dad and granddad's footsteps and pursue Forest Service careers. They had attended different forestry colleges in the same region. Larry had gone to Colorado State and Jim to the University of Wyoming, following his Vietnam tour as a decorated combat Marine. He and Vicki had also met and married while in college. Her degree was in education, and like Peggy, she had worked for pay until their first boy, Kevin, was born. There were many similarities but also a number of distinct differences between the two Weaver brothers. While both had strong work ethics and good senses of humor, Jim was more outgoing and somewhat less serious in his approach to his job—and to life. The two brothers had grown closer in recent years, their earlier rivalry maturing into a strong friendship.

Peggy roasted a turkey for a midday dinner the day before the hunt, complete with all the trimmings normally associated with Thanksgiving, including cranberry sauce and pumpkin pie. She said it was like a holiday celebration having everyone together, and besides this would assure plenty of leftovers for several days, which meant more time to visit and play with the little boys. Hunting camp meals would be simple too, mostly homemade but prefrozen dinners in plastic bags to reheat on a propane stove. Breakfasts would be the usual bacon and eggs or hotcakes and sausage, or variations thereof. The hunters would pack sandwiches for lunch, but they didn't intend to spend a lot of time fixing supper; they weren't there to eat, but to hunt.

The four hunters fit comfortably into Larry's red, dual-cab, four-wheel drive, one-ton pickup. They pulled his slant load, three-horse trailer with Gifford and Cougar and left for camp shortly after dinner. They planned to be in place and ready to get started at daylight opening day.

There were two other camps in the vicinity of the Sandstone Allotment corral, but still plenty of room for the horses since there were several separate pens. They unloaded Gifford and Cougar, and Ernie fed them hay and oats while the others made camp in a good, level area at the edge of the big aspen grove nearby. They set up the nylon tent where Larry and Jim would sleep in bedrolls on low canvas cots. Ernie and his grandfather would sleep in the horse trailer, also with bedrolls and cots, after Ernie made sure it was well cleaned out with a flat-blade shovel and stiff push-broom. A large tent fly was extended from the trailer-top hayrack to nearby trees, providing cover for the camp kitchen.

All but Ernie were still full from the big turkey dinner, so a light supper of half a sandwich was adequate. Ernie ate two turkey sandwiches and a big piece of pumpkin pie, which he said would tide him over until breakfast. His grandfather marveled at the "bottomless pit." They turned in early.

Larry fried bacon and scrambled a skillet full of eggs, and they were finished with breakfast a full half hour before sunup.

Jim and Ernie rode the horses the first day, planning to make a big circle from camp, about twelve to fifteen miles total if need be. Larry and his dad walked down a ridge from camp for about a mile, and then they dropped into a broad drainage, which was the North Fork of Elk Creek, covering both sides upstream for another mile or more. Then they turned west and crossed into another small drainage. They had all left camp just at daylight. Rifle shots were heard in the distance less than a half hour later, heralding the start of elk season. They saw fresh tracks but no elk.

Within four miles north of camp, riding upwind in a westerly direction, Jim and Ernie sighted a small group of about 15 elk, including three or four bulls, moving generally toward them at an angle to the south. They dismounted quickly, pulled rifles from saddle scabbards, tied the horses to sturdy trees with halter ropes and waited quietly for a minute or less. The little herd topped the ridge ahead of them about 150 yards, stopped and looked nervously around, but just briefly. Jim motioned to Ernie to take the big bull on the right. They both fired their 30-06s from a squatting position within a second of each other.

It was a clean and open shot for both of them. At 150 yards, the rifle scopes made those two bulls look very large indeed. With crosshairs centered on the chest just behind the front leg, it was a simple matter of squeezing-off a single round for both hunters. As the two bulls fell, the others dashed off to the south and were out of sight in an instant.

The horses had been standing quietly until the sound of the shots caused them to move around and nicker. By then it didn't matter.

Although still flushed with excitement, Jim and Ernie approached the downed bulls cautiously. They knew full well that there was danger of a wounded bull rising up and causing great damage with swinging antlers. But that wasn't the case this time. Jim's bull was still. Ernie's was breathing until another shot in the neck, just below the skull, finished him off. They tagged the antlers and took each other's pictures. Both bulls were nice six-pointers, with Jim's appearing slightly larger.

At this point, Jim explained an elk hunter's ritual to his nephew. With his hunting knife, Jim carefully removed the "ivories," also known as wolf teeth or tusks, from his bull's mouth and put them in his zippered vest pocket. Ernie, greatly impressed, did likewise.

The two hunters spent the rest of the morning, or most of it, field dressing* their prizes and hoisting them from tree branches well off the ground, using ropes and small pulleys

from their saddlebags. They left the hides on the carcasses to keep the meat cleaner. Jim was careful to put the livers in ziplock plastic bags in to save this delicacy from the "gut pile."

Jim stayed with the hanging elk while Ernie rode Cougar and led Gifford back to camp to change to decker packsaddles with manties, square canvas tarps and ropes. While Ernie was gone, Jim quartered his bull, with hunting knife and a folding meatsaw, and got it ready to pack out.

Ernie rode into camp at noon, soon after the two pedestrian hunters came into camp to have lunch. They had seen a good many tracks but no elk.

"How'd it go, pal?" Larry asked. "You must have scored, or you wouldn't be back here without your Uncle Jim."

Ernie, trying to sound casual, but failing to conceal his excitement, said, "Oh, we got a couple of 'em down, big bulls, six-pointers, musta' weighed close to a thousand each, 800 or 900 pounds at least."

"That's wonderful, Ernie!" his grandfather exclaimed. "You must be really excited, your first elk and all. Did you get the ivories?"

"You bet I did, grandpa," Ernie replied enthusiastically, fishing into his vest pocket to show them off. "And yeah, I guess I'm a little excited. It may be just starting to sink in."

"That's great! I'm proud of you," Larry said. "Let's eat a quick lunch, and then I'll go back with you to help pack them out."

"That will be fine with me," Lawrence said. "After this morning's hike, I'm ready to sit down awhile this afternoon. I'll guard the camp and keep watch in case some big bull elk comes strolling in."

Ernie pulled his sack lunch from his saddlebags and, realized that Jim's lunch was still in Gifford's saddlebags.

"That's okay," his dad said, "He'll be ready for it by the time we get back there."

They resaddled with the deckers and got on, their seats on manties between the rings, and rode the four miles to where Jim was waiting.

"Hey, nephew," Jim said, pretending anger, "you ran off with my lunch and I'll bet you ate it for me too, didn't you?"

"Gosh, I'm sorry about that, Uncle Jim," Ernie responded. "But you know, I really was hungry after the long ride back to camp. That second lunch really hit the spot." Then with a big smile, Ernie removed Jim's lunch from the folded manty behind him on Cougar's decker saddle and tossed it to his uncle. Larry laughed at this exchange, while Jim grumbled under his breath to complete the act.

"I'd say they were both close to 800 pounds on the hoof," Larry said, "a couple of really nice bulls. Congratulations, guys!"

They mantied* the quarters of Jim's bull, rubbed some strong smelling ointment on the horses' nostrils to mask any blood smell, and hung the hindquarters on Gifford and the front ones on Cougar, with the antlers tied on top.

Larry volunteered to stay this time and quarter the other elk while Jim and Ernie led the "packhorses" and their cargo back to camp.

"I think I can do it, dad," Ernie said, "and I don't mind trying. I've done several deer, you know, and it's just a matter of cutting and splitting."

"Fine with me," Larry said, "but let me help you get started while Jim eats his lunch."

Larry and Jim led the horses, packed with elk meat, into camp at 3:30 P.M.. "At this rate, it's going to be 'dark-thirty' by the time we get back with the other one," Jim commented.

"I'll have supper ready," Lawrence said. "How about elk liver and onions with Dutch-oven spuds, instead of the planned rations tonight, as a sort of celebration of a successful hunt?"

"That would be great, dad!" Larry said. "Ernie's not big on liver, but on this occasion it may be different."

They quickly unloaded the packs, hung the quarters from a nearby tree, refolded the manties, and Jim and Larry headed back, riding on decker saddles.

Ernie had done a good job of quartering his elk, but he hadn't tried to saw-off the antlers. "I didn't want to botch that job," he said.

Larry started to manty the quarters while Jim helped Ernie saw the antlers off. They repeated the packing job as before, and began the four-mile-hike back to camp, leading the packed horses. They estimated this bull at 750 pounds when on the hoof.

"By the time we get back to camp," Larry said, "I figure I'll have walked about fourteen miles today, maybe a little more. Good thing I'm wearing packer boots, instead of the pointy-toed, 'cowboy' variety."

"Eight miles of walking for me and just four for Ernie doesn't seem so bad then," Jim said and then chided, "but hey, you're a tough forest ranger; you can take it!"

It was nearly eight o'clock when they got back to camp at dusk. They unloaded, hung the meat, unsaddled the horses and scratched their backs with a curry-comb, then fed them. Then they sat down to the promised "elk liver banquet."

"Not half bad," said Ernie. "Grandpa, you're a pretty good cook."

A propane lantern lit the camp, but it was extinguished soon after supper. It was a cold night, well below the freezing point, which helped cool the hanging elk quarters.

The next morning's start was later by an hour. Sourdough hotcakes with link sausage was their breakfast. This time Jim was the cook. Then Larry and his father, rifles in scabbards, rode off in the general direction of yesterday's successful hunt. Jim and Ernie were camp tenders that day. They read from books that Lawrence had brought along, and listened to a pro football game on a portable radio that afternoon. The Broncos beat the Raiders, so they were happy about that.

The hunters rode back into camp at 5:30. "We saw lots of tracks, but no fur," Larry said. "Is supper ready?"

"What do you think we are, your hired hands?" Jim asked in jest. Then he uncovered a Dutch oven sitting on a pile of charcoal that had been placed on a garbage can lid in keeping with the "leave-no-trace" camping style.

They ate a precooked meal, which all agreed was quite good. There was time for a hotly-contested pinochle game that evening by lantern light, with Ernie and his grandpa getting the best of the two brothers.

"Anytime you guys want more lessons, just let us know," Lawrence said, with a wink in Ernie's direction.

They had planned a three-day hunt unless they finished earlier, but it was agreed they would break camp and go home the third morning. Two nice bulls could surely be construed a successful hunt.

They awoke that last morning to find about five inches of fresh snow, a normal elk-hunting occurence. Larry and Jim removed their gear from the tent and shook it off so that it might dry in a short time. The tent fly had kept their kitchen reasonably dry, and for that they were greatful.

As they finished breakfast of fried eggs and ham with Lawrence as cook, Larry looked up, and there in the snow-covered meadow 200 yards below the corral stood a young bull elk, his nose deep in the snow and grazing peacefully. Both Larry and his dad reached for rifles, but Larry said in a hushed tone, "Go ahead, dad, you've come the farthest for this hunt."

"No, you go ahead," Lawrence said. "I've had more than my share in past years."

"Well, either Alphonse or Gaston had better shoot before he decides to flee the scene!" Jim exclaimed in a hushed tone.

Lawrence Weaver set his rifle aside, and Larry realized that his father was serious. He sighted through his scope as the bull looked up and started moving slowly away, and squeezed off a round. The bull dropped in his tracks.

It was a four-point bull weighing probably 550 to 600 pounds. Larry checked to assure that he was dead, then cut his throat to assure proper bleeding and dug-out the ivories. He then began the process of dressing him out. While Jim and Ernie broke camp, Larry and his dad dressed and quartered the young bull. Ernie, with guidance from his father, sawed-off the antlers.

The load on their return trip was considerable, with nearly 1,200 pounds of elk meat, antlers and hides, added. They could put much of the camp equipment, including the still-damp tent, the stove, cots and bedrolls, in the front of the trailer, with the horses in the last two spaces. Twelve elk quarters fully loaded the pickup bed. Three sets of antlers were tied on the hayrack on top of the trailer.

After a final inspection of the camp area to assure that the Weaver family hunting party "left no trace," they started back to town, just before noon, with Ernie munching an apple and some trail mix. They were glad to have a good, graveled road to drive on this snowy morning.

There had been a rain shower but no snow at the lower elevation of Elk Creek. After unloading the horses and unhooking the trailer, and showing the others the load of elk carcasses, Larry and Jim drove to Henry's Market to see about hanging the elk quarters in the big coolers and arranging to have them cut and wrapped. They dropped off the hides at the tannery and leather store for tanning. Ernie had already expressed plans to make elkskin gloves for the whole family, and perhaps some vests too.

The women and kids were eager to hear the details of the hunting trip, at least the kids were; the women might not have been quite so anxious, having heard many hunting stories before.

"I'd say you guys did pretty well," Grace said. "Seventy-five percent is an impressive success rate."

"We were lucky, Mom," Jim said. "And there were at least two other nice bulls in the bunch that Ernie and I came upon the first morning."

"The luckiest part, I think, was when the other bull came nearly into camp the last morning," Larry said. "Looks like we'll all be eating elk meat for awhile."

The two traveling families stayed another two days to visit and give Ernie and his grandpa a chance to join Jill and their grandma playing with Kevin and Kyle. Jill took them for a horseback ride, much to their delight. She rode Gifford and led Cougar with both boys sitting up high on Larry's big saddle. Grace read them books and Lawrence told them stories until bedtime each night. Card games of bridge, pinochle and hearts were in progress much of the time.

The butcher at Henry's was able to cut, wrap and freeze enough elk meat to fill four big coolers for the visitors to take home. They made plans to come back at Christmas time and get some more.

And so, after a successful elk hunt and a wonderful family get-together, the visiting Weavers went home, and life at the local Weaver household was back to normal. But it didn't stay that way for long. It was soon business as usual for Larry on the Elk Creek Ranger District, or perhaps not exactly as usual, another crisis was about to loom on the horizon.

The next night at about midnight, an explosion rocked the Powder Bowl Ski Area. Although it was about twenty five miles from Elk Creek, several people in town later claimed they had heard it. Powder Bowl's manager, Roger Jones, called Larry at 7:00 A.M., shortly after his crews arrived to start hanging chairs on the lower lift cable in preparation for the coming ski season.

"It looks like the bull-wheel at the base of the Dark Cloud lift was the main target," the manager said. "Anyway, it's twisted into a pretzel and the building around it is demolished. Without that lift, the start of our ski season will have to be delayed indefinitely, and our plans for expansion put on hold also. It looks like your friends from Wilderness Plus were serious when they objected to our expansion."

"I'm sorry to hear it, Roger," Larry said. "I'll get hold of the deputy sheriff and come right out there."

Larry called Virgil Craft and arranged to meet him in fifteen minutes at his office and they would go to the ski area. Then he called Phil Ortega in the Supervisor's Office, knowing that Phil usually gets to work early.

"I'd suggest you call the U.S. Marshal's office and give Carl Hess an alert," Phil told Larry. "And I can also call the U.S. Attorney's office here in the city. I'll let the Office of General Counsel in the RO know about it too. Would you like for me to come over? I had planned to be on the South Fork District today, but I can cancel that if you want me there."

"I don't think it's necessary, Phil, at least not yet. But thanks, I'll keep you posted," said Larry. "How about the FBI, do you think we need to notify them, since the explosion was on federal land?"

"I wouldn't bother, Larry," Phil said. "In my experience, they wouldn't come to help, unless it was a real headline event. They'd probably just ask for a copy of our final report, if and when the case gets solved, so they can take credit for it."

After calling and leaving a message for Assistant U.S. Marshal Hess, Larry picked up Deputy Craft at his office, and they drove to the ski area.

"This is a familiar-looking road," Virgil joked, "seems like we've driven up here before, and not too long ago."

They drove into the Powder Bowl parking lot, and the first person they saw was Roger Jones.

"Wow, what a mess!" Virgil said with a low whistle. "Someone really did a number on this place.

There was a shallow crater where the bull-wheel used to be and a twisted mass of metal and cable fragments for 100 feet or so up the hill. Virgil quickly enclosed the area with crime-scene barrier tape and called the sheriff's office in Centerville to ask them to send someone out to check for residual traces of explosive. He asked Roger Jones if there had been any provisions for security in the area before the present time.

"We keep a night watchman up here during the ski season," Roger said, "but not this time of year. And I suppose the crew truck and our vehicles have obliterated any tire tracks into or away from the area."

"You might be surprised," Virgil said. "Sometimes our technicians pick up clues you'd never suspect were there. Roger, have you had any phone calls recently, warning that something like this might happen?"

"I've been getting crank calls fairly regularly since our expansion plans were first announced," Roger replied. "I'm sure it's a campaign by Wilderness Plus to discourage me. No threats of violence though."

The sheriff's office technician, Dan Norwood, was there within three hours and set to work. "It was ammonium nitrate, a common fertilizer, also used as an explosive," Dan said. "No doubt about it." Then after checking the tire treads on the crew vehicle, Roger's car and Larry's pickup, he started down the road looking for tire tracks. He found a set at the edge of the road leaving the area that were distinctly different from the others, and he took a plaster cast of them.

"Well, I'll be damned!" Roger exclaimed.

Later that afternoon, Virgil called Duane Selzer, president of Wilderness Plus.

"Explosion at the ski area?" Duane said in a puzzled tone. "Don't know a thing about it. I suppose you guys figure our group is responsible just because we've been vocal in our objections to plans for expansion. Well, I can tell you that's not how we operate."

"We're not accusing you of anything, Duane," Virgil said. "Just wanted to know if you knew of anyone who might have been involved. I hope you'll let us know if you hear of anyone bragging about it."

Duane said he would.

Several days later, in taking the plaster cast of tire tracks around to tire stores in the area, Deputy Virgil Craft struck gold. A dealer in Centerville had recently sold a fairly unique set of mud-grip truck tires to the same individual who had bought several hundred pounds of ammonium nitrate at the Centerville Feed Store. When Craft and Marshall Carl Hess confronted him with this set of facts, the guy admitted that he belonged to an environmental extremist group that operated primarily in the Pacific Northwest, infamous for such activity. He and two "friends" were arrested and brought before U.S. Magistrate Horace Enfield for a preliminary hearing. In less than a week after the explosion, three suspects were in the Adams County jail awaiting trial.

"This has got to be a new record in crime-solving for us," Virgil Craft commented. "These guys are a unique combination of environmental zealots and amateur terrorists."

"Well, it's nice to be successful now and then," Larry said. "You and Dan Norwood were really impressive in getting to the heart of this case. Roger Jones still can't believe it. He also can't believe that Wilderness Plus wasn't involved."

"That reminds me," Virgil said, "I need to call Duane Selzer and let him know how it all came out. I expect he'll want an apology for my suspecting his organization. Oh well..."

Ike Elliot ran a feature on Deputy Craft in the following week's Bugle and complimented the Sheriff's Department for their efficiency and diligence.

When Larry called Phil Ortega to report the conclusion, Phil said, "Here's one the FBI won't get credit for, too bad!"

CHAPTER XII

TRANSFERS

Larry Weaver and Tom Cordova were called as witnesses in the court trial of the Cannabis growers to be held in Centerville the week after elk season. Deputy Sheriff Virgil Craft and Forest Service Special Agent Phil Ortega were also involved, along with Assistant U.S. Marshal Carl Hess.

It turned out that the seven who were arrested in the raid were actually hired workers. One, the guy who had tried to escape up the hill, acted as foreman. He had been hired by two Centerville "businessmen" to grow, cultivate and harvest the crop. His payment was to be on a percentage basis after the owners had marketed the product. The other six were pick-up laborers, hired by the hour, but paid very well.

The foreman was willing to identify his bosses in a plea bargain arrangement with Assistant U.S. Attorney Katherine Dunlop. After conferring with the district judge in Capitol City Judge Enfield handed down a sentence of five years in a federal prison. The six workers plead "no contest" and were given two years each. The criminal trial, which took place in District Court, was heard by a jury as it turned out. It was for the two businessmen or entrepreneurs.

Their attorney made a case for mistaken identity, the wrong people incriminated by the foreman, but the judge would have none of it. The foreman had kept good records, including taped telephone conversations with his employers.

Larry and Virgil testified about how they found the garden, surveillance procedures and about the raid. Tom told what he had seen from his observation post. Carl Hess elaborated about the raid itself, and showed photographs of the scene and the plants. He also showed the confiscated plants samples. None of this was refuted. The defendants' attorneys simply maintained that their clients weren't involved.

It was the foreman's testimony that was critical. He told in great detail how he had been contacted and hired by the defendants. He explained how they had provided the seed and equipment for planting, and how he had been given essentially a blank check to procure the irrigation pipe and hire the needed workers.

The lead defense attorney challenged this testimony as tainted, given falsely in exchange for a lighter sentence. Katherine Dunlop, however, held all the trump cards. Her summary was complete, detailed and irrefutable. The jury found the two entrepreneurs guilty as charged, and the judge gave them ten to twenty years each, plus a $50,000 fine.

"This was a good case," Ms. Dunlop told Carl, Virgil, Phil and Larry, "almost open and shut from the start. Your thoroughness was impressive. The arrest was good and clean. Thank you and congratulations!"

"Sometimes the good guys win," Virgil told Ike Elliot, in response to the editor's request for a quote on the outcome of the case.

The next morning, Larry called Beth Egan into his office. "Personnel in the SO called me a few minutes ago with a job offer for you," he said.

"I don't understand how that can be," Beth replied. "All I've applied for have been ranger jobs."

"Well, that's what they called about," Larry said. "You've

been selected to be the District Ranger for the Cedarville District on the Blue Mountain National Forest. Congratulations!"

"What about Ben?" Beth asked. "Did he get an offer too?"

"No, Ben's still waiting," Larry said. "This is your job offer, Beth, it has nothing to do with Ben."

"Oh yes it does," she said. "Ben is way ahead of me, and more qualified by a mile! This should be his offer, not mine. I applied just to test the water, to make my name known for future reference. This isn't right, Larry. I can't accept it."

"If that's the issue, let's get Ben in here and repeat the conversation so he can hear it," Larry said, and he walked down the hall and came back with Ben Foster.

"Beth has an offer for a ranger job, Ben, and she says she can't take it because it should be yours."

"Hey, that's absurd," Ben said. "If it's your offer, Beth, you take it. And let me be the first to congratulate you. I'll get mine in due time, don't you worry. Just take it and run, no questions asked."

"I figured you'd say that," Beth told him, "but it's not right, Ben. They picked me because I'm a woman, not because I'm the most qualified."

"Woman or not, Beth, you're a qualified candidate, or you wouldn't have been offered the job. You have the 'people skills' necessary and you're an excellent organizer and communicator. That's really more important nowadays anyway. So take it and don't apologize." Ben meant what he said, it was obvious.

"He's right, you know," Larry said. "Do you want to talk it over with Richard before you give me your answer?"

"Richard is supportive of my career, you know that," Beth said. "As an auto mechanic, he can get a good job wherever we live. I'll talk to him, but he'll agree if I tell him I want the job; I know he will."

"Then tell him," Ben said, "and let's get started accelerating your training plan in the time we have left before you have to report. Tom and I can devote nearly full time to it if we need to."

"I guess that answers any questions as to how Ben might feel about it," Larry assured her. And with that, the process was set in motion for Beth Egan to become the Cedarville District Ranger.

Just after "quiting time" that afternoon, Chet stopped by Larry's office for a confidential discussion.

"It's none of my business, Larry, none whatsoever," Chet said, "but I've gotta' ask you something about this ranger job that Beth has been offered."

"Sure," Larry replied, "what's on your mind?"

"Well, I guess it concerns the concept of 'affirmative action'," Chet said, shifting his chaw to the other cheek. "Being a minority myself, I've always assumed affirmative action was a good idea, an opportunity for people to get ahead who otherwise might not have much of a chance. Now don't get me wrong, Larry, I'm a big supporter of Beth's. She's a bright young woman with lots of potential. But there's no way in the world she's more qualified than Ben to get a ranger's job. If that's what affirmative action is about, then I guess it's not such a good idea after all."

"I can understand and appreciate your concerns, Chet," Larry said. "But there are some things that Beth has going for her that may not be too apparent. You're looking at her experience in working with a variety of resources, and I agree she's a little short there. But Beth is very intelligent, she's well-organized, an excellent communicator, and she works well with people. Those are the primary attrubutes that they're selecting rangers on nowadays, Chet, not just how much timber or range experience she's had. She can get staff help with those activities as long as she understands the basics. Affirmative action was originally designed to improve training opportunities for women and minorities so that they might be able to compete better for higher-level positions. It also sought to assure that more women and minorities were on promotion rosters available for selection. Unfortunately, affirmative action seems to have become more of a 'quota' system lately, and that's wrong! I can see the reason for your confusion and concern. But I can tell you this, Chet, Beth is qualified for this job, and we're going to work at making her even better qualified, especially in the resource area, in the time we have before she leaves. She and Ben had a good discussion about it and he's very supportive. We need to be too. Does that answer your questions?"

"Yeah, I guess so. Thanks for taking the time to explain it, Larry," Chet said. He shifted his tobacco chaw back to the other cheek, grabbed his hat and headed for the door.

Beth spent the next two weeks improving her timber qualifications so she might more effectively oversee that aspect of her new district's activities. She spent two days scaling logs under the supervision of Clark Brightfeather. Tom gave her a thorough review of the cruising and marking* guidelines as well as the sale preparation process. She was already familiar with the National Environmental Policy Act standards and requirements and with the administrative appeal process. They went over every detail of the Bear Hollow timber sale, including the documented public involvement that Beth had been heavily-involved with at the time.

"Cedarville isn't a big timber district, but I think you're ready to handle whatever they might have," Larry told her, after reviewing the training accomplishments that she and Tom reported.

The same routine was next followed with Ben in the range, watershed and recreation activities. That took six days.

Beth spent two days with Mildred Bronson reviewing the ranger district budget and accounting process, property inventory, purchasing, contracts and other business management activities. These were items that Beth had been exposed to, but not responsible for, as a ranger must be, and it was important that she understand it thoroughly from that viewpoint.

She spent two more days with Joe Garza on fire suppression and prescribed fire.* They went over care, maintenance and the use of fire handtools as well as the dozers and pumpers. Joe put extra emphasis on fire safety.

"After the Dry Gulch Fire and the fatality in the crew just above ours, I have a special appreciation for fire safety," Beth commented.

Another two days were devoted to evaluating and upgrading Beth's horsemanship skills. Chet made sure she knew how to manty a load* and hang it on a decker saddle. He also reviewed the process of tying a diamond hitch and a double diamond* on a patient Molly, who was carrying panniers* and a top load. After catching, saddling and loading horses in the trailer, they took a ride on a nearby forest trail and talked about horse safety.

"I don't suppose Larry would agree to my taking Badger with me to the Blue Mountain," Beth said, rhetorically.

"I don't suppose so," Chet answered. "We don't want to break up a set. Maybe you'll have Foxtrotters at Cedarville; I hear they're pretty progressive there. If not, I suggest you buy some and start converting to 'em."

"Good idea," Beth replied.

In nearly five weeks of concentrated training, Beth felt more secure in dealing with those ranger district functions that she had not been directly responsible for in her previous experience.

Glen Romero called Larry and said the Sportsmen's Club

would like to give Beth a farewell party. He said that she had done a lot to promote wildlife and fisheries habitat improvement on the district, and his group appreciated it very much.

"I'm flattered," Beth said, when Larry told her. "I wasn't expecting any party at all, maybe an extended coffee break on my last day here."

"These people like you, Beth," Larry told her. "I'm sure the whole Kiwanis Club will want to be there too."

So it was settled, and arrangements were made by Glen and the Sportsmen's Club social committee to reserve the big room at Barney's Cafe.

Kent Maluski acted as master of ceremonies, and he was in rare form, witty and clever. The Sportsmen's Club and Kiwanians "roasted" Beth with good-natured kidding and exaggerated accounts of various incidents from her tour of duty on the Elk Creek District. They gave her several "gag" gifts, including an oversized ranger's hat and a huge laundry basket altered to resemble a fishing creel.

Serious gifts included a flyrod and reel from the Sportsmen's Club, a tooled leather briefcase from the Kiwanis Club, and a framed, enlarged photograph of a small elk herd in the early morning in Big Meadow in the Trappers Cache Sheep Camp Wilderness. Chet had taken the picture on the regional forester's pack trip with the governor in September.

Rita cried. Jill hugged Beth and thanked her for being her role model. Ernie hugged her too, to the surprise of his family. And he thanked her for all her help with his Eagle Scout project.

Glen Romero made a brief serious speech about Beth's commitment to wildlife needs in the forest multiple-use program, and he thanked Beth and Richard for being an important part of the community.

When it was Beth's turn to talk at the end of the evening,

she thanked everyone for the fine sendoff. She said how much she had enjoyed working with Kent and the Fish and Game Department, with Glen and the Sportsmen's Club, and being an active member of the Kiwanis Club.

Then she said that the past two years on the Elk Creek District had been the most rewarding experience she could ever imagine. She thanked everyone for their help, guidance and support, and then she thanked each district employee individually—Larry, Tom, Ben, Chet, Joe, Mildred, Rita, and Clark. She said that she and Richard would never forget the great people of Elk Creek and her "family" on the ranger district. Rita cried again.

The next day, Larry called the forest personnel officer to request a vacancy announcement to fill the district's wildlife biologist position. He had delayed doing this in order to save some money in his budget, figuring that he, Ben and Tom could handle her duties among them until a replacement for Beth came on board.

The personnel officer, Vera Potter, said she would get it out right away, and then she said she thought the Forest Supervisor wanted to talk to Larry. "Hold on a minute and I'll transfer you," she said.

"Good morning, boss," Larry said, when Frank Johnson came on the line, "what's up?"

"I understand Beth Egan is on her way to the Blue Mountain," Frank said. "How did she feel about the move?"

"A little apprehensive," Larry replied. "She didn't feel as qualified as she thought she should have been. And she hated the idea of getting a district ahead of Ben Foster."

"I can sure understand that," Frank said. "Most new rangers begin by feeling a little unsure of themselves. And there's no doubt that Ben is better qualified, overall. But she got picked for the Cedarville job, and she shouldn't feel bad about it. Ben's time will come."

"That's what we told her," Larry said. "I was hoping maybe you were calling with a ranger's job offer for Ben..."

"No, as a matter of fact, I'm calling about you, Larry," Frank said, "and it's a unique situation."

"What do you mean?" Larry asked.

"Well, it's the first time I've ever had three job offers to present to one person at one time," Frank said. "Apparently you did as I suggested and started applying for vacancies right after your performance rating session."

"That's right, I did," Larry said. "I applied for a staff job on a National Forest out on the coast and a deputy forest supervisor job in Idaho. And I also put in for a ranger job on a National Recreation Area, one that has a well-rounded multiple-use workload. All three were a pay grade up from mine. I figured if I was going to move, it may as well be with a promotion."

"Well, they've selected you for all three!" Frank said. "I've never heard of such a thing. I guess what it boils down to, Larry, is that you have your choice of three jobs."

"That's really kind of a nice problem," Larry said. "Let me talk it over with my family and get back to you."

"That will be fine," Frank said. "I guess there's no big hurry. If you could give me a decision by the end of the week we can let them know, and they can go back to the drawing board on the other two."

They hung up the phone, and then Larry called Peggy. "Let me give you something to think about today," he said, "and we can discuss it and talk it over with the kids when I get home this evening..."

"I'll bet we're moving!" Peggy interrupted in an excited tone.

"Well, maybe so;" Larry replied, "I've had three job offers, honey, all three that I applied for a while back, the staff job, the deputy supervisor's job and the NRA ranger job. Frank said we can have our choice."

Peggy sighed, "I never heard of such a thing! I thought you got a job offer and that was it."

"I thought so too," Larry answered, "but I guess it can be done this way too. Anyway, we'll talk it over this evening and we'll decide what to do."

That evening after supper, Larry and Peggy sat down with Ernie and Jill to discuss what Peggy referred to as, "A very important matter."

"What's up, Mom?" Ernie asked. "Sounds serious."

"It is serious," Peggy replied, "it's about our family's future, our next move at least, and we all need to be together on this. Your father has received three job offers, a very unusual situation, and we have to decide which one to take."

"Cool," said Jill, "it's neat to have a choice. What are the jobs?"

Larry described all three positions and told about the locations of each. "We can use the 'choosing by advantages' decision-making system on this," he said. "We use it to resolve a lot of tough problems on the district. In fact, it's a process used throughout the region and even by other agencies, I understand. It will help us identify our best choice in a systematic way."

Larry set-up a grid that they could all see, with the three jobs on the top line and spaces to list advantages and weigh their importance under each alternative.

"We'll have to be able to keep our horses and have a place to ride them," Jill exclaimed. "And a 4-H program is important too."

"Those are good ideas, sweetie, but all three have that," Larry said, "so there are no advantages to list."

"How about a college in the state with a good forestry school?" Ernie asked.

"Another good item, but again all three have it, so there are no advantages, one over another."

"Close to our families," Peggy said. "Our folks are both getting older and we don't want to move too far away."

"That's important all right, honey," Larry said. "I'd say the ranger job has a slight advantage over the deputy supervisor position, and both have a big advantage over the staff job on the coast." And he noted the advantages on the chart.

"Career potential, dad," said Ernie. "Which job would help take you higher up the ladder in the Forest Service organization?"

"Well, I'm not sure how important that one is to me," Larry said, "but we'll list it. Here the deputy has an advantage over the ranger, with the staff somewhere in between, I suppose." And again he noted these advantages on the chart for all to see.

They talked about several other potential issues, but dropped them as being relatively unimportant or the fact that none had relative advantages over the others.

Then Jill spoke up, "Dad, I think the most important thing of all is what job you like best and want to do. You're a ranger, dad. Don't you want to stay a ranger?"

"Out of the mouths of babes..." Peggy observed.

"You're right, sweetie," Larry admitted. "When all is said and done, the ranger's job is the one I'd be most satisfied with, no doubt about it. In fact, I guess I'd have to say it's the job I've wanted all my life."

"If that's all the advantages we need to list," Peggy asked, "then shouldn't we be deciding on which are most important?"

"You're right," Larry said. "Following the process we need to assign numbers, after we agree on which are the most important advantages."

"Why don't we give the ranger job the biggest number on

the chart, since that's clearly the most important advantage we've talked about," Ernie said, "and let's move to that National Recreation Area."

"He's right, you know," Peggy said, and Jill nodded agreement.

And with that, the decision for Larry Weaver to take the NRA ranger's job was made by the Weaver family.

When Larry called back with his decision, Frank Johnson said he really wasn't surprised, although he thought Larry was missing a bet in turning down the deputy job.

"I'm a ranger, Frank," Larry said. "Jill reminded me of that as we were talking it over as a family."

Peggy started the laborious job of packing. They got big boxes from the moving company in Centerville, and everyone helped out. They discussed the logistics of the move itself. A big moving company van would haul most of their possessions, but some things, such as firearms and frozen elk meat, would have to go in the pickup bed and in the back of the Suburban. Larry would pull the horse trailer with Gifford and Cougar, and there would be room for a few things, like camping gear, in the front stall. Peggy would drive the Suburban and follow. They would use two-way radios to communicate enroute.

For the first time in several moves, they were going to government housing, which was described to them as "very nice." It even had a barn, corral and horse pasture near by, a place to keep the horses. This met Jill's main requirement. All these features eliminated the need for an advance house hunting trip, and allowed them the time they needed to try to sell their house in Elk Creek, without using one of the Realtors in Centerville or paying a commission on the sale. Although the government would pay for such costs, Larry was conscious of the fact that eventually the district budget would absorb the expense involved.

Larry announced the news of his pending move to the district workforce, and they received it with mixed emotions. They knew it was inevitable that their ranger would be moving on. He had told them that the supervisor had encouraged him to start applying for vacancies. But they were sorry to see him leave, and at the same time happy for his promotion and the opportunities it presented.

Larry called Ben aside. "Are you going to put in for this job, Ben?" he asked. "With your familiarity with the district and the respect the employees here have for you, it seems a natural."

"I don't think so, boss," Ben replied. "I've been here four years. It's probably best that my first district be somewhere else. Besides, you're a tough act to follow."

"Now about your going-away party," Mildred said the next day, "it's only fair that you be given some choices."

"We just had a big party for Beth," Larry replied. "We don't need to impact the people with another one so soon. How about some kind of open house here at the office, with cookies and coffee, and let it go at that?"

"No way!" Mildred said, indignantly. "We're not going to let you and Peggy slip out of town without ceremony. Let's get serious."

"Okay, how about a potluck?" Larry said. "That way, people could come, if they wanted to, without shelling-out big bucks for an average restaurant meal. We've already given Barney plenty of business anyway. Father Carlos would probably let us use the St. Agnes social hall."

"There you go taking over," Mildred admonished, in a kidding tone. "I was trying to get your ideas, not turn the whole thing over to you. But you know, I think we can make a potluck work."

Mildred had five weeks to work on party preparations before the transfer's effective date. Larry had this same time to wrap up unfinished business at Elk Creek and get ready for the move.

Since the move would be before Christmas, plans for another family get-together were changed. Larry's parents and brother made quick trips back to retrieve their shares of frozen elk, to help lighten the move somewhat.

As word spread throughout the community among the Lions Club, the Kiwanis Club, the Sportsmen's Club, Chamber of Commerce, St. Agnes parish and other congregations in town, it soon became apparent that Barney's Cafe would not have held the crowd that would be there anyway, and neither would the St. Agnes social hall. Finally, Mildred called Principal Bruce Matthews to talk about using the junior high gymnasium. Mr. Matthews did not hesitate, saying he would advise the school board, but since they'd all be there he couldn't see a problem.

For a going-away gift, the district employees bought Larry a popup tent for great convenience on packtrips. He had grumbled about how long it took to thread poles through the sleeves of his old, nearly worn-out pack tent. Another beautiful Chet Wagoner photograph of a Wilderness scene was enlarged and framed as a gift for Peggy.

Mildred made all the arrangements for the party. She took reservations for over 250 people by the cutoff date, and they were still coming in up to the day of the party. Frank and Vivian Johnson were coming from the SO, and so were Don Hendricks and his wife, Lucille, and Georgia Kenley and her husband, Vern. Rangers Tony Angelo and Barbara Williams with spouses, Ann and Rob, would be there also, along with the other three Rio Verde rangers and their spouses. Law Enforcement Agent Phil Ortega was on detail out of the region, to his regret, and could not attend. State Fish and Game Director Bert Edwards and his wife made reservations early. Governor Clyde Winston sent his regrets, good wishes and congratulations. Beth and Richard Egan drove all night, 390 miles, to be there.

Ben and Tom got their heads together and decided that this shouldn't be the same old routine going-away party, with speeches and platitudes.

"I think I'll write a play, a skit for the occasion," Ben said. "You want to help?"

"A play about what?" Tom asked.

"How about a 'typical day' in the life of Ranger Weaver?" Ben said. "We could involve lots of people as 'actors,' and use satire and exaggeration on a whole variety of topics and issues. It could be a parody of some of the past year's major events on the district."

"Sounds good," said Tom, "let's get with it."

Over 300 people made up the final count. Mildred had long since given up trying to coordinate the potluck menu and instead concentrated on lining-up extra tables and chairs, mostly from churches around town. The junior high school gym was full to overflowing.

Father Carlos asked the blessing. But before that, he commented about the Weaver family. "These are good people," he said. "They participate in activities of the community and help make it a better place. They have done the same for our parish. They will be sorely missed by all of us. May God's blessing go with them."

It turned out there was plenty to eat. The crowd passed through six serving lines in a relatively short time. Mayor Braggs commented about what a fine event it was, "bringing the community together like this."

The skit was a riot! Luckily, with the size of the crowd, they had microphones and a good loudspeaker system on the stage at one side of the gym, so that everyone could hear, even if not everyone could see as well as they'd have liked. It was all in good fun; the satire came through and no one was offended, at least not that the authors were aware of.

Ernie played the part of his father, the ranger, in his office. That was funny to start with. Mildred was herself, announcing the arrival of visitors, one at a time, coming to see the ranger. Most had concerns or something to complain about. Every staff member played a role. In some cases, the "visitors" played themselves.

Clark Brightfeather, playing the role of Bill Crawford, came in to pound on the ranger's desk and demand more timber for the Alliance Sawmill. There was a scattering of laughter from the crowd.

Then Joe Garza, as Duane Selzer, president of Wilderness Plus, came in to demand that all timber harvest stop and the entire district be made Wilderness. The crowd burst out in louder laughter still.

A slightly-embarrassed Rita Vigil, as Ruth Osborne, complained about moving porta-potties on the field tour. The real Ruth Osborne, demonstrating her good nature, chuckled in the audience.

Mildred came to the ranger's "office door" and said, "Forest Supervisor Hanson is on the phone. He wants you to run a raft on the Middle Fork River for at least a month."

Ernie, as the ranger at his desk, threw the papers he was working on into the air, grabbed his hat and started for the door.

"It's not until next week," Mildred said, and the "ranger" sat back down, looking disappointed. The real ranger and his wife laughed aloud.

Tom Cordova was banker Hamilton Braggs, who was irate about mule damage to his beautiful yard. The mayor, Harriet Braggs, in the audience forced a laugh, as did her husband, the banker.

BLM Area Manager Steve Underwood, playing himself, came in to ask the ranger to assemble every horse and rider on the entire forest to help with a gigantic roundup of wild horses. Again, Ernie grabbed the ranger's hat and started out, only to be told, "not just now."

He was followed closely by Ben Foster, as editor Ike Elliot, complaining that the ranger and area manager were withholding important news from him and his newspaper. The 6' 4" Ben Foster playing the part of the 5' 6" editor brought some chuckles from the audience. Ike didn't think it was very funny, but he was glad to be included.

Deputy Virgil Craft, playing himself, came in to tell the ranger that marijuana was now growing in every clearing on the district. Joe Garza, as Duane Selzer again, followed him in to announce that Cannabis had been declared an endangered plant and it all must be protected. Duane, in the audience, laughed at "himself."

Barney Shultz, playing himself, was announced by Mildred as being irate and demanding to see the ranger. Barney came in waving his arms and said, "This is an outrage! I just heard that your going away-party is going to be a potluck at some public facility, a warehouse or something. It should be at my cafe. There's plenty of room and besides, I need the business!" The crowd of 300-plus roared.

Glen Romero and Kent Maluski, as themselves, came in together demanding that the district put more priority on wildlife and fish, and get rid of all the livestock.

They were closely followed by Sandstone Grazing Association range rider Hank Eden, also himself, with a

counter-demand that all the deer and elk be removed so there could be more forage for his cattle.

Next, Tom, in a dual role as Lions' Club President George Meredith, said, "Ranger Weaver, the Lions and Kiwanis Clubs of Elk Creek have passed a joint resolution calling for your father to be the permanent speaker, every week." Larry and George in the audience both laughed.

When Mildred announced that the Honorable Governor Clyde Winston was "here to see you," Frank Johnson stopped laughing and looked up with interest. Chet Wagoner, playing the role of governor, came in and said, "Ranger Weaver, I've decided we should change the name of the Trappers Cache-Sheep Camp Wilderness to include the names of every member of this state's congressional delegation, living and dead, past and present. I figure it will take about thirty six hyphens and 5,000 board feet of lumber for the new signs." Frank nearly fell off his chair laughing; so did Bert Edwards.

The next time Mildred came in, she said, "Beth Egan is on the phone, boss. She says this new ranger job is for the birds and she wants her old, cushy job back." Beth and Richard laughed the hardest at this one.

And finally, Mildred announced, "Mrs. Ranger Weaver is here to see you, sir, shall I tell her you're out?"

Peggy stopped laughing for a moment, and she looked up to see her daughter, Jill, playing the role of her mother, squeeze past Mildred screaming, "Our son, Ernest, has been expelled from school! What will we do?"

Ernie, as his father, had said nothing up to this point in the program, his acting limited to facial expressions and body language, shaking his head and murmuring inaudible phrases as the various actors said their lines. But this time he leaped from his chair, and gesturing dramatically, said, "Don't worry about it, dear, I've just found out we're being transferred! Maybe the kid won't find out where we're going."

Rita carried a sign that said, "THE END," across the stage.

The crowd applauded for nearly two minutes until the "actors" came back onstage to take a bow. Then they applauded some more. Even though most of them did not understand or grasp the significance of every segment, it was all funny and taken in good spirit by everyone, including those being portrayed on the stage. Ben and Tom felt a sense of accomplishment that their brain-child had been a success.

It was Larry's turn to talk. He thanked everyone for coming and for bringing dinner with them. "It's very humbling to see the size of this crowd," he said, "and to see the display of affection for my family and me. We couldn't have had a better assignment these past seven-plus years, or a more supportive community. I'm not even going to try to single out those who should be thanked, there are just too many of you. We thank you all! We appreciate your friendship. Thank you for your efforts to understand what we try to do in managing the National Forest—your land. We can't always satisfy everyone, but the important thing is for us to make these lands and their resources available for your use and enjoyment, and also produce to their full potential for the good of the people and the future. Please continue to give your support to the district staff and to my successor, whoever it might be.

"I want to give special thanks to those of you who traveled some distance to be here tonight, from as far away as Capitol City and a place nearly 400 miles north of here called Cedarville.

"Now about that skit," Larry continued. "I don't know who wrote it, but I have a sneaking suspicion," and he glanced in Ben and Tom's direction. "I know I haven't laughed so much or so hard in a long time. It depicted, in a very funny way, a lot of things that happen and have happened in running this district. You're all good sports to laugh and enjoy the humor in the conflicts that they showed. Anyway, thank you for that. I saw Principal Matthews videotaping it. I sure would like a copy." Bruce Matthews nodded in the affirmative.

"Now, on behalf of my family, Peggy, Ernie and Jill, I thank you all, everyone of you. We'll never forget you. Elk Creek, the town and the ranger district will always have a place in our hearts." As Larry sat down, the crowd stood up and applauded Ranger Larry Weaver and his family.

Before leaving, Larry and Peggy shook hands and/or hugged everyone there and thanked them individually for coming. Rita cried.

Clark Brightfeather asked Peggy to turn around and sit down. Then he fastened a beautiful squash blossom necklace around her neck and said, "You are my friends. Thank you."

Larry said, "Clark, it's beautiful, but we can't accept such a gift. Thank you for the thought, but..."

"What do you mean 'we,' Kimo Sabe?" Clark said with a very stern look on his face. "It isn't for you. It's for my friend, Peggy. You are just my ex-boss. You should stay out of this deal."

"Thank you, Clark," Peggy said, wiping a tear from her cheek, "Its lovely; I'll treasure it always!" And she gave him a big hug.

"Isn't that the necklace you were working on when I stopped by the mill last spring?" Larry asked.

"Yeah," said Clark.

"I remember suggesting you enter it in the State Fair," Larry said.

"I did," Clark replied.

"Did you win anything with it?" Larry asked.

"Blue ribbon," Clark said.

"You never mentioned it," Larry said.

"Nope," was Clark's matter-of-fact reply.

The next day at the office, as Larry was cleaning out his desk and bookcase of personal items, or trying to, people kept stopping in to say good-bye and wish him well. Many of them had been at the party the night before; a few had not.

Virgil Craft told Larry that he would have made a "hell of a law enforcement officer." This was the highest form of compliment the deputy could bestow.

Kent Maluski thanked him for his attention to wildlife needs and for helping him get better acquainted with Bert Edwards, his boss's boss. Larry thanked Kent for their good relationship and also for being such an encouragement to Ernie in his Boy Scout work.

Hank Eden stopped by to tell Larry and Ben that he had submitted his application for membership in the Society for Range Management. He also mentioned that he had been looking at Foxtrotters, hoping to buy one or two before next grazing season.

"You won't be sorry, on either count," Larry told him.

Steve Underwood said he'd miss their professional relationship and also their personal friendship. He thanked Larry again for helping with the wild horse roundup and for his good advice in dealing with mustang overpopulation problems.

Ruth Osborne thanked him for all he had done to help her and the League of Women Voters to understand the forest better. Then she stopped to tell Rita that she enjoyed her part in the skit.

County Commissioner Sam Turner, State Representative Fred Graves and Mayor Harriet Braggs came in together to thank Larry on behalf of the people they represented. "We'll have a time finding another ranger like you," the Mayor said.

Ike Elliot told him he wished he'd done more stories

about the forest in the Weekly Bugle, and he promised to do more in the future.

George Meredith said that Larry had been a good Lions Club member even if his attendance record wasn't the best. He said he hoped Larry would have a chance to be in the Lions Club at his new location.

Duane Selzer and Earl Ashworth told him that despite their differences they had always appreciated his courtesy, honesty and willingness to listen to their point of view on behalf of Wilderness Plus.

Larry thanked them and said, "What I'd like you to know is that your group plays an important role in keeping the district and its priorities on track. You get a little over-zealous sometimes in opposing uses of the resources, but that often counter-balances the commercial interests who sometimes might like to overuse those same resources. We need the public looking at and commenting on what we do in managing their land. Believe it or not, fellows, it's been fun working with you."

Bill Crawford came in and said, "I wasn't sure about you at first, ranger, maybe for quite awhile, but I finally came to realize that you were trying to manage the forest by using timber harvest as a tool, which is a damned good idea. And I think, despite pressures from above, you were trying to keep our little company in business. Well, that helps our industry as well as the local economy. In fact, I've come to the conclusion that you're a goddamn good ranger. I'm sorry to see you leave."

Mid-afternoon, district personnel had coffee together in the conference room for the last time with Ranger Weaver. Ben, Tom, Mildred and Rita were there as usual. Chet came in along with Joe and Clark. And Beth stopped by on their way out-of-town, while Richard went to gas up their car.

"At the risk of sounding mushy," Larry said, "I want you to know that this has been the best district crew that anyone ever assembled. I'll miss you all. Thank you!"

Chet raised his coffee mug in a toast. "Mildred and I have been through a bunch of rangers on this district. But I've got to tell you, Ranger Lawrence E. Weaver, the Third, you're the best one we've ever had."

Mildred nodded her head affirmativley, while the rest applauded Chet's words. Rita cried.

Larry excused himself to take a phone call from Supervisor Frank Johnson, and came out of his office smiling. Then he returned to the conference room and shared a final bit of news with his staff.

Next he placed a quick phone call to Peggy to tell her the same information. "Selling our house might not be such a problem after all, honey," he said.

The last visitor of the day was grazing permittee Alex Pierce. He and Larry had battled the whole time Larry had been on the district about the condition of the Horse Mesa Allotment and about Alex's resistance to an improved rest-rotation management plan. While Larry had been able to work with most permittees, an obstinate Alex Pierce was the exception. He insisted on doing business the way his father and grandfather had always done, season-long grazing, salt on the water, let the cows manage the range. By grazing some thirty percent above his permitted numbers one year, he had been forced to take a cut in his permit and was put on notice that the entire permit might be canceled if there was a reoccurrence of excess numbers.

During the past year, with prodding by Larry and Ben, Alex had reluctantly agreed to work on implementing the management plan, but he grumbled that it was being forced on him.

"I just stopped by to make sure you were really leaving," Alex said. "You cut my permit and forced me to follow that crazy plan. In all honesty, I can't say I'm sorry to see you go."

"I'm sorry you feel that way," Larry said. "What we've tried to do, whether you realize it, is keep you in business and also get your allotment in acceptable condition. Your range is already starting to improve with just one year of rest-rotation. And I didn't really cut your permit, Alex. You did it to yourself by trespassing."

"Nevertheless," Alex replied, "I'm glad to see you leave, ranger. I don't think we can do any worse, whoever replaces you!"

"Well, as a matter of fact, I can give you a newsflash on that subject, and I'm not so sure you'll be very happy about it," Larry said. "I just talked to the forest supervisor, and he told me that my replacement has been selected. His name is Jim Weaver. He's my brother and he's a lot tougher than I am."

THE END

CAST OF CHARACTERS

(Alphabetical order by last names)

Aldrich, Dave—Recreation Staff, National Forest with Middle Fork

Anderson, Ted—Middle Fork River Manager

Angelo, Tony—Granite Peak District Forest Ranger

Angelo, Ann—Tony's wife

Ashworth, Earl—Wilderness Plus Resource Director

Barker, Joyce—Regional Information Director

Braggs, Harriet—Mayor of Elk Creek

Braggs, Hamilton—The Mayor's husband, a banker

Brightfeather, Clark—Elk Creek Ranger District Scaler

Brightfeather, Cleo—Clark's wife

Brill, Vince—Vice Presidental Staffer

Bronson, Mildred—Elk Creek Ranger District Business Mgt Assistant

Carlos, Father—Saint Agnes Parish Priest

Cordova, Tom—Timber, fire, minerals Staff, Elk Creek District

Cordova, Angie—Tom's wife

Craft, Virgil—Deputy Sheriff, Adams County

Crawford, Bill—Alliance Sawmill Manager

Crawford, Mary—Bill's wife

Donahue, Ed—Range, Wildlife Staff, Rio Verde National Forest

Dunlop, Kathrine—Assistant U.S. Attorney

Eden, Hank—Sandstone Association Range Rider

Edwards, Bert—State Fish and Game Department Director

Egan, Beth—Wildlife Biologist, Elk Creek District

Egan, Richard—Beth's husband

Elliot, Ike—Editor, Elk Creek Weekly Bugle

Enfield, Horace—U.S. Magistrate

Fisher, Jack—BLM Rider

Foster, Ben—Range, watershed, recreation Staff, Elk Creek District

Foster, Jean—Ben's wife

Garza, Joe—Fire Crew Foreman, Elk Creek District

Garza, Yolanda—Joe's wife

Gomez, June - Waitress, Barney's Cafe

Graves, Fred—State Representative

Hanson, Ralph—Forest Supervisor, National Forest with Middle Fork

Harrison, Karen—Regional Forester

Hendricks, Don—Timber Staff, Rio Verde National Forest

Hendricks, Lucille—Don's wife

Hess, Carl—Assistant U.S. Marshal

Jameson, Betty—Governor's Communication Director

Johnson, Frank—Forest Supervisor, Rio Verde National Forest

Johnson, Vivian—Frank's wife

Jones, Roger—Powder Bowl Ski Area Manager

Kenley, Georgia—Recreation, Lands, Minerals Staff, Rio Verde NF

Kenley, Vern—Georgia's husband

Lopez, Bob—BLM rider

Maluski, Kent—State Fish and Game Officer; Scoutmaster

Matthews, Bruce—Junior High Principal

Meredith, George—Lion's Club President

Morris, Elaine—Middle Fork District Ranger

Murphy, Gene—Forest Service Researcher; Research Natural Areas

Norwood, Dan—Sheriff's Department technician

Ortega, Phil—Law Enforcement Special Agent, Rio Verde NF
Osborne, Ruth—League of Women Voters President
Pendleton, Cecil—U.S. Senator, deceased
Pierce, Alex—Grazing permittee, Horse Mesa Allotment
Potter, Vera—Personnel Officer, Rio Verde National Forest
Romero, Glen—Sportsmen's Club President
Russell, Paula—Regional Ecologist
Salazar, Henry—Proprietor, Henry's Market
Selzer, Duane—Wilderness Plus President
Shultz, Barney—Proprietor, Barney's Cafe
Small, Jimmy—Governor's Staff Assistant
Turner, Sam—Adams County Commissioner
Underwood, Steve—BLM Area Manager
Vigil, Rita—Receptionist, Elk Creek Ranger District
Vigil, Ray—Rita's husband
Wagoner, Chet—General District Assistant, Elk Creek RD
Wagoner, Gladys—Chet's wife
Weaver, Lawrence, Jr.—The Ranger's father; Retired Ranger
Weaver, Grace—Lawrence's wife; the Ranger's mother
Weaver, Jim—The Ranger's brother; FS Range Conservationist
Weaver, Vicki—Jim's wife
Weaver, Kevin—Jim and Vicki's young son
Weaver, Kyle—Jim and Vicki's younger son
Weaver, Larry—District Ranger, Elk Creek Ranger District
Weaver, Peggy—Larry's wife
Weaver, Ernie—Larry and Peggy's son
Weaver, Jill—Larry and Peggy's daughter; Ernie's sister
Williams, Barbara—South Fork District Ranger

Williams, Rob—Barbara's husband
Winston, Clyde—Governor

Un-named:
Chief of the Forest Service
Other Regional Forester
The Vice President
The Vice President's wife
The Vice President's daughter
Vice Presidental staffer who fell in the water
Media Video Operators (2)
Secret Service Agents (4-plus)
River Outfitters, Boatmen (several)

ORGANIZATION CHART

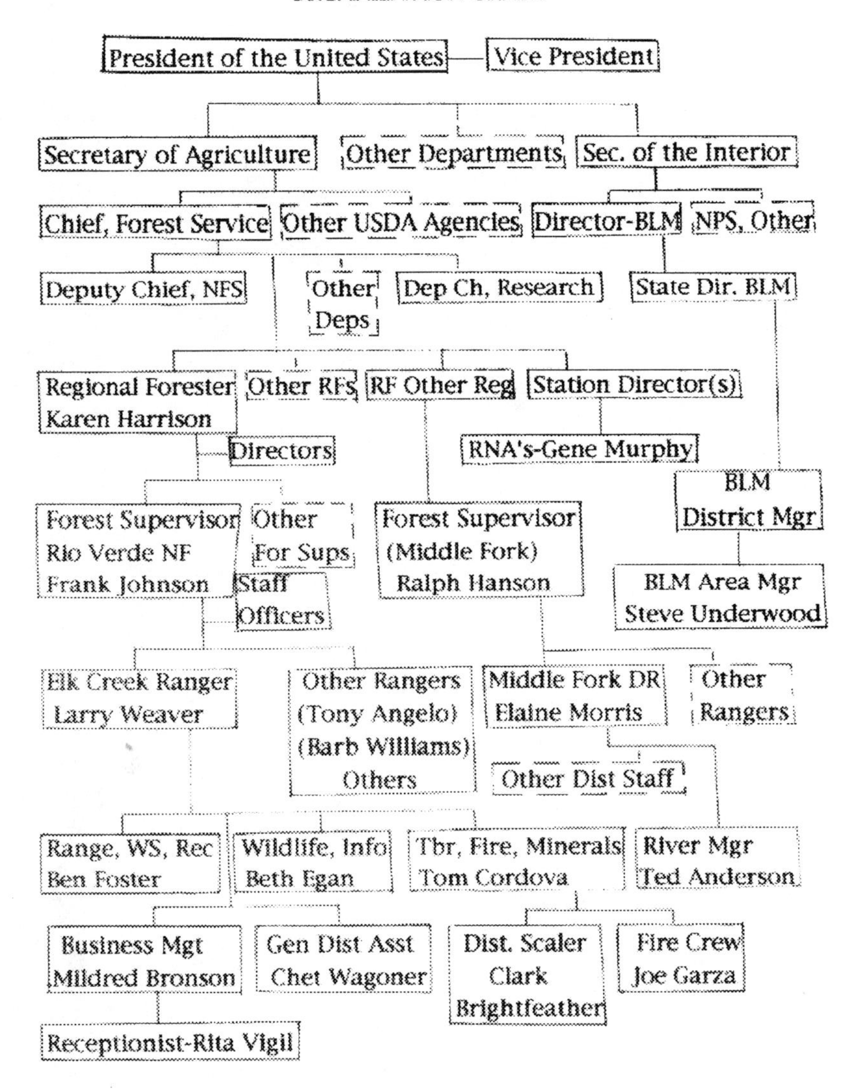

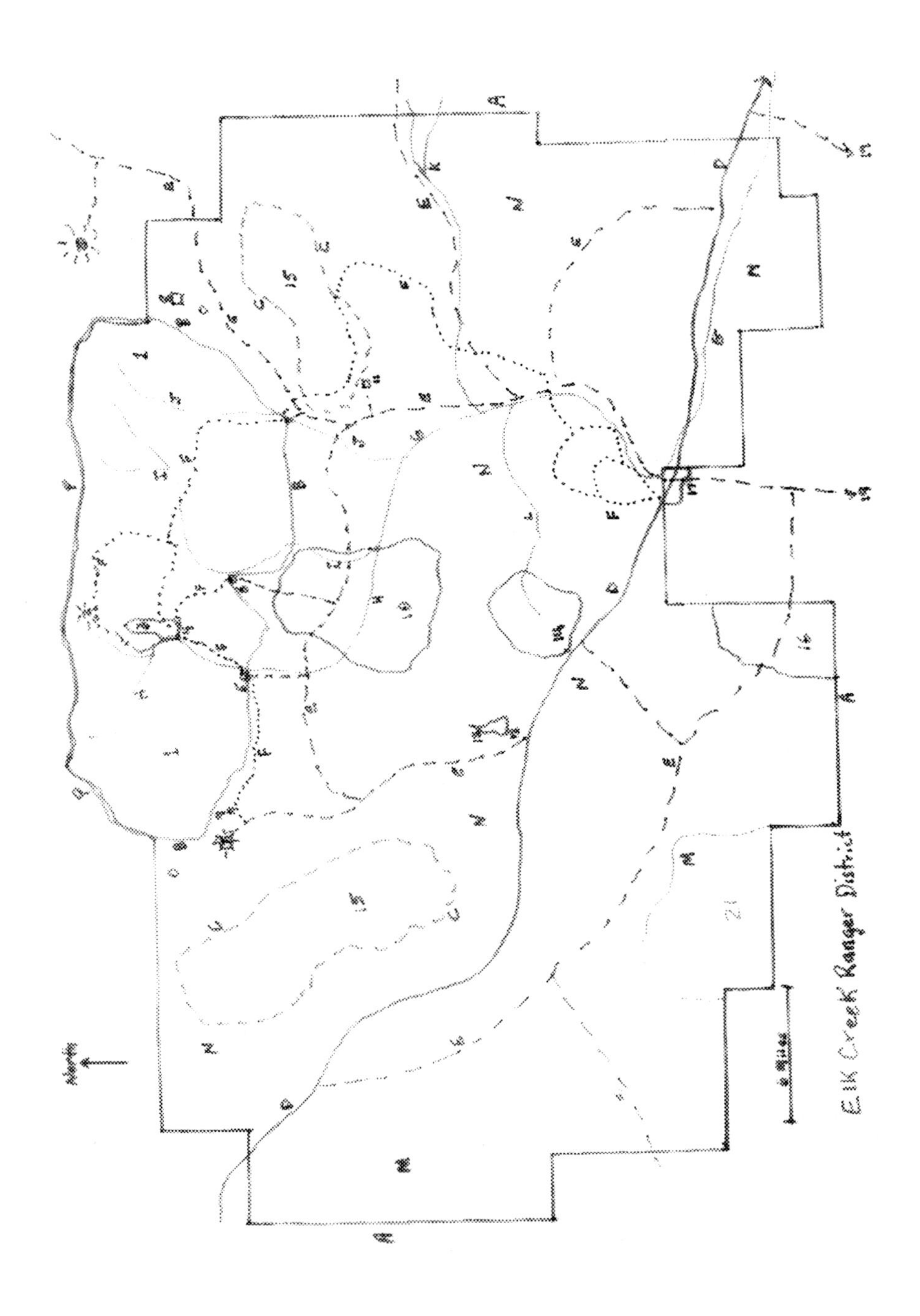
Elk Creek Ranger District

MAP LEGEND
ELK CREEK RANGER DISTRICT

A—District Boundary
B—Wilderness Boundary
C—Roadless Area Boundary
D -U.S. Highway
E—Forest Road
F—Forest Trail
G—Elk Creek (stream)
H—North Fork, Elk Creek
I—Smith's Fork, Elk Creek
J—Middle Fork, Elk Creek
K—East Fork, Elk Creek
L—Bear Hollow Fork, Elk Creek
M—Pinyon-Juniper Vegetation Type
N—Ponderosa pine-Douglas fir Vegetation Type
O—Spruce-fir Vegetation Type
P—District boundary within Wilderness (not Wilderness bdry)

1—Trappers Cache/Sheep Camp Wilderness
2—No Name Peak (10,500 feet)
3—Big Meadow
4—Campsite at Big Meadow (8,500 feet)
5—North Fork Trailhead (7,100 feet)
6—Smith's Fork Trailhead (6,900 feet)
7—Powder Bowl Ski Area (8,400 feet)
8—Spruce-Fir Research Natural Area Candidate
9—Cannibus Garden
10—Sandstone Grazing Allotment
11—Oil Well Dry Hole
12—Moose Lake

13—Campground at Moose Lake
14—Bear Hollow Timber Sale Area
15—Roadless Areas
16—Horse Mesa Grazing Allotment
17—Elk Creek (town)
18—Highway to Centerville
19—Roads to Rock Creek Valley
20—Granite Peak Fire Lookout (8,500 feet)
21—Diamond Fork Grazing Allotment

(Other features on the Elk Creek Ranger District, such as developed recreation areas, campgrounds, etc., not mentioned in the story, are not shown on the map.)

GLOSSARY OF TERMS

Allowable sale quantity—amount of timber a forest may offer for sale in a given year

Appraisal—determination of value of timber in a sale

BLM—Bureau of Land Management, U.S. Department of the Interior

Board foot—measurement of timber, 1 foot x 1 foot x 1 inch

Broke—trained or started, as a young saddlehorse

Browse transects—areas where edible, shrubby vegetation is measured, usually to determine annual growth

Buck-and-pole fencing—rustic wooden fence made of poles and posts that are crossed on the ground surface

Butt and breast height—places on a tree where marking for harves is done, at the base of a tree and 4 1/2 feet up

Cannabis—generic name for plant that produces marijuana

Carryall—crew-carrying vehicle, seating 9 to 12, usually 4-wheel drive

Chaparral—thicket of shrubs or thorny bushes, usually evergreen

Community allotment—designated grazing area used by several livestock operators

Concessionaire—someone with contract to operate a recreation area

Contained—status of a wildfire that is effectively stopped and about to be controlled

Controlled—status of a wildfire that is no longer a threat to spread

Cruise and mark timber—the processes of doing a field inventory before a timber sale and designating individual trees to be harvested either by paint or removing some bark with an axe

Decker—type of packsaddle with two steel rings for hanging bundled cargo; a sawbuck is another type where hitches are used

Diamond hitch/double diamond—types of hitches usually used to fasten cargo on a sawbuck packsaddle

Driptorch—device used to spread fire by dripping burning kerosene, usually in a backfire, or in slash burning

Eartags—colored metal or plastic tags placed in the ears of cattle for identification or to show they are authorized on an allotment

Equipment agreement—contract whereby personal property is used as if it were govern ment property

Field-dressed—the butchering of a game animal in the woods

Fire bags—previously-packed personal gear and firefighting clothing

Fire cache—location for fire fighting tools

Fire line—area cleared of vegetation or combustible material to stop an oncoming fire for lack of fuel

Fire salvage—the harvest of trees killed or damaged by fire

Forest officer—a permanent employee of the Forest Service

Gabion—wire basket filled with rocks for streamside stability

Harden—process of making an area, such as a trail, less subject to erosion, usually by paving or place ment of rocks or gravel

Hydraulics—rapidly-shifting river currents

Inventoried roadless areas—the formal listing of portions of a forest with no roads, usually 5,000 acres or more

Latigo—leather strap to fasten saddle to horse or mule

Mantied load—a pack of cargo tied to a decker saddle in a bundle using a canvas tarp called a manty

One-way gates—gates made of long poles like a funnel slanting into a corral that allows horses to enter but not exit

Packer boots—high-top, high-heeled, lace-up leather boots for work or horseback riding

Panniers or pannier boxes—sacks or containers for hauling cargo on a packsaddle

Prescribed fire—a fire set on purpose or planned to reduce fuel or achieve other management purposes

Production/utilization cage—device used to protect grassy area from grazing so that measurements may be made

Pulaski—fire-fighting hand tool, combination ax and grubbing hoe

Release—process by which a roadless area is no longer considered for Wilderness classification

Reversal—place in river where current shifts rapidly

Riparian—wet meadows or streamside areas

Roll-up table—small square table with screw-in legs that can be rolled up and packed on a mule or raft

Rout (sign letters)—engraved or cut-out lettering on wooden signs

Seabags—zippered rubber bags used by river floaters to carry their personal gear

Sinker—a log that sinks to the bottom of the mill pond

Slant-load horse trailer—a trailer where horses are loaded sideways on an angle providing greater stability

Slash disposal—treatment of waste vegetative material as in a timber sale, usually by burning or scattering

Smokejumpers—elite firefighters who parachute in to control forest fires in remote areas

Sustainable—the ability for natural resources to keep producing

Sweepboat—large rubber raft with long oars operated from a standing position, used to float rivers

Withdrawal from mineral entry—legal process whereby an area is not available to be mined

Woods crews—timber company employees who harvest trees

REFERENCES

CHAPTER V THE PARADE

Forest Trails and Tales, a behind the scene account of a career with the US Forest Service" by A. Joel Frandsen
Sunrise Publishing, Orem, Utah, 1999.

A Good Lookin' Horse, Cowboy Poetry and Other Verse
by Stan Tixier, Eden, Utah, 1993.

CHAPTER VI THE SPEECH

BREAKING NEW GROUND by Gifford Pinchot
Island Press, 1974.

CHAPTER IX THE PACK TRIP

Horses, Hitches and Rocky Trails; the Packer's Bible by Joe Back
Johnson Books, Boulder, Colorado, 1959.

Packin' In On Mules and Horses by Smoke Elser and Bill Brown
Mountain Press Publishing Company, Missoula, Mountana, 1980.

CHAPTER X THE FLOAT TRIP

Handbook to the Middle Fork of the Salmon River Canyon by James M. Quinn, James W. Quinn, Terry L. Quinn and James G. King
Commercial Printing Company, Medford, Oregon, 1981

CHAPTER XII TRANSFERS

The Choosing by Advantages Decisionmaking System by Jim Suhr
Quorum Books, Westport, Connecticut, 1999

About the Author

Stan Tixier has worked at every level of the U.S. Forest Service, including serving as a staff officer at the regional and national levels. He was a district ranger, forest supervisor, and regional forester. Stan is now retired and living in Eden, Utah, where he and his wife Jan raise, train, and occasionally sell Foxtrotting horses. Stan is also well-known as a cowboy poet.

CEDAR FORT, INCORPORATED
Order Form

Name:____

Address: ____

City: ____________________ State: ________ Zip: ___________

Phone: (   ) ____________ Daytime phone: (   ) ____________

Green Underwear

Quantity: ____________ @ $14.95 each: ___________

plus $3.49 shipping & handling for the first book: ___________

(add 99¢ shipping for each additional book)

Utah residents add 6.25% for state sales tax: ___________

TOTAL: ___________

Bulk purchasing, shipping and handling quotes available upon request.

Please make check or money order payable to:
Cedar Fort, Incorporated.

Mail this form and payment to:
Cedar Fort, Inc.
925 North Main St.
Springville, UT 84663

You can also order on our website **www.cedarfort.com**
or e-mail us at sales@cedarfort.com or call 1-800-SKYBOOK